$\mathcal{B}$ is for Bonnet

SHELLEY SHEPARD GRAY

B is for Bonnet

KENSINGTON
PUBLISHING CORP.

kensingtonbooks.com

KENSINGTON BOOKS are published by

Kensington Publishing Corp.
900 Third Ave.
New York, NY 10022

All Kensington titles, imprints, and distributed lines are available at special quantity discounts for bulk purchases for sales promotion, premiums, fund-raising, educational, or institutional use. Special book excerpts or customized printings can also be created to fit specific needs. For details, write or phone the office of the Kensington Special Sales Manager: Attn. Special Sales Department. Kensington Publishing Corp., 900 Third Avenue, New York, NY 10022. Phone: 1-800-221-2647.

Library of Congress Card Catalogue Number: 2024944363

KENSINGTON and the K with book logo Reg. US Pat. & TM Off.

ISBN: 978-1-4967-4887-4
First Kensington Hardcover Edition: February 2025

ISBN: 978-1-4967-4888-1 (trade)

ISBN: 978-1-4967-4889-8 (ebook)

10 9 8 7 6 5 4 3 2 1

Printed in the United States of America

For the members of the Buggy Bunch. Thank you for your continued enthusiasm and friendship.

Lord it's good that we're here. —*Matthew 17:4*

You only live once, but if you work it right, once is enough. —*Amish proverb*

B is for Bonnet

PROLOGUE

June
Cleveland, Ohio

Dr. Mason's office was decorated in shades of gray. Dove gray walls. Black-and-white artsy-looking photographs and charcoal prints surrounded by silver frames. The flooring was some kind of fake wood done in a muted mushroom color, and the furniture was constructed of chrome, glass, and gray suede.

Jonny Schrock guessed some fancy interior designer believed the monochromatic template made patients feel more at ease.

It had the opposite effect on him. With each passing minute, his dark mood intensified. He couldn't wait to get out of there.

"Jonny Schrock?"

"Yeah. That's me," he said, jumping to his feet.

"Hi. I'm Danielle," she said when he reached the doorway. "I'm so sorry, but Dr. Mason had an emergency this morning. He's running late."

"I understand." Feeling like he was a convict just granted an early parole, he tried not to smile. "I'll call to reschedule later."

"Oh, there's no need for that. He'll be here, but it's probably going to be another fifteen minutes. We just didn't want you to have to wait in that room any longer," she explained with a smile. "Come with me."

And just like that, his spirits took a nosedive again. Following her down the narrow hallway, he entered the examination room.

"Have a seat. And here," she added, moving to a small cabinet that hid a tiny refrigerator, "have some water. It's warm out."

"Thanks."

When the door closed, he opened the bottle of water, drank half and then kicked out his feet. Now he figured he could play on his phone or just sit and stew.

For some unknown reason, he chose to do the latter. No matter how much he usually enjoyed scanning social media pages or texting his friends, his mind wasn't on anything but the reason he was there. Three days ago, Dr. Mason's assistant had called. It seemed the doctor had looked over his test results, found a problem, and wanted to speak to him in person.

He was twenty-two years old. As far as he was concerned, he was in his prime. He was well-built, not anywhere close to being overweight, and had never had a serious problem beyond breaking his arm when he slid into second base during an intense baseball playoff game in high school.

Honestly, he had no idea how a routine checkup had come to this.

"You're freaking out for no reason," he muttered as he leaned back in his chair. "It's probably nothing."

Crossing his feet in front of him, he pretended to believe that, but it was a hard sell. From everything he could tell, Dr. Mason was a busy man. He wasn't going to ask a guy to come to his office to discuss test results if there was nothing to talk about.

The door opening brought him to his feet.

When he saw that it was Dr. Mason and not Danielle, his already rapid pulse sped up.

"Sorry about the wait, Jonny," Dr. Mason said as he strode forward to shake hands. "It couldn't be helped."

"I didn't mind waiting."

"Since we've had more than a couple of patients coming in with either the flu or strep, I thought you might be more comfortable in here." He smiled slightly. "I don't want you to leave here feeling worse than when you came in."

"I appreciate that."

Dr. Mason motioned to the chair Jonny had just vacated. "Have a seat," he said as he sat down on the other side of the desk. He put on a pair of glasses as he opened the folder.

Then he looked Jonny in the eye.

"Jonny, when we asked for blood work, I expected some relatively good numbers. You seem to be in good health, you exercise, and your weight is good. Unfortunately, your cholesterol is through the roof."

It took a moment for the doctor's words to sink in. But when they did, Jonny breathed a sigh of relief. "Oh, boy. I was afraid it was something really bad, like you thought I had cancer or something."

Dr. Mason didn't crack a smile. "We didn't see any signs of cancer, but what we did find isn't good, son. Everything you complained about—feeling worn down, thirsty, and blurry vision—those are all signs that you're prediabetic. You're going to have to make some changes."

Jonny still wasn't sure why the doctor looked so worried. The "pre" part of his diagnosis meant that nothing bad had actually happened. "Don't I just have to stop eating cheeseburgers or something?"

"You do need to stop that. But your numbers are so high, I'm worried that something else could be going on." Looking up from the chart, he asked, "Do you have a history of heart disease in your family?"

"I don't think so. My parents are fine."

"What about your grandparents? Any idea about their health?"

"Both sets of my grandparents are Amish." Didn't that mean that they were healthy?

Dr. Mason's expression still didn't ease. "That doesn't mean you aren't at risk."

"I guess not. But, um, I haven't heard about anything."

"Let's focus on your parents. How are their cholesterol levels?"

"I'm not sure." Especially because he'd barely talked to either of them ever since he and his siblings had decided to think about becoming Amish.

"I suggest you call your parents and talk to them about that."

Yeah, like that would break the thick wall of ice that had formed between them. "I will. No problem."

Dr. Mason's eyes narrowed. "Son, I'm serious. You could have a heart attack."

Jonny chuckled. "I'm only twenty-two."

"Twenty-two-year-olds can have heart attacks. It's rare but not unheard of. This is serious."

"I understand."

"No, I don't think you do. Your cholesterol is 267. It should be around 180."

"That's almost a hundred points higher."

"Exactly." Dr. Mason started spouting off numbers about LDL and HDL and triglycerides. And then he handed Jonny the report and a packet of papers. "You have two months to get your numbers down. Read this and follow the guidelines, Jonny."

"Can't I just take a pill or something?"

"If we can't get a handle on it, that's an option. But the root of the matter is your lifestyle. You are going to need to make some big changes and follow the recommended diet."

"I'll do my best."

But instead of appearing pleased, Dr. Mason appeared even more concerned. "Jonny, I want to see you two months from today. We're going to do a blood draw again and see what we find out. If your lab results aren't better, then we'll need to do an EKG just to make sure you're not at an immediate risk."

"Yes, sir."

"Have that conversation with your parents, son. Talk to Martin, and your sisters, too. I wouldn't have brought you in here if I wasn't concerned."

"I will, but no one's ever mentioned anything."

"Let's hope that the next time we meet it will be a better conversation."

"I hope so, too."

Dr. Mason stood up. "Make sure to book your next appointment before you leave." When Jonny hesitated, he lowered his voice. "I'll be asking my assistant to give you a call in two weeks to see how you're doing."

"In two weeks?" What could they possibly need to know so soon?

"She'll be asking what changes you've made, son. I expect to hear that you've made quite a few."

"Yes, sir."

Three hours later, Jonny was sitting in his apartment and feeling like the bottom had just dropped out of his life. After a brief phone call with his mom, who'd said that she always had low cholesterol, he'd called up his dad.

And gotten the surprise of his life.

"Dad, are you sure your brother had a heart attack at thirty?" And died?

"I'm afraid so."

"I don't remember you speaking about that."

"Probably because it happened when you were little, Jonny. Just a toddler. And, to tell you the truth, thinking about my brother not being around still makes me sad."

He vaguely remembered once overhearing his grandparents talking about Hank. "I bet it was devastating for them."

"It was. It was hard on all of us. Hank was a good guy," his father murmured, emotion thick in his voice. "It's good you got checked and asked your mom and me about our health histories."

"I'll let the doctor know about Hank."

"Good. That's important. Don't worry about doing whatever he needs you to do, son. If he wants you to get some more tests, don't hesitate, okay? You're still on my health insurance, and it's top of the line. That's what it's there for."

Health insurance. He hadn't even thought about it.

Or the consequences of not having it.

"Thanks, Dad," he muttered, his mouth suddenly feeling like it was full of cotton.

"No need to thank me. I'm your father."

"But still . . . I appreciate it."

"Are you still entertaining this Amish nonsense?"

And just like that, all of the good feelings he'd been experiencing vanished in a heartbeat. "It's not nonsense."

"I know Kelsey fell in love and became Amish, but that doesn't mean that all four of you need to do the same. I know you and I have had our differences, but we can work them out, right?"

"Dad, me wanting to be Amish doesn't have anything to do with you and me. There's something about living more simply in Walden that appeals to me. I want a change of life."

"Living without electricity or a car isn't as idyllic as you might think. Are you still going to live there for the next couple of months?"

"I am. I found a job at a bicycle shop." Though he hadn't thought about his health when he'd interviewed, he figured getting more exercise could only help his cholesterol levels.

"You know I'd rather you go back to college, Jon."

They'd already had this conversation. Several times. "I know, but I don't want to enroll in another semester until I'm sure about my future." Jonny clenched his fists and reminded himself that his father was simply concerned.

"I guess not." His father sounded frustrated.

"Dad, I appreciate your help, but I'm not going to change my mind. If you can't accept it, you need to let me know."

"I'm trying, son."

"Do you want me to handle all this on my own?"

"No. Of course not." He sighed. "I know things have been hard ever since Mom and I decided to divorce. But I still want a relationship with you, son."

"I want that, too."

"Well, maybe this diagnosis from Dr. Mason is the Lord's way of forcing you and me to start talking."

Jonny thought that was a pretty far-fetched notion, but he didn't completely disagree. "Maybe so."

"When are you moving?"

"In one month." After his next blood draw.

"I'd like to see you before you leave. We can have lunch or something."

The invitation sounded awkward. Almost as awkward as accepting it was. "Okay."

"I love you, Jonny. Don't forget that, okay?"

"I love you, too, Dad."

"Follow the doctor's directions."

"I will."

"Good."

After they hung up, Jonny realized that his world really had just turned on its side. Now he was tied to their father in a way that Martin, Beth, and Kelsey weren't. And, if he didn't get better, he would need to be on insurance for the rest of his life. No way did he want to chance having a heart attack without being completely covered.

And that meant that he couldn't follow in his grandfather's footsteps and farm.

He didn't know what to do.

But as he thought about calling Martin or Beth and sharing everything, he frowned. Martin and Beth were older and sometimes shrugged off his concerns. It didn't matter if it was him worrying about being a freshman in high school, going to take his driver's test, or when Courtney Bellerman broke up with him and broke his heart. They'd always acted as if he was exaggerating things or worrying too much.

They weren't always wrong, either. Sometimes he actually was guilty of making a mountain out of a molehill.

Then there was everyone's attitude toward their parents. Jonny knew all of them liked being a united front. The last thing he wanted to do was risk one of them saying that he shouldn't take their father's insurance.

It was probably a lot better to keep things to himself. At least until he had something to worry about.

What would probably happen was that he'd try to eat a little better, his cholesterol numbers would go back to where they were supposed to be, and all of this would be in the past.

Exactly where it needed to stay.

CHAPTER 1

Two months later
August

"Ah, Jonny. Here you are, and as on time as ever," Brandon Matts said as he entered the Landen Bicycle Shop.

Jonny glanced at the clock behind him. It was only a quarter to eight in the morning. The store technically wasn't supposed to be open until nine, but here he was.

As was one of the store's best customers. Because of that, Jonny bit back a comment about Brandon taking advantage of him and joked instead. "Can't think of a place I'd rather be—besides sipping coffee on my back porch while in my pajamas."

Brandon chuckled like Jonny had just spouted the best joke ever. "I knew I could count on you for a laugh."

"Glad to be of service. What may I help you with?"

"Well, I was hoping you could help me look at some of your new portable charging stations."

"I can, no problem." Setting down his mug, which held

the very last of the coffee from the pot he'd made that morning, Jonny turned to a cabinet filled with portable chargers.

He'd been fussing with some new ideas for chargers. Because electric bikes used only a small amount of electricity at a time, it was easy and cost-effective to use solar power. He'd been testing different manufacturers in his spare time and felt like he'd come up with a couple that were both inexpensive and reliable—all with his boss Alan's approval.

He set the two most popular models on the counter. "Here you go."

Brandon didn't pick up, either. Instead, he turned his head this way and that, studying each as if it could snap at him with a little bit of encouragement. "Tell me the difference."

"This one is the basic model. It will likely charge a bicycle in an hour or two." Then Jonny picked up the bigger choice. "This one has more solar panels, a bigger portable battery source, and the connector is a little more user-friendly."

After he told Brandon the prices, the man whistled low. "The second is also almost double the price."

"It's got more bells and whistles and does more." He shrugged. "Quality costs money."

Brandon snorted. "You sure you want to be Amish? I'm starting to think that you could be a good used car salesman."

Jonny fought off a smile, but just barely. "Hey. Just because I'm trying to make a living doesn't mean I don't belong here."

"I canna say you're wrong about that." Staring at both, Brandon at last picked up the larger model. "You say this is easier to use?"

"I think so." He pointed to the connector, showed how the tubing retracted easily, then demonstrated how everything worked on the less expensive model.

"It seems I would be a fool to go with the cheaper one."

"Not necessarily. It works just fine."

"I might have to use it more often and be more frustrated with it, too."

"It's up to you." Jonny picked up his cup of coffee and took a sip, hating that he'd reached the bottom of the cup so fast. Now that he was on his new, low-cholesterol diet, a lot of his vices had gone out the window. He'd begun to really appreciate a good cup of coffee in the morning. It, along with his oatmeal or whole wheat toast and fruit, were his healthy substitutes for bacon and eggs.

"What's wrong, English? Out of *kaffi* already?"

"*Jah.*" Smiling at himself replying in Pennsylvania Dutch, he said, "The two cups of coffee my coffee maker makes always go down too fast."

"Hmm."

"I know." Pointing to the small coffee maker in the corner, he added, "I should go out and buy another coffee maker."

"I've got a better idea. You should head down to the Trailside Café. It's about two miles down the way," Brandon said, pointing to a narrow, seldom-used road. "You know it?"

"No. I didn't think anything was down there except for a couple of houses." All in need of a bit of repair.

"That's true, except now there's a coffee shop in the old barn on the Kramer property."

"So, you're saying there's a new coffee shop in an old barn?"

"*Jah.* Sure. I was there before I came over here." Brandon smiled. "If you're feeling blessed, she might even have a batch of apricot squares left."

"I don't think I like apricot." And he was pretty sure apricot squares weren't part of his new low-fat diet.

"If you don't, it's because you haven't given her squares a

shot." Looking a little dreamy—quite a feat for an Amish man in his midthirties—he continued. "Those things are a little taste of heaven, right here in Holmes County. They're almost as good as Treva's *kaffi*."

"You sound like a billboard."

"I'm a fan, that's what I am." Looking back down at the counter, Brandon sighed. "All right, Jonny. You wore me down and won me over. I'll take the more expensive charger." Pulling out his wallet from a pocket, he glared. "I suppose you're gonna charge me tax, too."

When Jonny had first started working at the shop, he'd been taken aback by some of the Amish men's dry sense of humor. Now he understood that give-and-take was part of the transaction. "Try as I might, the government makes me pay taxes just like everyone else."

"Figures." Slapping a hundred-dollar bill on the counter, he smiled. "Pleasure doing business with ya."

"I enjoy it, as well," Jonny replied, as he handed him change out of the cash box. "You need a bag or do you have one?"

"I've got a canvas carryall right here." After sliding the cardboard box holding the charger into his bag, he held out his hand. "Wishing you a good day, Jonny."

"To you, as well."

"Go visit Treva and get yourself a cup of coffee. It will improve your mood, English." He winked. "She's got chocolate and orange scones, too, if you don't have a mind to live on the apricot side of life."

Jonny couldn't stop his lips from twitching. Brandon certainly did have a way of turning a phrase. "Yes, sir."

Brandon tipped his hat and went out the door. A couple of minutes later, he and his bike had moved out of sight.

Jonny checked the clock again. It wasn't even eight yet. Alan, his boss and the owner of the Landen Bicycle Shop,

had told him to come and go as he saw fit because their customers didn't usually come in during normal business hours.

It was yet another reason he was glad he'd approached
Alan for a job. Even though his dad was going to pay for his
medical insurance untilo he was twenty-six, Jonny had always been a planner. And that meant that he couldn't ignore
the fact that his body was going to need checkups every six
months for the next couple of years. Being diagnosed with
prediabetes and the beginning stages of hypertension did
that to a person.

After weighing the cons of leaving against the advantages
of another cup of coffee—a freshly brewed cup that was actually good—the coffee won. He was tired and already having doubts about living with his grandparents.

Ironically, he didn't find living Plain as difficult an adjust-
ment as living with his grandparents. They were good people
but set in their ways. Jonny had essentially lived on his own
for quite a while. When he was in high school, he'd switched
back and forth between his parents' houses all the time.
They'd made sure he had what he needed but hadn't come
close to watching his every move. He was the youngest of
four children, and his parents had busy lives. He was used to
being independent and being by himself a lot.

Things were completely different at the farm. Not only
did his *mommi* and *dawdi* enjoy eating breakfast and supper
with him, they also wanted to visit about his day. Sometimes
for a whole hour. Sometimes two.

He loved them but needed some space.

And yes, some caffeine, because he was still having a difficult time adjusting to his grandparents' normal schedule.

Decision made, he put Alan's "BE BACK SOON" sign on
the door, locked it, and hopped on his bike.

Pedaling down the road that Brandon had mentioned, Jonny
took a moment to appreciate the many changes that had re-

cently taken place in his life. Eighteen months ago, he'd sat with his two sisters and older brother, commiserating on their collective discontent.

Being the youngest, he'd kept his mouth closed for most of the conversation. He'd been a college sophomore and bored with classes, though he'd known a lot of people who felt the same way.

His sisters and Martin had described a whole lot of other problems, though. And it wasn't just dissatisfaction with jobs or current relationships. It was a yearning for a completely different way of life.

They'd yearned to live like their grandparents did. He'd been so swept up in their dreams—and the idea of doing something collectively—that he'd gone with his siblings to talk to their *mommi* and *dawdi*. Eventually, it was decided that only Martin and Kelsey would live "Amish" at first, because they'd learned that there was a whole lot more to becoming Amish than a simple desire to live off the grid.

Martin and Kelsey had learned a lot that year. Martin had mixed feelings, while Kelsey felt like she'd fit in from the very start. She'd even married an Amish preacher!

Now it was his turn to live Amish.

He'd quit college and moved in with Josiah and Sylvia with little worries. And then, just as he was working in a field, he saw a group of Amish men and women about his age riding electric bikes on the hills around the farm.

One conversation led to the next, and eventually, he'd gotten hired at the Landen Bicycle Shop. Alan was New Order Amish, had an affinity and a heart for mission work overseas, and was eager for Jonny to take over the business.

It truly felt as if the Lord had paved the way for him.

He was still waiting for his heart to catch up, though. He didn't want to simply find living Amish easy. He wanted to yearn to be Amish. He wanted to feel as if he was going to honor the Lord by living Plain.

He hadn't had the nerve to share his thoughts with anyone, however. It felt too selfish and maybe too self-centered to share his goals with his grandparents.

He'd also begun to realize that his thoughts weren't exactly in line with Martin's and Beth's. Martin and Beth were feeling torn not only about becoming Amish but also about their jobs and their relationships with their parents. He might be wrong, but he didn't want to do anything to make them feel like their struggles weren't important or valued.

Richard, Kelsey's preacher husband, had once told him that each man and woman had to take his or her own path in life. He'd reminded Jonny that the Lord was with him and that was whom he should look for to be by his side.

Jonny believed Richard, but he also wasn't sure his faith was that strong. He needed his grandparents' and siblings' support in addition to God's.

Sometimes he wondered if God got frustrated with him, because He'd obviously been the one to give Jonny such a wonderful family in the first place.

A pair of passing walkers pulled his attention back to his need for coffee . . . and there was the Trailside Café. Down a little path next to an Amish house with a large front porch and gorgeous garden. The store truly was in a converted barn, but that was where the easy description of it ended.

It was like nothing he'd ever imagined finding on an Amish farm. The owners had put in a glass-and-metal garage door in the front that replaced the barn's door. It let in lots of light and allowed customers to be greeted by steel beams, metal and wooden tables and chairs, and gorgeous primitive-looking quilts hung from some of the rafters.

Honestly, it looked like a place one would find in Aspen, Colorado, or Lake Tahoe. Somewhere expensive and trendy. Not on a farm off a bike trail in Walden, Ohio.

To his surprise, there were two cars and a number of bicycles parked nearby. Perhaps it wasn't as far off the beaten path as he'd thought.

He slowly rode his bike to an area off to the side and parked it on one of the many black iron bike racks. Their design was yet another unexpected and strangely cool feature.

When he entered the red barn, he was greeted by the scent of coffee, the sound of laughter and conversation, and a bakery window with three different kinds of baked goods.

Also behind the counter was an incredible-looking espresso machine—one that looked like it would be found in a fancy coffee shop in a high-end area of a major city.

There was also a line of people, a golden retriever on a leash, a dark grey cat curled up on the top of a couch, and a whole lot of framed prints of inked drawings of people and animals. The prints were a nice contrast to the quilts hanging from the ceiling and the stained-concrete rust-colored floor.

Every bit of it looked fantastic and inviting. Brandon had absolutely not been exaggerating about the place.

Hopefully, the coffee wouldn't be a disappointment.

"Bennett! Here you go," a woman called out as she entered the area from a back room. "A whole pan of apricot bars, just for you."

"Just for me and my whole office," a woman corrected. "Even I couldn't eat a whole pan of these beauties."

"At least not in one sitting, ain't so?"

"You got me there. Thanks, Treva. You've just made me look like a hero."

"Surely not." Treva's green eyes sparkled underneath perfectly formed dark eyebrows and wisps of raven-colored hair that was gathered at her nape and covered by a white *kapp*.

"It's true," the woman said. "Thanks again for making them special."

"Thank you for ordering them." She popped a hand on

her hip, looking just like a saucy barmaid in a pub out of an Irish movie or novel. After taking the woman's money, she moved to stand in front of the coffee machine. "Now, who's next?" She scanned the area. Seemed to take in each person individually.

And then settled on him.

Their eyes met. Jonny felt his insides twist and settle. Just as if his entire being had simply been waiting to meet her.

Man, where had that thought come from?

"Hi," he said. Because he couldn't think of anything better.

She blinked, giving him a better look at her long eyelashes. "Hi. You're new."

"Yes," he replied. "I am."

Her full lips parted. For a second, Jonny could've sworn he'd spied a look of longing in her eyes.

"I'm next, Treva," a woman in her fifties or sixties called out. "Sorry, you didn't see me. I was looking at the pastry case."

"I'm glad you were looking, Joan. What would you like today?" She smiled. "If you're wanting to try something new, my coconut butterscotch bars are delightful."

"I bet. But . . . I better stick to my usual. A large cup of coffee, black, and an orange and chocolate scone."

"Gotcha."

Standing five people back, Jonny heard conversations begin again. He opened the door for the woman holding the dish of apricot bars and even leaned down to pet the golden retriever when it nudged his leg.

He felt like he was in a different place. Like Brigadoon or in the middle of the Harry Potter World at Universal. Somewhere that he'd stumbled upon but immediately felt as if he'd been there before. Or, at the very least, that he wanted to be there for a little while longer.

Somewhere that was familiar but unexpectedly different. But someplace that made him feel good. And wanted.

The only problem was that he feared it was the beauty of the woman behind the counter that made him feel that way. Sure, she was striking, but it was her personality that had made him entranced.

Treva seemed to be an artless combination of sweetness and spice. That appealed to him. He wanted to watch her make coffee, listen to her talk to everyone in line, and linger nearby for hours.

Just to hear what was going to come out of her mouth next.

As Treva continued to wait on each customer like they were doing her a favor by asking her to make them lattes, he was barely able to look away. He was captivated.

He hoped she didn't already have a boyfriend or husband, but how could she not? She was Amish, and the Amish guys he knew weren't idiots. They'd do everything they could to capture her smile.

He knew he was going to try, just in case everyone in the entire Walden area was blind.

CHAPTER 2

It was as if the Lord had taken all the best parts of a man, mixed them together, and came up with him. As Treva stood behind the counter and patiently waited for the couple to pick out their choices, she couldn't help but eye the gorgeous man standing behind them.

He wasn't Amish. At least, she didn't think so. He was dressed kind of Plain, but it wasn't a real match. Instead, he looked like he was balancing two worlds, which was a ridiculous thing for her to even be thinking about. Was it even possible to be both Plain and fancy?

She hadn't thought so. Reuben certainly hadn't.

Annoyed that her ex-boyfriend had crossed her mind even for a second, Treva smiled at the couple on the other side of the counter.

"Are you still deciding?"

"I'm afraid so, hon," the lady said. "Everything looks so good." As if she was suddenly aware that there were people behind her and her husband, she turned to the perfect man standing behind them. "I'm so sorry. I won't be but a second more."

"Take your time. I'm good."

Oh! Now that he was standing closer, she noticed that he had a deep, scratchy voice! Unable to help herself, she glanced at him again.

She should be ashamed of herself, but how could she help it? He was standing right in front of her.

"I'll take the scone . . . no, the coconut thingy . . . no, the cinnamon roll." The lady sighed. "Maybe we should get all three, Steve?"

While the lady's husband weighed in, Treva looked at the stranger again. He was wearing an expensive pair of sunglasses, a loose pair of jeans, and a plain white-colored shirt. There was no reason he should have caught her attention the way he had.

Or . . . maybe there was.

His blond hair under a ball cap was gorgeous. It was that perfect shade of blond—warm and golden instead of brassy. The scruff on his cheeks and jaw was one shade lighter. Somehow it served to make him even look more masculine.

Or maybe it was his tan.

Or maybe it was the fact that he was wearing worn-looking white Converse tennis shoes without socks.

He was so very different from either her Amish customers or many of her English ones, with their phones and trendy outfits. Unexpected.

"Treva, did you hear me?"

"Hmm? Oh, sorry. *Nee*. What did you want?"

"One of each of your scones. Chocolate-orange and blueberry."

She immediately put one of each in the bag in her hands. "Here you go. Is that it?"

"Yep. Well, two black coffees, too, dear."

"Coming right up." Focusing back on her job, she tallied

the two coffees and two treats, gave them the total, then set everything on the counter for the couple to take.

And then there he was.

Her mouth went a little dry. "What would you like?"

His lips twitched. "Coffee, please."

"You need to be more specific."

"Pardon?"

"Do you want a latte? Espresso? A cup of coffee? Black? Cream, sugar, Equal? Large or small?" She winked at him. "We need specifics around here."

The corners of his lips turned up. "All right. I'll have a latte. Large."

"Sorry, but I still need more information. What kind of milk? Regular, low-fat, almond . . . ?"

"Low-fat milk." He leaned forward slightly. "Do you need to know anything else?"

He was almost flirting!

Or, maybe he actually was. It had been so long, she'd almost forgotten how to flirt. "All I need to know now is what you want to eat." She smiled. "Maybe an apricot bar? They're the specialty around here."

"Thanks, but no."

"All right, perhaps a cinnamon bun?"

"Just coffee."

Feeling a little let down that he didn't want to try anything that she'd made fresh that morning—though she didn't know why—Treva nodded. "All right. You can wait here or over to the side if you'd rather. It's just me this morning, so everyone has to be patient."

"Understood." His lips curved up again. Not to a complete smile but to the hint of one. Enough to make her wish that he didn't have his sunglasses on.

Before she found herself staring at him any longer, she

quickly turned and got to work on his drink. Behind her, the door chimed and more voices filled the space.

"Hiya, Treva!"

Waiting for the man's milk to heat, she turned around. And wished she hadn't. "Hi, Mamm."

As she turned back around, she could feel her mother make her way to the front of the line. "Excuse me. So sorry. Don't mind me. I'm her mother."

After a few folks murmured their greetings, her mother moved around the counter. "Honey, I came to see how I could help you."

"There was no need. I'm doing just fine." Well, she had been before her eager mother had burst into the room. She loved her mother dearly, she truly did. But Treva was trying to prove to her family that she could run this coffee shop on her own and do a good job of it, too.

She couldn't do that if her *mamm* was constantly attempting to help.

"I know you have everything well in hand, but I had a few hours to spare." Without waiting, she washed her hands, and said, "Did you want anything besides your coffee, young man?"

"No thanks."

"Are you sure? My daughter makes all of these treats herself. She gets up before dawn so they're fresh."

He took off his sunglasses, revealing a set of blue eyes framed with thick eyelashes. "That's great, but I'm good."

Her mother seemed immune to his charms. All she did was frown. "Are you sure . . . ?"

Practically feeling the new tension in the air, Treva hurried to pour the hot milk into the espresso.

"It's impressive that she gets up early to bake, but I'll just take the latte."

"I bet if you just tried—"

Treva finally intervened. "Mamm, don't. He said he didn't want anything else."

"I'm just saying that a lot of men prefer the scones," her mother said. "Or sometimes she makes a breakfast popover with ham and cheese."

Wariness edged into the man's blue eyes. And who could blame him? Her tiny mother had become the Doberman of coffee shop workers—never taking no for an answer.

"I'm so sorry about her," Treva said. "Here's your coffee."

"How much is it?"

Feeling embarrassed about her mother's pushy behavior, she whispered, "It's your first time here. It's on the house."

"I'll pay." When she was about to protest, he said in a firm tone, "I insist."

"All right. In that case, it's four dollars." They shared a smile. "I hope you enjoy your latte."

"Me, too."

She stared at him. There had been something telling in his tone. As if one simple cup of coffee meant something to him.

"Hey, Treva!"

Turning to the next customer, Treva attempted to regain some of her pep. "Hi, Monica. What can I help you with?"

"Four scones, two of each flavor."

"I'll get them, dear," her mother interrupted. "You can get this handsome man his change."

This was awful. She was in a terrible, terrible nightmare, where the most perfect man she'd ever seen had wandered into her life and her mother had scared him away.

"How much change do I owe you?"

"I gave her a twenty."

"So I owe you sixteen back."

"It would seem so," he said in a low tone. It sounded serious, though his eyes were lit with interest.

Almost as if he saw something in her that he liked. Which she should probably not care about because she'd sworn off men.

At least she intended to. For the next five years.

"Here you go," she said. Then, figuring she'd already made a cake of herself, she said, "Are you new here in town or just riding through?"

"I'm new."

"Where you from?"

"Cleveland." He shrugged. "Thereabouts."

"Well, welcome to Walden."

"Thank you. My name's Jonny."

"I'm Treva."

"And this is your place?"

She couldn't help but lift her chin. "It is. It's small and it's also on my family's farm, but it's all mine."

"Congratulations. I like how you decorated it."

"Thank you. I like it, too."

"I reckon owning one's own business isn't easy."

"It isn't, but then again, neither is working for someone else."

He grinned. "Point taken."

"No offense taken, I hope."

"Not at all. Glad to meet you. I'll be back."

"Thanks. I mean, I hope so." Oh no! She sounded desperate and slightly creepy! "I mean, if you like the coffee, you should come back."

"I'm sure I will."

"Next person in line, please," her mother called out.

Effectively snuffing out any hope of more conversation between her and the mysterious Jonny.

He smiled at her. Thankfully, looking amused instead of horrified. Then, with a slight wave of his hand, he walked back out.

"How may I help you?" Treva asked the woman in line.

"Did he give you his number?" the customer asked.

She blinked. "Pardon me?"

"Come on, Treva. He was staring at you like you were the main attraction in here and not your magical coffee or amazing baked goods. It was something to see."

She'd thought so, too. Not that she'd ever admitted it, though.

"So . . . did he ask for your number?"

"*Nee.*"

"That's too bad. I was hoping I was witnessing love at first sight or something and that you slipped him your phone number."

"That didn't happen. And I'm Amish, *jah*? So I've got no phone number to give him."

"Bummer." She leaned closer. "Well, I hope he comes in again, because man, is he cute. Okay, he's better than that, right? He's hot as a wildfire." She waved her hand like it had just gotten singed.

Treva giggled at the woman's silliness but couldn't find it in her heart to disagree. Mainly because she was right. Jonny was truly something more than merely cute. Hot.

Which she definitely should not be thinking about. "What would you like?"

"It's been a hard decision, but I decided on a large mocha latte with a chocolate scone."

"Chocolate mood today?"

"Always, but you know how crazy-good those scones are. Seriously, you should box them up and sell them for fifteen dollars for six."

"That much?"

"It's not that much. Not for the grated orange zest and that chocolate you like to use. You should give packages of your baked goods a try, Treva."

"I might."

"I'll look for boxes next time I come in."

"Well, today's order will be right up. Mamm, get Hailie a chocolate scone."

"Coming right up. Do you need anything else, dear?" she asked Hailie.

"Thanks, Mrs. Kramer, but I better not."

"I understand."

Hailie smiled at her mother the way everyone did except for her. Like she was Betty Crocker and their long-lost favorite aunt all rolled into one. It was as sweet as it was aggravating.

"Thanks, Mamm." As Treva turned back to the machine, she had to admit that everything really was moving better now that her mother had arrived. Why did she fight her mother's assistance so much?

Was it because she was trying to prove herself to her clients and her family? Or was it more of a matter of her trying to prove her worth to herself?

Ever since her first small business had failed—right around the time that she and Reuben had broken up—she'd been having a hard time with her confidence. Now even the simplest ideas made her think twice.

So did every future business decision. It was like her regular, comfortable personality had gone walking and in its place was a new, quiet version of herself.

A tentative one. Almost shy.

Treva didn't know if she liked this new version or not. Sure, she was more thoughtful and spent a lot less money. Those were good things.

So was the fact that her heart was carefully coddled and safe.

But did she miss being a little more impulsive and free-spirited?

She did.

She missed the girl she'd once been. She seemed almost a stranger now. She didn't know if it was possible to ever get her old self back.

She reckoned it wasn't. Too much time had passed, and it seemed much healthier to look forward instead of behind.

But sometimes she wished things were different. Or at least she was.

CHAPTER 3

Even though their long talks and many questions sometimes wore him out, Jonny loved his grandparents with his whole heart. Josiah and Sylvia were in their early seventies and so smart. They were also easy to be around and kind. They had a knack for encouraging him to ask questions about living Amish without making him feel either embarrassed or like he was prying into their lives.

They also were fairly spry and didn't need help with much except maybe splitting logs for the wood-burning fireplace in the living room.

All in all, Jonny thought living with them was great. He hardly even noticed that they didn't have electricity anymore. Life was simply easy at their house.

Except when it came to suppertime. He was starting to dread the meal.

He was embarrassed about that, too.

In his defense, he had some pretty good reasons for his feelings. The first had to do with timing. Supper was promptly every evening at five thirty. Him needing to work late didn't come into consideration. As far as his *mommi* and *dawdi* were concerned, they'd eaten most of their meals at five thirty and it had served them well.

It didn't serve his hours at the bike shop all that well, however.

They didn't care about that.

More than once, Jonny had found himself pedaling home as fast as he could to sit down at the table on time. And yes, they noticed if he was five minutes late.

As far as Jonny was concerned, he was a little too old to be stressed about getting to a dinner table on time every single night.

The second reason dinner was difficult was because his grandmother was ignoring his new dietary needs. Completely.

This had come as a surprise.

He'd explained to both of them about his need to eat more vegetables, chicken, whole grains, and fish. His *mommi* had patted his hand and said she'd understood.

Then she'd ignored everything and continued cooking the way she had for fifty years.

No matter how many times he'd reminded her about his new diet, she'd refused to make any changes. She also got her feelings hurt if he either tried to make a heart-healthy substitution (such as steamed broccoli instead of cheesy broccoli-rice casserole) or didn't eat big helpings of calorie- and fat-laden food. It was maddening.

His *dawdi* was no help at all. Not only did he seem unconcerned about Jonny's doctor's instructions, he also never took Jonny's side when he complained that every item on the plate was filled with butter or covered in sauce. Actually, the most his grandfather ever did when his grandmother started on her guilt lecture was give Jonny a sympathetic look.

The final reason supper was beginning to really bother

him was because of how long the meal took. Not only was it a large meal, it also was his grandparents' time to visit and relax. Jonny understood and appreciated that.

But sometimes a meal lasted almost two hours. Add to that helping in the kitchen to clean up everything, then any chores outside or in the barn . . . well, it made for a long evening.

And he'd already worked a long day.

If he was going to remain at their house, Jonny knew something had to be done. He just didn't know how to broach it.

All that was why he was currently sitting in his chair, in need of a shower because he hadn't gotten home in time to take one, and staring at a plate of mashed potatoes, gravy, fried fish, creamed spinach, and rolls.

And could barely control his irritation when his lovely, very sweet—but very stubborn—grandmother directed a question at him.

"How was your day, dear?"

Jonny paused with his fork halfway to his mouth. "It was good. Things at the shop are going well."

"Did you do anything interesting?"

"Not really."

"Hmm."

He glanced at his grandfather, who was paying close attention to his plate of fried perch.

His *dawdi* didn't care for fish, a sure sign that something was on his grandmother's mind but she was taking her time to meander over to it in the conversation.

"Why do you ask?" he finally asked.

His *mommi* refolded the napkin in her lap. "Oh, no reason."

"Okay." He popped the fork of mashed potatoes in his mouth at last. Even though he knew he shouldn't be eating them, happiness exploded in his mouth. "You really do make the best mashed potatoes, Mommi."

"I'm surprised you noticed. You hardly put any on your plate."

"I'm not supposed to be eating foods with butter and cream," he reminded her. Yet again.

"A little bit now and then won't hurt ya." She leaned forward. "But I would still like to know what else you did today."

He put his fork down. "Mommi, I got up early, did chores, worked at the bicycle shop all day, and hurried home to have supper with you and Dawdi. I love you, but I'm hungry and in need of a shower. I'm also too tired to try to figure out what you're needing to know."

Her eyes widened. "Jonathan, I don't need to 'need' anything."

His *dawdi* grunted. "Sylvia, give the boy a break, *jah*? It's obvious that he's got no conversation left today."

Jonny shot his grandfather a grateful look as he shoveled in another bite of fish.

"Fine," his grandmother said as she rearranged the napkin on her lap. "I heard from Rachel Lapp. She spotted you at Treva's Trailside Café. Was Rachel imagining things?"

"*Nee.* I did go over there."

"Well, what did you think?"

"The coffee was good."

"And the apricot bars? Did you love them?"

"I didn't eat one."

She frowned. "Why not?"

Jonny didn't know if he could go through his dietary needs yet again.

Placing his fork down, he realized that he was barely holding his temper in check. "Why is what I ordered a conversational point? Are you really discussing my every move with Rachel Lapp?"

Hurt filled her eyes. "It wasn't like that."

"It sounds like it was."

After an exaggerated sigh, she said, "Fine. Some people—"

"That would be Rachel," his *dawdi* said.

"Thought that there were some sparks happening between the two of you."

"I ordered some coffee. I paid money for it. She handed me both after I paid, and we chatted for a minute or two. Then I rode back to the shop. That's the end of the story."

"You sure?"

"Positive."

When his grandfather started laughing, she scowled at him. "Stop laughing, Josiah."

"It's kind of hard not to. You are playing matchmaker to our handsome grandson, who likely hasn't ever needed help finding a girl to date his entire life."

"That's not exactly true," Jonny said.

"Close enough."

His grandmother picked up her fork again. "All right, Jonny, I'll let this subject go. But I do hope you visit Trailside again."

"I probably will. The coffee was great."

"The owner is great, too. Give Treva a chance, dear. And eat your supper. You've hardly touched a thing." Reaching for the plate of fish, she said, "How about another piece?"

Jonny's stomach clenched. He had a feeling it was going to be easier to fall in love with Treva than to convince his grandmother to change her cooking habits.

"Pick your battles, son," his *dawdi* said as he reached for the plate of fish. "It will make suppertime a whole lot easier for you."

Jonny reckoned his grandfather had a good point.

CHAPTER 4

It was half-past six in the morning, and Jonny's sudden appearance had scared her half to death.

He was also laughing at her reaction, which Treva didn't think was very nice. She couldn't fault his laughter too much. She'd probably jumped a foot in the air.

"How about you announce yourself next time?" she chided, though she knew it made no sense. She had a business, and the barn door had not only been slid open, but all the propane-powered lights also were on.

His eyes flared. "Okay, if that's what you want," he murmured as he walked toward her.

She was acting like a shrew. "It isn't. I'm sorry for snapping at you. Please ignore me."

He studied her face. "Are you all right, Treva?"

"I'm fine." She rubbed her head. It smarted, though she hadn't actually hit it very hard against the shelf she'd been under when he'd appeared next to her feet. "I'll survive."

And just like that, the last bit of humor in his expression evaporated. Striding to the opening on the side of the counter,

Jonny reached for her. "I'm sorry," he said in a gentle tone as he cupped both of his hands around her arms. "I truly did think you'd heard me walk inside. I promise, I wouldn't have laughed if I had thought you were actually hurt. Would you like me to look at it? Do you have a bump on your head?"

"I don't think so."

His blue eyes peered at her a moment. Then, before she even knew what he was about, he reached for the pin on her *kapp*. "I think we better check."

Shocked, she drew back. "You canna take off my *kapp*!"

"Um, sure I can. I'll hand you the pin and look at your head real quick. After we make sure you're none the worse for wear, you can put it back on."

He was making it sound like it was no different than examining a hurt finger. She thought differently. "I think not."

He frowned. "I'm not trying to do anything weird. I have a sister who's now Amish. I'm familiar with *kapps*."

Jonny really was being sincere. Which made her reticence feel more foolish. "It's not that I think you are being . . . weird. It's more the fact that my head feels fine now." She wasn't lying, either. It almost did feel okay.

Taking a step back, he nodded. "Understood."

Smiling at him more softly, she said, "I think my pride is more injured than anything."

"There's no reason for you to be ashamed of hitting your head. I am sorry I scared you. It was wrong of me not to announce myself. Like I told you earlier, I thought you heard me come in."

"I didn't expect you to be here so early." And there it was. She'd now made it obvious that she took note of when he was there. "Um, I mean, most people don't usually walk in until after seven." She felt her face heat up as she prepared for him to tease her about that, too.

He was still studying her. "I got up early to help my grandma with the eggs. I had intended to help her with some washing, but she shooed me away." Sounding aggrieved, he added, "Mommi told me that she was not too old to carry a load of clothes out to the line."

"That sounds like Sylvia." Treva didn't know her well, but she knew enough about the woman to know that she was full of pride and still able-bodied.

Still standing so close that she could smell the hint of soap on his skin, Jonny continued. "When I left the farm, I couldn't handle going to the bike shop before seven."

"Why is that?"

"Someone would show up."

She wasn't following him. Studying his face, she noticed that he had a faint scar near his lip and yet again had scruff on his cheeks. "And the problem is . . . what?"

"That the shop actually has business hours. I've been ignoring them because I like being there, but I've started to think that maybe there are other, better ways to be spending my free time than working ten hours a day."

Ten hours was too much, though she was pretty sure she put in that many hours from time to time, as well. "That's a dilemma."

"Maybe it is, maybe it isn't. I don't know. Things have been a little crazy in my life. I've started to think that I worry about all the wrong things."

"Or you'd simply like to have more free time?" she hinted. After all, she was beginning to think the very same thing.

"Yeah. Maybe that, too." He smiled.

"Perhaps you need to adjust your hours? You know, open later and close earlier? Or even close in the middle of the day for a spell?"

"Maybe. I'll ask Alan." He continued to gaze at her, no longer looking for bumps or bruises but seeming to be fixated on her lips. For one moment—or maybe it was only five seconds—her breath caught. Then he seemed to realize that he still had one of his hands on her arm and was standing mere inches from her.

He stepped back. "So, um, you're sure that you are all right?"

"*Jah.*"

He walked back around to the front. "When you're ready, I'll be needing a coffee."

"I'm ready. Unless you'd like to try one of my scones or other treats?"

"No thanks. Just coffee will do me."

She nodded. Just before she turned away, Treva caught a look on his face as he stared at the three containers of freshly made baked goods. He was looking at them with such a look of distaste, it brought forth yet another wave of insecurity through her.

What was going on? Did he just not like bakery goods, or was it something more personal? Also, why was she feeling a little offended that he didn't want to ever try at least one?

Shaking off the thoughts, which didn't make any sense, she pinned a smile on her face. "What would you like to drink this morning?"

"A large latte with almond milk."

"Okay."

She got to work on his drink, thinking that he wasn't the only customer who seemed to be enjoying fake milk. But after his first visit, he was the one who never wavered.

"Are you unable to have dairy products?"

"What do you mean?"

"Oh, I was curious about your liking for almond milk. I thought maybe you were allergic to dairy products or something." Yet again, she was wondering why she was so attuned to him.

"I'm not allergic to dairy."

"Ah." Of course, the moment she spoke, she wished she'd kept her mouth shut. Why was she acting like she understood when she didn't? Furthermore, why did his preferences even matter?

They didn't.

Well, they shouldn't.

After frothing the almond milk, she added a nice foam topping, carefully put on the lid, and handed the cup to him. "Here you go. I hope you have a nice day."

"Thanks." He pulled out six dollars from his pocket and set them on the counter. Once again, giving her a tip in addition to the price.

She took the money. "Thanks."

But instead of quickly moving away, he took a sip of his drink and then kind of leaned against the counter. Like he had all the time in the day. "So, what do you do when you aren't serving coffee or baking?"

"I help out on the farm."

"And what else?"

He was staring at her in such a way that she wished she had a better answer than she did. But she didn't. "I sleep, I suppose." And yes, she was starting to wish she was a lot more interesting.

By now she knew enough about him to realize that he was still English, was thinking about being Amish, and managed a bicycle shop. He also had a confidence about him that made her believe that he had even more important things hidden underneath the surface that she didn't know about.

"That's a shame."

His gaze was kind, but that didn't stop her from blushing. She hated feeling inadequate. "I'm not sure what you're wishing I said."

"I wasn't wishing for you to say anything. I'm just surprised, that's all."

"Why?"

He fussed with the navy blue ball cap on his head. Took it off, pulled back the chunk of hair that had started to curl over his brow. Put it back on. "Well, you're young. Aren't you supposed to be enjoying life?"

"I am young, but I also have started my own business. I have more and more people coming in every week. I'm enjoying that."

"Of course. You're right. Sorry if I made you uncomfortable. That was the last thing I intended." He sipped his drink. "This is great. Just like last time."

A little part of her deflated some more. For the first time since she'd started her business, she couldn't care less about the quality of her coffee. "I'm pleased you are enjoying it. Have a good day."

"Yeah." He paused, then kind of thumped his hand on the counter. "You, too."

Just as he walked out the door, Treva's best friend, Emma Jane, appeared. "Hiya." She directed a sweet smile Jonny's way.

He stopped. "*Gut matin.*"

"My name is Emma Jane. I think we met the other day at the deli?"

"I remember. You were buying turkey."

"And you were buying roast beef." She chuckled. "You are sounding more Amish with each passing day."

Watching the exchange, Treva clenched her teeth. She couldn't believe that Emma Jane had met Jonny and had never said a word!

And now, here he was, smiling at her in a bashful, adorable way—all while she was watching from behind a counter.

"Thanks, I think."

Just as Jonny started to turn away, Emma Jane reached out and touched his arm. "How goes your bike shop?"

"It's not mine. But it's going well. You should come in sometime."

"I might . . . but I'm not sure I need an electric bike."

Treva felt her insides tighten. This conversation wouldn't end—and Emma Jane was flirting with him! Though a part of her knew she should turn around and at least pretend to fuss with the espresso machine, she continued to watch.

Jonny's beautiful blue eyes warmed. "I sell other things. Water bottles, packs for your bike, guidebooks."

"Maybe I'll surprise you one day and come inside."

"I hope you will." After flashing Emma Jane another smile, he sauntered out without sparing Treva another look.

Her stomach sank.

Emma Jane, to Treva's dismay, didn't come in right away. Instead, she remained where she was, no doubt just in case he wanted to speak to her some more.

Or perhaps, admire the way he looked getting on his bike.

Treva supposed she couldn't blame the girl. After all, she was standing behind the counter doing pretty much the same thing. In fact, she'd just realized that if she tilted her head just so, she could watch Jonny slip on his helmet, then peddle off.

What did that say about her?

She wasn't sure, but she had a feeling the description would involve words like *desperate* and *infatuated*.

"Treva, hi."

"Hiya." And yes, her voice was flat.

Emma Jane didn't appear to notice. "So, this is the second time I've seen that handsome Jonny Schrock. What do you know about him?"

She hurriedly picked up a rag and began wiping down the already-clean counter. "Not too much." Only now did she know his last name. Added to the list was that he liked almond milk and had a strange aversion to baked goods.

A sweet frown marred Emma Jane's perfect brow. "That still doesn't ring a bell. Is he related to Sylvia and Josiah Schrock?"

Treva knew Emma Jane was in a different church district than the Schrocks. "*Jah*. I'm pretty sure he's their grandson." Actually, she knew that for a fact.

"And he works at Landen Bike Shop. For how long? Is this just a passing fancy?"

She didn't know. Of course, she didn't know, because all they ever talked about was his preferences for milk and snacks. And today's bump on her head. She mentally rolled her eyes. No wonder he'd seemed so smitten by Emma Jane!

"I have no idea what his long range plans are, Em. You'll have to figure that out for yourself."

"I will. Alan Wilson owns the bike shop, right?"

"I think so. We haven't talked about that."

Emma Jane blinked before staring at her hard. One long look telling a whole story. "Treva."

And . . . there came her awkward blush again. When was she ever going to get over Reuben and feel good about herself again? "Em, would you like a coffee?"

"*Jah*, but in a minute." Still looking thoughtful, she glanced back out the window before facing Treva again. "Wait. Did he have a sister who married a preacher and turned Amish?"

"I don't know. Maybe."

"Come on. You've got to remember all those goings-on as much as I do. Remember how they had their grandchildren living with them, and the woman ended up turning Amish and marrying the preacher, Richard Miller?"

"Kind of."

But not really. The Amish community in Holmes County was a large one. Not only were there more than forty thousand Amish in the population, but there also were many different denominations of Amish. Conservative like the Swartzentruber Amish all the way to the most liberal Beachy Amish. In addition, each group was divided into several church districts. All that meant that it was impossible to know everyone who wore a *kapp* or drove a buggy.

Or rode an electric bicycle, it seemed.

"How do you know so much about them, Emma Jane?"

Looking embarrassed, she said, "My sister. She had her heart set on Richard Miller for a while—especially after he'd been asked to join the lot. She told me all the gossip about Kelsey Schrock and her family."

"Oh."

"I know. Her interest in Richard bordered on infatuation. It didn't serve her well."

"Hmm." Knowing that she'd likely save that thought for another day, Treva picked up a mug. "How about that coffee now?"

"Danke. I'll take a caramel coffee. Iced. To go."

"You got it. Want any treats?"

"I better not. My waistline is starting to look a little wide, I think."

"I doubt that. You are as pretty as ever."

Emma Jane's cheeks bloomed. "Thank you, Treva. You are looking well, too."

Treva smiled at her longtime friend while she waited for the shot of coffee to dispense. Then thought of something else.

"What happened with your sister?"

"What do you mean?"

"Has she found another man yet?"

Emma Jane shook her head. "Unfortunately, *nee*. She's broken up about it, too. And frustrated, if you want to know the truth."

"Why's she frustrated?"

"Well, she keeps saying yes to dates or to men who come calling. But within ten or fifteen minutes, she knows that nothing good is going to come of them meeting each other. The good ones are hard to find, you know."

Treva did know that. Not wanting to dwell on her own past, she attempted to put a positive spin on things. "I bet one of these days she'll feel differently. There are still a lot of good men around, you know."

"Are there, though?" Looking a little bitter, Emma Jane added, "Forgive me, but a lot of the good ones get snapped up too early. I wish I had realized that back when I was fifteen. I would've tried harder to catch Aaron."

Even though Treva usually tried to watch her words, she couldn't prevent a dose of plain speaking. "Aaron isn't much of a catch, Emma Jane."

Her lips turned into a sweet frown. "Sure he is. He's well off and has a nice house."

"He also doesn't shower regularly." Maybe a lot of people didn't, but Aaron really was a person who should.

She pulled in her bottom lip. "I reckon that would be a problem."

"More than a problem, I'd imagine."

"Maybe I'd get used to it?"

Stirring a generous amount of caramel into Emma Jane's drink, Treva chuckled. "You can't be serious."

"Of course I am. You're oblivious to it because you had Reuben."

And just like that, reality returned as she was reminded about what she'd lost. "Hmm."

"I'm sorry. That wasn't very kind of me to bring up."

"There's no reason to apologize for the truth. It's the truth. I did have Reuben for a while."

But then he jumped the fence for an English girl who drove a red convertible.

He never looked back, at least not at Treva.

Though, sometimes when she was feeling especially thoughtful, Treva found herself wondering if he'd left her for the pretty Englisher or the fancy red car.

She still wasn't sure which had been more enticing. It didn't matter, though. All she'd ever cared about was that she hadn't been reason enough for him to stay.

CHAPTER 5

Staring at the e-mail from Martin, Matt Schrock tried not to be disappointed. But it was hard. Out of his four kids, he'd thought he had retained the best relationship with his oldest. Sure, they didn't talk every week or even see each other once a month. But honestly, he'd thought they were still pretty close.

Now it was glaringly obvious that they weren't close at all. Worse, that they hadn't been for some time and they weren't even in danger of not "being close"—they were in danger of having no relationship at all.

Matt had been fooling himself.

Staring at the e-mail, Matt knew he had to face the truth. If he and Martin did have a decent relationship, his eldest would've called him. Especially because—last he'd heard, anyway—Martin wasn't even currently living Amish. Nope, he was back in his condo near downtown Cleveland.

He hadn't called. Instead, he'd e-mailed a three-paragraph note to Matt's computer because he didn't want to speak to him. Didn't want to have a conversation. After reading the short note again, he set his phone down.

"This is nothing more than the result of the seeds that were sown," he muttered to himself as he wandered into the living room and sat down in front of his TV.

For the first time in months, he didn't automatically reach for the remote and click on his seventy-seven-inch big screen 5G television. He knew all about the TV's bells and whistles because he'd investigated every component before he'd purchased it.

For weeks, he'd visited different retailers and compared televisions, prices, warranties, and speaker systems. By the time he'd bought the thing—and the mount for the wall, the wireless speakers, and the new suede sectional—he'd barely thought about anything else.

Except work.

In the midst of all that, he'd completely forgotten Beth's birthday.

When he had remembered and then had finally called two days late, his daughter's voice had been cool and distant. Of course, he hadn't told her that he'd been focused on television shopping instead of remembering the day of her birth. But he also hadn't attempted to make up an excuse. He'd learned over the years that half-baked excuses were neither believed nor appreciated.

By the time he'd hung up, even the promise of the check that he'd sent her and the roses that were supposed to arrive hadn't thawed their conversation enough to feel like he was in her good graces again.

When he'd told Ashley—the woman he'd been dating—she'd been completely confused. Not by how he could forget one of his children's birthdays, but by why he was feeling so guilty. She'd honestly thought he'd been estranged from his children.

He'd broken things off with her soon after.

He didn't regret ending things with Ashley. She had been a nice person. They'd met online, had a lot in common, but he'd known from the start that she wasn't destined to be anyone special to him.

None of the women he'd dated had ever meant anything to him compared with Helen.

His ex-wife and mother of his four children.

From what he'd gleaned over the years, Helen had been struggling for a while, too. She'd been just as self-absorbed and created just as many fissures in her relationships with their children as he had.

Not lately, though. Kelsey had told him the last time they'd talked that Helen was dating someone pretty seriously. She'd finally moved on and was finding happiness. He was glad for her. He really was.

Just as importantly, he didn't envy the new man in her life. Helen was a good person and she'd been a good mother when their house had been crazy and chaotic and loud. Four toddlers and a golden retriever had been a recipe for mess and fur and exhaustion. Back then, he'd worked long hours, always half afraid they wouldn't have enough money to pay for the diapers and clothes and formula and everything else four kids under six had needed.

When he'd come home, she'd kiss him lightly, allow him to change, then hand him a child. Or two. Sometimes he'd resented it—feeling like she didn't care that he'd worked nine hours and then commuted another half hour home in rain or snow.

Looking back on it, Matt knew he'd do a lot of things differently. He had a feeling Helen might, too. Most of all, he would now treasure those days a little harder. Back then, he'd felt needed and loved.

Now those moments were far harder to come find.

He wished things between him and Helen had worked out. Sometimes he even considered trying to give their relationship a go again, but too much time had passed.

He appreciated the woman she'd been and the woman she'd become, but he also knew that the two of them would never be able to go back in time. Their divorce had been too contentious, and the years after hadn't done either of them any favors. He'd been angry, resentful, and adrift. Helen had been the same. To his shame, there had been many times when it had been his turn to have the kids that he hadn't been all that present.

So many years had passed.

It was no wonder that all four of their children had turned to his parents for guidance and comfort. They'd been bright lights in some of the kids' darkest days.

"At least Jonny called you," he said to the silent room.

He had. The boy—who really wasn't a boy any longer—had needed him for his insurance.

And he'd been so desperate to keep things going between them he'd promised that Jonny could stay on his insurance another four years. Until his twenty-sixth birthday.

"Maybe you'll remember that one," he told the empty room.

After flicking on the fancy TV that no longer seemed all that special, he scanned the channels. Five minutes later, after finding nothing of interest, he turned it back off, encasing the house in silence once again.

The type of silence he'd grown up with.

The type of silence he'd once been used to—before the kids came and the divorce and his need to fill the emptiness with work and money and stuff and women.

Feeling despondent and at a loss about what to do, he walked around his place. Straightened a crystal vase that didn't need straightening.

Contemplated reading a book.

Then he noticed the mailman had just driven by, so he walked out to get it.

His mailbox was down the street. The houses in his development were large—four and five bedrooms—but had small lots. What lot he did have was covered in well-manicured grass and landscaping that someone else took care of.

He worked so much, the low-maintenance lifestyle worked for him. He didn't want to spend his Saturdays or Sunday afternoons mowing, pulling weeds, or trimming bushes. It had made perfect sense when he'd bought the place, especially because he already had a cleaning service that stopped by every two weeks and cleaned his house top to bottom.

Now, though, he couldn't help but think what his father would have to say about his choices.

No, he didn't have to wonder at all. He knew exactly what his *daed* would think.

That he had his priorities twisted into knots. A good life was not working sixty, seventy, and eighty hours a week. It wasn't having a sizable bank account. It wasn't about being so exhausted that he had no energy to do anything other than sleep.

And it certainly was not having a home that was simply an afterthought, a place to sleep before going out the next morning to work again.

But over all of that, his father would remind him that his most precious belongings were the four children he'd fathered.

He would be right.

"Arff!"

Caught up in his musings, he was taken aback by the fluffy dog barking at his feet. No leash was in sight, but it did have on a fancy black leather collar. Where was its owner?

His hand still half in the metal mailbox, he glanced around. "Arff!!"

He looked down at the dog again. "What, buddy?"

"Ar . . . Arff!" He followed the noise with a low growl that sounded goofy instead of menacing.

"You're pretty tough, aren't you?"

The dog continued to expectantly stare at Matt. Obviously waiting for him to do something.

What, he didn't know.

"I'm so sorry! Just ignore him! If you don't bend down and pet her, he'll realize you're not a friend and walk by."

There was something about the instructions that didn't exactly set well with him. Even though he'd never been a big fan of small, yappy, fluffy dogs, he knelt down on one knee. "Hi . . . what's your name?"

To his surprise, the dog sat down and craned its neck. Matt pulled at the tag on its collar and then read it again to make sure he hadn't read it wrong. "Alfred? Your name is Alfred?"

"Arff!" the dog barked again. This time a tail wag accompanied it.

"Well, good to meet you."

"Alfred, come here, you bad dog," the woman said.

There wasn't much of either anger or irritation in her voice, though. Instead, she sounded almost resigned. After she hooked a black leather leash to the collar, she stood up. "I'm so sorry about that. Did he ruin your slacks?"

"Hmm?" He looked down and noticed his slacks did have two faint, dusty prints around his knee, but it wasn't anything that couldn't be quickly wiped off. "Oh, I'm good."

"You sure?"

"Positive."

She still didn't look convinced. "Let me know if you need me to pay for a dry cleaner bill."

"Do I really look like that kind of guy? The type who would make someone pay for a dry cleaning bill for a pair of paw prints?"

Her eyes, which he now realized were a honey-colored brown, looked him over. "I'm not sure. Maybe."

"Really?" He was kind of offended, though he had no idea why.

"You do look pretty dressed up and neat." She waved a hand around the road. "Just like these houses with the perfect lawns and professional landscaping."

Taking her in, he saw that she was wearing black leggings, designer tennis shoes, and some kind of loose light-gray-and-violet top. Casual but put together. That look, together with her dark brown hair, was noticeable.

He would've remembered meeting her before. "You don't live here?"

"No. I'm house-sitting." Looking down, she smiled. "And pet-sitting Alfred."

"Do you do that a lot?"

She raised a shoulder in kind of a half shrug. "Often enough. I usually pet- and house-sit one week a month."

"What do you do the other weeks?"

A guarded look entered her eyes. "I'm sorry. We haven't even met. Why are you asking?"

Because he wanted to know more about her, and his curiosity had nothing to do with either pet- or house-sitting. "I guess I'm just curious. My name is Matt, by the way. Matthew Schrock."

"Matthew Schrock, like the head of Matthew Schrock Financial Services?"

"Yeah." Because that was who he was. But his business definitely wasn't something that most people were even aware of. "Any reason you know of it? Were you a client?"

"No, but my father was."

"Want to tell me your name now?"

"Sorry." She held out a hand. "My name is Kennedy Graham."

Shaking her hand, he noticed that his light grip wasn't needed. She was a woman who had a fondness for a good grip. "It's nice to meet you. Who is your dad?"

"James Graham."

He didn't have such a big client list that he couldn't recall the name. Or the man's trademark lopsided grin. He'd told Matt once that it was because he'd fallen out of a tree when he was a kid, busted open his lip with his teeth, and had to have surgery to fix the damage. It had left him with a slight scar on his upper lip and an uneven smile. "James . . . Jimmy, right?"

Kennedy nodded. "Yes."

Belatedly, he remembered that Jimmy had gotten cancer in his forties, battled it again in his fifties, and died in his early sixties. He'd been concerned about his daughter and wanted to make sure that she'd been taken care of.

"I'm sorry for your loss."

"He died a long time ago, but thank you."

"Jimmy was a really good guy." He wished he could think of something else to add, but he couldn't.

Her gaze softened. "Dad was the best." She stared at him a moment longer, then finally glanced at the dog. "Well, I better go take this escape artist home."

"Are you going to be staying here awhile?"

"Three more weeks."

"Three? Wow."

"Alfred's owners are on a cruise around South America. It's twenty-two days."

"Must be nice."

"The destination or the vacation?"

That caught him off guard. "I'm not sure. All of it, I guess."

"Dad used to say that money wasn't to be wasted . . . but it also liked to take a spin every now and then."

He grinned. "I need to write that down and share it with some of my clients, if you don't mind."

"I won't mind if you tell them Jimmy said it," she said, teasing him.

"I'd be happy to give credit to him. It's a good saying."

"Yeah," she said softly.

He smiled at her again, realizing that the laugh lines around her eyes revealed that she was older than she'd looked at first glance. There was something about her that struck a nerve with him. He wanted to be around her again. Wanted to know her better.

When was the last time he'd felt so strongly about a woman?

Obviously bored, Alfred shifted and groaned.

"Well, I'll let you go," he said. "I live four houses down on the left. Number 882. If you need anything, don't hesitate to knock."

"Thanks, Matthew."

Her eyes were pretty. All of her was. Feeling more flustered, he cleared his throat. "Call me Matt. Everyone does." Everyone who mattered to him.

"I will, then." Kennedy smiled at him again before turning away.

After watching her for almost a minute, he realized that his mail was still in his mailbox and the door to it was still wide open. His keys were still inserted in the lock.

Quickly, he pulled out the mail and closed the compart-
ment. But as he turned around, he realized he could not care
less about what bills or flyers were in his hands.

All he seemed to be able to think about was Kennedy and
her dad. And how Jimmy's world had been his daughter and
she'd known it.

He wanted that.

CHAPTER 6

Jonny's question about her interests outside of work had hit a nerve. She hated that she'd drawn a blank. That was why, she supposed, Treva found herself analyzing her life and likes whenever she had a moment to spare.

While it was awkward at first, she'd soon gotten the hang of things and was almost enjoying the experience.

There were many things she enjoyed about running the Trailside Café. Too many to list, she reckoned. But if she had to pick her very favorite parts, they involved working behind the counters, making coffees, baking breakfast treats, and interacting with a variety of people. Though each took a lot of effort in order to do well, none of them seemed like work. She truly enjoyed owning her own business and making her childhood dream of owning a cute café a reality.

Unfortunately, she was learning the best thing about her job was also the worst. The problem about having a job she loved was that she didn't want to ever leave. Ever.

She enjoyed visiting with her customers. She enjoyed working on the baked goods and organizing the little sacks she'd recently bought to put them in for customers wanting treats to go. She found satisfaction when some of her patrons didn't choose to take their coffee and run but decided to relax in the small seating area.

She even loved doing the dishes and making sure everything looked picture-perfect before she locked the door late each afternoon.

The drawback of all that was that her aunt and mother seemed to fear that she was substituting a vibrant, fulfilling business for a good life.

She used to find that a little offensive. Couldn't they be the same thing? And if they weren't, what was wrong with her choices?

After all, if she were a man who showed so much care to his office or place of business, she didn't think anyone would think a thing about it—except to maybe pat him on the back and tell him good job.

Right?

But after visiting with Emma Jane, as well, Treva had begun to believe that her *mamm* and Aunt Ruth weren't foolish after all. Maybe she had given the Trailside Café not only all her time but also her heart. Maybe she had been so upset about Reuben that she'd substituted a thriving business for him.

Instead of attempting to form a good relationship with another man.

That was why Aunt Ruth was currently making cappuccinos and lattes and Treva was riding her old, rickety bike down the bike path near her family's farm.

Okay. She supposed that even if she wasn't willing to confess all her thoughts to either Emma Jane or her family, she needed to be honest with herself at the very least.

There was something about Jonny that she couldn't stop

thinking about. She was sure it had something to do with his looks. He was handsome in a way that was impossible to ignore. Every time he'd entered her café, he'd drawn admiring glances from women of all ages and backgrounds.

Treva knew she'd be lying if she pretended that she hadn't done the same thing.

But there was something else about him that was more interesting and special than just a good jaw and physique. Maybe it was his story—the way not just him but also his brother and two sisters were all experimenting with living Amish. That took a determination and a way of thinking that not everyone had. It was hard to dream of a different path when one was surrounded by folks who were delighted to never drift too far from either the left or right.

But what she thought was making her heart beat a little bit quicker was the faintly bleak look in his eyes. Something in his life had been hard, and he was doing a good bit of work attempting to either forget or come to terms with it.

Kind of like the way she was with Reuben.

Maybe Jonny wasn't suffering from a broken heart, but she kind of thought that something worrying was on his mind.

Treva didn't want to pry into his business or private life, but her sympathetic nature did want to try to help him in some way. Probably because she knew what it was like to have all her dreams shatter. She knew better than most that not every broken shard was picked up easily. Sometimes there were still tiny slivers of glass that poked into one's skin from time to time, causing an unexpected twinge or making one bleed.

As she'd hoped, the Landen Bicycle Shop was open. Parking her bike outside, she forced herself to walk inside the shop, even though she wasn't exactly sure what she was going to say she needed from Jonny.

It was a bad plan, but that couldn't be helped. She'd always been good at math and businesslike concerns. Not long-term relationship goals.

Opening the door, she stepped in with a smile.

But was brought up short by the scowl on his face.

"That's not what I said, Beth," he said.

She froze, looked around, then realized he was talking on his cell phone.

When he saw her, he sighed. "Hold on," he said into the phone before raising his chin. "Hi, Treva." He flashed a quick smile. "It's good to see you."

"Hi. Um, do you want me to come back?"

"No."

He didn't sound like he meant it. Or maybe he just sounded angry? She wasn't sure. "Um, okay."

Hearing her hesitant response, he gritted his teeth. "I meant, please don't leave. I'll be right with you."

She nodded and smiled, but she really wasn't too happy. How could she be? So far, her impromptu visit was turning out like nothing she'd imagined.

Now, though, it would seem rude to leave. So, she loitered around the door.

Returning his attention back to whomever was on the other side of the phone line, Jonny said, "I've got a customer here. I've got to go." After another pause, he grunted. "I hear what you're saying, but you don't know the whole story, and now isn't the time to talk about it."

Treva tried to look interested in the collection of bike helmets on the shelf in front of her, but it was impossible to ignore Jonny's strong, clear voice.

"Uh huh. Okay. Yep. I know, Beth. Okay, fine. Love you, too. Bye."

He was in love? Now she was even more embarrassed.

She turned back to him just as he tossed his phone on the counter. When his blue eyes met hers, she blurted, "Tough phone call?"

"Yeah." Running a hand along his face, he groaned. "I'm sorry you had to hear that."

"There's nothing to be sorry for. It was your business, not mine."

"I get that, but I would still rather not have the world hear me arguing with my sister."

Beth was his sister. Suddenly, things were looking better again. "Older or younger?"

"Older." He grunted. "I'm the youngest of four, which means I'm *always* the youngest."

"I'm guessing that also means that they like to tell you what to do?"

"Yep. It can be annoying. No matter which of the three I'm talking to, they think they know better."

"That sounds frustrating."

"It is." Leaving the phone on the counter, he stepped closer. "Do you have older or younger siblings?"

"My situation is worse than that. I have none. I'm an only child."

"Oh, I'm sorry . . . Unless you're glad about it?"

"I don't have any feelings one way or the other," she said. "It's just how it is."

"That's a good attitude. I need to think more like that."

"Maybe look at the bright side? They'll hit fifty before you," she said, teasing him.

He stared at her, then grinned. "True that." Walking toward her, he rubbed his hands down the sides of his jean-covered thighs. "It's nice to see you in here. I was beginning to think you'd never take me up on my invitation to come see me."

"I've been busy. I decided it was time to take a break."

"What can I help you with?"

"I'm not sure. I just wanted to peek inside."

"I'm glad you did." Gesturing to the cluster of bicycles in the back corner, he said, "This is just a small portion of the bicycles we have for sale. If you are interested in any style in particular, I can pull out some others."

"Oh, I don't think I'm going to be needing a new bike."

"Yours is in pretty good shape?"

Thinking of its condition, she winced. "It's fine, but I wouldn't exactly say that it's in good shape."

Looking concerned, he asked, "What's wrong with it?"

Everything. "Nothing. I mean, it works." Barely.

"That's not telling me much, Treva. Where is it? Or did you walk?"

"I rode it. It's parked outside."

Before she could stop him, he opened the door and stepped outside. Then turned right back to her as he started laughing. "Treva, you can't be serious."

"About what?"

"You know what. This bike of yours must be fifteen years old."

He was calling out to her from outside. Walking to the door, which was propped open, she folded her arms across her chest. "It is old. But, like I said, it still works." And why was she sticking up for this bike she'd never much cared for riding?

"That's a miracle because the tires look like they're about to disintegrate any moment. Where have you been keeping it? Hooked to a tree outside?"

"I'm starting to get a little offended. Don't you think you're being kind of rude?"

"Honey, sorry, but your bicycle doesn't have feelings. And you can't be that attached to it, can you?"

Honey? Feeling flustered, she sputtered, "Why not?"

"Because it's a mess. There's rust on the frame and the seat is cracked." Standing straighter, he looked her way again. "It couldn't be a comfortable ride."

It wasn't. Which was one of the reasons she didn't ride it much. The other was that she was always either serving customers coffee or baking treats to serve them.

But there was no way she was going to tell Jonny that. It made her seem too pathetic, like she didn't have any social life. Okay, so she didn't, but he didn't need to know that!

"It's not too bad."

Walking inside, he looked like he was about to say something but abruptly changed his mind. "Hey." In a soft tone, he continued, "Treva, I'm sorry if I hurt your feelings. I didn't mean to do that."

"I came over here to check on you. Not have you check out my bicycle—and make fun of it."

He pursed his lips. "I'm sorry if you thought that's what I was doing. I didn't mean to be mean. I . . . well, as far as bicycles go, yours is pretty bad."

She would have been offended if she didn't agree. "I know."

"Do you want to look at some of the new ones? You could give one a test ride . . . just to see the difference?"

"*Nee.*"

"Oh. All right."

Had she just inadvertently hurt his feelings? "All my money is going into my business right now."

"Of course." He ran a hand through his hair as he walked back to the counter. When he stood on the other side of it, she felt his loss.

He cleared his throat. "Why are you checking up on me?"

"Emma Jane reminded me that you're one of the Schrock

siblings intending to become Amish. I wondered if you needed any help."

His brow wrinkled. "Help with what?"

"You know." She waved a hand. "Being Amish."

After a moment's pause, he asked, "Who's Emma Jane?"

He didn't remember Emma Jane! The question shouldn't have made her as happy as it did. "She's *mei* friend. She was walking in when you were walking out the other morning. You two spoke for a bit."

He frowned, then his expression cleared. "Oh. I had forgotten about meeting her." Pressing his palms on the counter's surface, he said, "So my family has become a source of gossip?"

"Well, there's been talk. But not in a bad way."

"Gossip." He frowned. "What do you think about what we're doing?"

"About becoming Amish?" When he nodded, she said, "If you want the truth, I think it sounds really hard. Deciding to be baptized in the faith isn't an easy decision, even for someone raised in an Amish home."

Yet again, their conversation seemed to be going at cross-purposes. "Jonny, I'm sorry, but once again the words I say seem to be coming across in ways I never intended. I didn't mean to say I thought what you were doing was wrong. I only wanted to help."

"How? Do you think I need advice about how to be a better Amish person?"

"Of course not."

His sarcastic tone continued. "Or maybe you don't think my grandparents are good enough role models?"

He wasn't letting it go—and seemed to be intentionally twisting and turning her words around. It wasn't fair, and she didn't think it was very nice, either. "I meant nothing of the kind."

"Or what about my new preacher brother-in-law? Is Richard Miller lacking in some way that you know of?"

She stepped backward. It felt as if all the anger and sarcasm that was shooting out of his mouth was taking a physical form and slicing her skin.

Or maybe it was simply her heart?

All she did know was that it was time to get away from him. His words were hurting her.

"I'm going to leave."

He raised his eyebrows. "What's your hurry? You could probably give me an Amish lesson now. There's no one in the shop."

She was near tears. Near tears and feeling as if her heart was breaking. "You know, Jonny Schrock, you might not need any advice about being Amish, but you could sure use some help when it comes to being a good person. I can't believe you just attacked me for offering my friendship."

He stared at her for a long moment. Seemed to be mentally weighing what she had said.

Then, unbelievably, he acted like she'd just made that up. "That isn't what just happened."

"No, that's exactly what just happened." Backing up toward the door, she said, "Don't worry, I won't make that mistake again."

"Hold on." Reaching across the counter, he said, "You're really upset."

She backed away. "Of course I am. You've been horrible."

"Hey, wait—"

But she didn't wait. There was no way she was going to do that. She didn't want to hear one more awful word he had to say.

So she turned and hurried to her bicycle. Halfway back to

the farm, the front tire burst. It caused her to fall and scrape her hands and arm on the path.

Then, to make matters worse, she had to walk the bicycle for most of a mile, all the way home.

She had a feeling the Lord had made that happen for a reason, but she wasn't quite ready to face that.

She didn't think she could take one more thing.

CHAPTER 7

It didn't happen all that often, but his sister Kelsey and her husband Richard came over for supper. His grandparents' sweet neighbor Patti—who also just happened to be Jonny's brother's girlfriend—joined them. As well as Martin. He'd driven down earlier, spent most of the day with Patti and then had appeared at his grandparents' doorstep an hour before supper.

Jonny had no idea all four of them were going to be joining them.

He'd had been so irritated about the way Treva's visit had gone, he'd taken a long bike ride, then had elected to make up the time lost by working on three more solar chargers to sell.

He'd been surprised to discover his sister and his brother there—and dismayed that everyone had been sipping coffee and catching up while they'd waited for him.

Though his grandparents hadn't said a word about his late appearance, both Kelsey and Martin had shot daggers at him. If they'd been alone, he would've said something about that.

He was pretty sure that if they'd been alone, they would've said something, too.

Deciding that silence was golden and that absence made the heart grow fonder, Jonny had rushed upstairs. Sure, he was clinging to clichés like they were actual words of wisdom, but he would take what he could get. He needed as much help as he could glean in order to make it through the next couple of hours.

By the time he'd taken a hot shower, put on fresh clothes, and stridden back downstairs, everyone was bringing serving platters to the table. He'd arrived in time to retrieve the last one from the kitchen counter.

"I'm sorry I got home so late, Mommi," he said, as he paused next to the island where she was standing. "I didn't remember you telling me that everyone was coming over for supper."

As always, his grandmother's grace and goodness shone in her eyes. Placing a palm on his cheek, she said, "You didn't remember because I didn't tell you. Our gathering came together this morning. Patti had come over, then Kelsey did, too. Next thing I knew, we were planning dishes."

"I see." Not really, though. The bicycle shop was only a fifteen-minute walk away. Plus, he had a phone and his grandparents were New Order. There was a phone in the kitchen. No one had felt the need to give him a heads-up?

As if she were reading his mind, his grandmother added, "Kelsey offered to tell you, but I told her not to worry because I had time to give you a call." She chuckled. "And then I promptly forgot about that promise."

"So you're not mad?"

"There's nothing to be mad about, Jonny. Don't fret so much. There's nothing to do about the past, anyway."

Like always, his sweet grandmother's voice and kind manner soothed him like few things did. He loved her kindness and loved how she continually made him want to be like her. Centered and forgiving.

"I told the girls you've been mighty busy at work, Jonny," their grandmother said, after they'd bent their heads for silent prayer.

"I have been."

Kelsey cleared her throat. "And busy doing other things, too."

Hearing something pointed in her tone, he felt himself go on guard as he took some broccoli, then passed the platter to the next person. "Hmm? What do you mean?"

"Well, I heard you've gotten to know Treva Kramer."

"I have." He glanced at Patti to see if she could give him a clue about where his sister was steering the conversation.

Unfortunately, she was busy putting spoonfuls of mashed potatoes onto her plate.

"Pass the gravy, Jonny," Martin said.

Feeling as if Martin knew exactly as to what Kelsey was referring, he said, "Hold on. I'll pass it in a second. As soon as I get the potatoes." After Kelsey sent them his way, he helped himself to both the potatoes and a small amount of gravy before passing them on.

"I also heard she visited you today."

It took a second for him to realize Kelsey was still talking about Treva. "Who did you hear that from?"

"It doesn't matter. Pass the rolls, Patti."

"Here ya go," Patti said.

"So, how was the visit?" Martin asked.

"Fine." Of course, that was a lie. Treva's visit hadn't gone well at all.

"What did you two do?" Kelsey asked.

"What does it matter?" he snapped.

"Why do you not want to talk about her visit, Jonny?" Mommi asked.

Making sure to temper his tone of voice, he turned to her. "It's not that I don't, it's more a matter of trying to fill my dinner plate."

Dawdi raised his eyebrows. "You have a bit of everything there is, son. Do you need more?"

"Of course not. I'm sorry." Even though the food was beckoning him with tantalizing smells, he ignored it and answered, "I just don't understand why Treva's visit to the bicycle shop is interesting." To the entire family.

"We heard you two have become friends," Richard murmured.

Glancing at his brother-in-law, Jonny noticed that he was looking apologetic. It was obvious that he felt sorry for Jonny's hot seat but wasn't going to go against his brand-new wife.

Jonny reckoned he would do the same thing.

Knowing that he was never going to be able to eat in peace until he gave his family the information they wanted, he said grudgingly, "I have gotten to know Treva, but I've gotten to know a lot of people. Treva owns a coffee shop, and I sometimes get coffee there in the morning."

"Did she ride her bicycle there?" Dawdi asked.

Jonny took the time to put a chicken leg on his plate. "She did," he said. "I'm not sure why any of this is notable, though."

"She got a flat tire on the way home," Patti said.

"Oh no. Is she okay?"

"I think she has a couple of scrapes, but she's good. Or so I heard."

"I'm glad to hear it." Tomorrow morning he'd go see her and check out her injuries himself. And maybe try again to encourage her to get a new bike?

"Why didn't you check her tires, Jonny?" Dawdi asked.

"I did, even though she didn't ask me to."

"And?"

He was getting frustrated, but he really wasn't sure why. "And . . . and I told her that her bicycle was old and needed to be replaced. Or, at the very least, repaired and taken better care of."

"Uh oh," Patti murmured.

"She didn't like hearing my opinion, but I wasn't being mean. I was speaking the truth." Finally getting enough food to fill up his plate, he picked up his fork. "She ignored my suggestions."

"So you let Treva leave?" Kelsey asked.

She sounded scandalized, which was ridiculous. "Uh, yeah. She's not a child. Of course I let her leave."

Mommi cleared her throat. "Jonny, dear. I canna help but think that you could've handled things better with her."

"I agree." Glad he had his ball cap off, he dragged a hand through his hair. "But we, ah, had a disagreement. It's not my fault that I'm human."

"Mmph."

Feeling like everyone at the table was giving him grief for a relatively minor fault, he said, "Next time I see Treva, I'll apologize. May we not discuss her visit to my shop anymore?"

Martin sat up a little straighter. "All right. How about this . . . Want to explain why you now seem to have some new, cozy relationship with Dad?" Martin said.

No way did he want to talk about their father. "No."

"Jonny," Dawdi murmured under his breath.

Things were going from bad to worse. "You're my brother, Martin. But that doesn't mean you get to start deciding how I deal with our parents." Or corner him in the middle of a meal to discuss them!

"I think it does, because Dad said the two of you are going to be talking a lot more often."

Why couldn't their father have kept his mouth shut? Immediately, shame coursed through him. That wasn't fair, and it was selfish of him to only be thinking of himself.

How was he ever going to be Amish if he was only thinking about himself?

As the silence continued, second by excruciatingly slow second, their grandmother entered into the fray.

"If Matt is reaching out to Jonny, that's *gut*, don't you think? We are all family."

"*Jah*, Mommi," Kelsey said in a small voice.

And, for once, Martin looked contrite. "You're right, Mommi. I . . . I don't know why I brought it up. It just took me by surprise. Sorry, Jonny. I didn't know you two were getting along so well."

There was that pinch of shame all over again. The only reason they were getting along was because he needed to stay on their father's insurance.

But because he'd promised himself not to tell Martin, Kelsey, or Beth about the doctor's words, Jonny couldn't completely explain himself. "I don't have to give you a report about who I talk to."

Martin blinked. "You're right. I'm sorry," he said again.

"Jonny was right," Dawdi muttered. "This ain't the place to discuss it."

"I understand," Martin said while Jonny said essentially the same thing.

As silence descended upon the table at long last, Jonny concentrated on his meal.

But it now tasted like cardboard.

Boy, when was life ever going to get easier? He really thought he would have had a handle on himself by now.

Instead, he was just as confused as ever.

CHAPTER 8

The second time Matt saw Kennedy, she was sitting on the front steps of the neighborhood's clubhouse. She was also bleeding.

"Kennedy, are you all right?"

"Um, kind of." Looking down at her legs, she wrinkled her nose. "I've been better, though."

Maybe on another day he would have appreciated her irreverent humor. At the moment, the only thing he felt was worry.

Rushing to her side, he felt more alarmed when he saw splatters of blood on both her white shorts and the pavement. "Oh, my word. What happened to you?"

"I tripped on the sidewalk and fell down hard." Frustration filled every word. "It was so stupid."

"Accidents usually are, right?" He reached for one of her hands and saw that she had some gravel embedded in her palm. The source of blood was her left knee, however.

Kneeling, Matt realized her injury wasn't merely a simple scrape. A significant flap of skin had been sliced. She must have skinned it on the sharp end of a rock or hit a piece of metal or something. Lifting his gaze, he took note of the tension in her eyes. She was obviously trying not to cry. "I bet you're hurting."

"I am. Next time I see a kid with a scraped knee, I'm going to feel a lot more sympathy for him or her!"

Unable to help himself, he tucked an errant piece of hair behind her ear. "Me, too." When her expression softened, he added, "We need to clean you up. You might need to get some stitches, too."

"Hopefully not."

Matt only noticed Alfred sitting on the ground when he helped Kennedy to her feet. Though the dog's eyes were alert, he didn't move a muscle. His leash was even resting on the ground. "That's some kind of dog. He's so well trained."

"He is a great dog, but he's still a dog," she said with a small smile. "He goes crazy whenever he sees a chipmunk."

"He doesn't like chipmunks?"

"Not even a little bit. Alfred turns into a vicious killer the moment he spies one rooting around in the flower beds. That's what got me into this mess," she said, as she took his arm. "One minute, we're going for our usual walk and I'm thinking about my grocery list, and the next Alfred's barking and yanking on my arm."

"He's full of surprises."

"He's a handful, that's what he is." Snapping her fingers, she said, "Alfred, by me."

Immediately, the dog stood up and walked to her side.

Matt rubbed the top of his head. He'd known enough dogs to not blame one for, well, being a dog.

Deciding to take her to his house, he reached for Alfred's leash, then proceeded to help Kennedy walk in that direction. It was a blessing that it wasn't very far at all.

She hobbled along next to him. "So, what are you up to today?"

"I was about to go for a run but remembered I had to put a bill in the mailbox. Then I saw you." Belatedly, he realized that the bill was still stuffed in his pocket. He hoped he remembered to mail it later.

As they continued to walk, Kennedy frowned. "Hey, we just passed my place."

"I know."

"Where are we going?"

"I've got a box of bandages and stuff at home. I figured you probably wouldn't know where it is at the neighbor's house."

"You guessed right. But are you sure you don't mind Alfred coming in?" Looking down at her knee, she frowned. "Or me? I seem to be dripping blood."

"I think we're safe. Most of my flooring is wood or tile, and I try to keep all chipmunks out of the living room."

Her pretty brown eyes warmed. "Listen to you, Mr. Schrock. You've got jokes."

"Not usually. I guess you bring them out of me."

"Good to know."

He smiled at her, determined not to tell her what was on his mind—mainly, that he was beginning to think that there was something about Kennedy that meant more to him than just a simple attraction.

When they got to his house, he reached for her elbow and Alfred's leash.

"Matt, I've got it."

"I know, but let me help you, anyway."

Her honey-brown eyes widened, but she didn't say anything. Instead, Kennedy leaned into him a little, giving him a reason to wrap a hand around her waist as they walked up the front porch steps.

When they were inside, he released Alfred, who headed directly for his kitchen like he visited all the time. Kennedy, however, didn't move. It was obvious she was uneasy. He wasn't sure if that was because she was in his space or was hurting more than he realized. He supposed it didn't matter. All he wanted was for her to feel comfortable around him.

Matt pointed toward the kitchen. "All my first aid stuff is in the bathroom. Why don't you have a seat in the kitchen? The light's good. I'll be back in a sec."

"Okay."

When he returned with a handful of towels, a plastic container filled with bandages and antibiotic salve, and an old bottle of antiseptic, her eyes widened. "You just happened to have all that on hand?"

"I have four kids. They're grown now, but for a while there, one of them was always getting hurt or into something." Remembering the phone calls and the tears, the harried visits to urgent care and the emergency room, Matt felt a little nostalgic. Funny, he never thought he would miss those days.

"Four?" She scanned the kitchen. "Where are they? What about their mom?"

"Helen and I divorced years ago, when my youngest was just a little boy. The kids are all grown and live nearby." Thinking about Jonny and Kelsey, he added, "Some are closer than others."

"But all are in Ohio?"

"Yep. I'm really glad about that," he said as he dampened one of the towels and started cleaning her knee. "It's nice knowing they are just a car ride away." Pausing, he scanned her face. "Doing okay?"

She nodded. "It stings, but it's not too bad. So, are you and your kids close? How often do you see each other?"

"They're grown adults, so not that often. Just a couple of times a year."

"Really?"

He felt like she was judging him, which was difficult, because they really didn't know each other. "They have jobs and other interests besides visiting their father."

"I'm sorry."

"Don't be. Kids grow up. Sure, I sometimes wish I saw them more, but there's nothing I can do about that. I'm glad they're independent." Of course, he wasn't quite telling the whole truth. Now that Martin, Beth, and Jonny were thinking about becoming Amish and Kelsey had just gotten married, their relationships were even more strained.

Kennedy was staring at him like he'd said something unforgivable. "What's wrong?"

"Nothing. Well, nothing other than I'm pretty surprised to hear you're a dad. I don't see a lot of pictures of them around the house."

"I've got a couple." Again, he felt judged. "Plus, now we take photos on our phones." Printing them out seemed to be yet another task he never made time to do.

"I guess that's true."

Huh? "You guess?"

"I'm sorry. I guess I thought I had you figured out because my father was such a fan of yours. I was wrong."

"Well, he did see me at work."

"True, but you don't seem to be the type to have four grown kids." She shook her head. "That didn't come out right. I meant, you don't look old enough."

"Helen and I married young," he murmured. Inspecting her knee, he said, "What do you think? Do you want to go to urgent care?"

"For this? No."

"You could have a scar," he warned.

"I'll be fine."

"Okay, then." After dabbing her knee again, he opened a box of large bandages and applied two to her knee. "How's that?"

"It's good, Matt, thanks."

Glad that the tension had eased between them, he murmured, "So, do you have kids?"

And just like that, shadows played around her eyes again. "I did. He died when he was twenty."

"I'm so sorry." Taking the chair next to her, he said, "What happened?"

"Car accident." She pursed her lips. "It was years ago, but sometimes it doesn't feel like it, you know?" When he nodded, she added, "I think that's why I started house- and pet-sitting for other people. Even after all this time, I find that I still need something to keep me busy so I don't descend into depression."

The pain in her voice was incredible. Not that he was surprised she still felt the loss, but that it still felt like a tangible thing.

Compared with the way he and Helen had treated their own kids—almost like they'd taken their love for granted—it made him feel humbled. Maybe a little shaken, too.

"Let's rinse your hands."

"I was about to wash them but then had no idea how to dry them without staining another towel."

"Towels are meant to be washed."

"Yes, but expensive white ones like this might stain."

"They're just towels, Kennedy. If they're too badly stained, I'll replace them."

"You must have been a great dad."

Matt knew Kennedy was simply being nice and offering a sweet compliment. As a nice gesture in return for him going out of his way to help her out. But the statement made him feel uneasy yet again.

He pushed off his regrets and focused on taking care of the gravel in her palms. With their hands under the faucet, he noticed that her nails were cut short and there were faint calluses on her palms. Maybe from all the dog walking? Maybe from life. He didn't know.

He did know that they were different from his wife's smooth, beautiful hands, with her long nails and graceful lines. They were also a far cry from his own mother's sturdy ones.

Realizing that he'd been holding her hands under the water a little too long, he cleared his throat. "I think all the dirt is out."

"Me, too."

Turning off the water, he flipped her hands over and dabbed at the cuts with the corner of a washcloth. "What do you think?"

After inspecting her palms, she smiled. "I think a couple of Band-Aids are all I need."

He pointed to the worst cut. "Sure you don't want to get that checked out?"

"Positive." After dabbing her hands a bit more, she held out her palms. "If you could help me with a couple of Band-Aids, I'll get out of your way."

He actually wasn't sure he was ready to send her away. "What plans do you and Alfred have for the rest of the evening?"

A guarded look slid into her eyes. "We have a couple of things to do."

"Oh, of course." After applying four Band-Aids to her hands, he walked her to the door. Alfred was already lying down in front of it.

He stood to the side and watched while she hooked up the leash to the dog. "Thanks again for saving the day."

"Anytime. See you around."

"Maybe so." When she smiled again, it looked forced. Then she was gone again.

Matt stood in the doorway and watched her leave.

Thinking about the way she'd questioned him about his kids and then had dropped the bomb about losing her own had made him feel sorry for her . . . but a little defensive, too.

She shouldn't have acted like he was doing something wrong.

But maybe he wouldn't be feeling like that if he hadn't been feeling the same way?

The truth was, he was living with regrets and he was feeling like he was caught in the middle of a knotted fishing net. He was afraid to misstep and then get stuck again—and forced to live with the consequences of that.

"No, you're tired of waiting by the phone and the mailbox hoping that one of your kids will reach out."

That's when he knew what he should do. No, needed to do. He was going to pack a bag and head down to Walden. He was going to walk on his parents' farm, help them as much as he could, and see Jonny and, hopefully, Kelsey, too.

He knew things might be awkward, but he also knew that he loved his family and they loved him.

He also might have left the Amish, but he knew how to live Amish. He might look fancy to Kennedy, but he'd grown up running barefoot for most of his childhood. Living Plain didn't scare him.

He was almost looking forward to unplugging and being out of touch for a day or two.

And a day or two was what he wanted. Not just a couple of hours. He wanted to go back and read, and see if he could find something that he'd lost too long ago.

See if it was possible to find it again.

And if it wasn't. If his parents didn't seem to be happy to see him or Jonny looked upset or Kelsey turned her back to him, then he would figure out what he needed to do to get back into their lives.

One step at a time.

All he needed to do now was drive down and show up. And if his parents didn't extend an invitation, he'd find a place to stay nearby.

He'd done harder things. For sure and for certain.

CHAPTER 9

He'd fallen asleep on top of his quilt with his tennis shoes still on. Feeling groggy, as if a thick fog had settled in his brain, he shifted. As Jonny pried open one eye and then the other, he continued to try to make sense of where he was.

It was daylight out. The sun was shining. Not night.

Turning to his side, Jonny reached for the small travel alarm clock he'd purchased soon after he'd moved into his grandparents' home. It was four in the afternoon.

He'd taken a two-hour nap.

When was the last time he'd napped on a Saturday afternoon? It had been years. Maybe when he was twelve or thirteen and had the flu? He honestly couldn't remember. It wasn't in his nature to nap. Not with being the youngest of four kids. His mom used to say that he'd been anxious to keep up with the others from practically the moment he'd been born.

Sitting up, he rubbed his face.

And then became aware of the voices floating up the stairs. Someone was over. By the tone of his grandmother's voice, he could tell that she was agitated.

Stressed out, more like it.

When he heard the voices lower and then rise again, he got to his feet. Still playing detective, he listened, attempting to figure out who was downstairs. Then he heard a low voice, each word spoken with care. That was his grandfather. So, his *dawdi* was in the room, too, and he seemed to have a lot to say. Definitely a rarity.

And then he heard it. Low laughter followed by a spurt of words. All of it sounding confident. His father was in the house.

His father had come to pay a call on his grandparents. Or maybe he was visiting Kelsey and Richard?

Or him? Jonny thought that was a long shot, but he supposed that could be the case. He hadn't called him in weeks, and his father had been concerned about the doctor's warnings.

Walking to the bathroom down the hall, Jonny closed himself in, arranged the blinds so he could snag a little bit more light, and turned on the faucet.

He was going to need to splash some cold water and wake up to deal with whatever was going on below. After wiping his face with a towel, he gazed at himself in the mirror. Wondering what his father was going to say to him.

In spite of his grandparents' suggestion, he hadn't gone "full Amish" yet. He had taken to wearing the cotton shirts his grandmother had made him, and he'd allowed his hair to grow a few inches. But instead of wearing the traditional pants, he was still wearing his favorite pair of Levi's and one of his two pairs of broken-in Converse sneakers. He figured he looked essentially the same. But different than he had when he'd been walking around his college campus. There was no doubt about that.

His father, being his dad and former Amish, would take note of every small change.

What Jonny didn't know was if he would comment on it.

No, that wasn't what was on his mind. He was wondering how he would feel about his father's reaction to him. He didn't have as many mixed emotions about his parents' divorce as the other kids in his family did. Martin and Beth had been especially traumatized by their parents' actions because they'd been forced to guide Kelsey and him through the mess.

Jonny knew that he had leaned on Martin a lot for most of his elementary and junior high years. He didn't have a strong memory of what life had been like when their mom and dad had been a couple, but he had known from an early age that there were two different sets of rules at each of their homes. And worse, those rules and parameters often changed, based on whatever new relationship each was in.

He'd found it confusing but accepted it as his "normal." Beth and Martin had resented their parents' actions—and the expectation that they would become Kelsey's and his adjunct mom and dad.

He turned off the sink. When he heard his father's laughter float up the stairwell, Jonny decided that the irony of the situation wasn't lost on him.

Now that he, Kelsey, Martin, and Beth had decided to distance themselves from their parents . . . their father had decided he didn't want to be forgotten.

He felt terrible for his grandparents. First, they'd had to deal with all of the siblings interrupting their lives . . . and now here was their long-lost son.

Deciding it was past time he'd joined them all, he picked up his pace. Maybe he couldn't make the situation better, but he was pretty sure that he couldn't make it worse. "Lord, please help me," he whispered as he trotted down the last four stairs.

"There you are," Matt said as Jonny appeared on the

stairs. "I was just telling Mamm and Daed that I was surprised to hear you were napping. You sure didn't do that when you were home."

No. No way was his father going to suddenly act paternal. Or act like he actually had lots of experience with Jonny being a kid.

Looking him in the eye, Jonny said, "I also wasn't working nine and ten hours a day five or six days a week, usually starting at seven."

Meeting his gaze, his father lifted his chin. "Still. It's new."

"I told your father that he was making too much out of nothing," Jonny's *dawdi* grumbled. "Taking a nap doesn't have to mean anything beyond being tired."

"I don't see anything wrong with sharing my opinion," Matt protested.

Jonny glanced at his grandmother. She was sitting in her rocker, but her back was ramrod straight. She was stressed.

He hated to see that.

"Dad, is this really how you've decided to say hello? I haven't seen you in months."

Finally, he looked embarrassed. "You're right." Walking toward Jonny, he hugged him tightly. "You look good, son. What are you, six foot now?"

"Six foot two."

His father smiled at his grandfather. "Jonny's towering over us, Daed."

Jonny's *dawdi*'s eyes warmed as he sat down in his usual brown easy chair. "You're right about that. Back when he was eighteen, I thought he'd stay my height, but it looks like the Lord had other plans. The boy is hungry all the time."

He was twenty-two years old. Hardly a boy. But he supposed if conversing about his size could settle the tension in the room, he'd go with it. "That's because Mommi's food is so good."

"I can't wait to eat one of your suppers, Mamm," his father said.

"It will be nice to see you at the table, Matthew. It's been too long."

He was staying in Walden? "How long are you staying? And where?"

For the first time his father looked a little unsure of himself. "Only a couple of days. I haven't asked your grandparents yet if I could stay here. Is there room?"

"There is, but it's in the girls' old room, Matthew. You'd have to sleep on either the twin bed or the pullout couch."

"Oh." He glanced at Jonny. "You're staying in my old room?"

"I guess I am." He took a deep breath and then said the right words, though he wasn't happy about it. "You are welcome to take that room while you're here."

"You don't mind?"

"I wouldn't have offered if I did." He inwardly winced. That wasn't quite the truth, but it was close enough.

His father shared a long look with him before shaking his head. "That was kind of you to offer, but I'll be fine in the girls' room."

"Are you sure, Matt?" his *mamm* asked.

"Of course." He grinned. "I've slept on worse."

But instead of making things better, his father's joke only seemed to create a new, unwelcome tension in the room. Jonny reckoned it brought back memories of when his father had first left this house. He'd snuck out in the middle of the night, aided by a group of men and women who helped Amish teenagers get jobs and housing for their first few months on the "outside."

Immediately, Jonny's dad walked to his mother's side. "Mamm, that didn't come out right. It was a poor joke. What I meant was that I don't want to be too much trouble."

"You aren't that, and you never were." Her voice softened. "Not even when you and Helen came with all four of your *kinner*."

His dad looked wistful. "Mamm, I love you, but you canna pretend that those visits were anything but disasters."

"It wasn't a disaster."

"I'm sorry, but it was," Jonny's *dawdi* said with a low chuckle. "Your brood turned our house on its side from the moment you pulled up in the driveway."

To Jonny's surprise, his father didn't disagree. "They sure did. The kids ruined the chicken coop's fence within a couple of hours."

"And threw a ball through the window," Jonny's *mommi* murmured.

"We also used all the hot water. Helen kept saying that she felt like she was never going to be able take a warm shower ever again."

Jonny's *dawdi* grinned. "But it was fun, wasn't it?"

"It sure was," his father agreed with a soft chuckle.

His grandfather turned to Jonny. "Do you remember that visit at all, Jon? You must have only been two."

"Sorry, I don't. I heard about it, though. Martin and Beth used to tell Kelsey and me about that visit. They said that our *daed* kept speaking Penn Dutch."

The three other people in the room smiled, but it was obvious that it was a sore subject.

His father cleared his throat. "Anyway, all I'm saying is that the guest room foldout couch is fine for tonight. If I end up staying longer, I'll move to a hotel."

"You don't have to do that, Matthew."

"I know I don't, but it might be for the best."

His grandmother nodded. "I understand."

Jonny had always wondered about what had really happened between his dad and grandparents, but none of them ever mentioned the exact reason his dad had run away. Feeling like he was prying, Jonny had never pushed, but he sure wished he knew.

Beth had told him once that no good would come out of pressing either of their parents for information about their dad growing up Amish, venturing out on his own, or the somewhat stilted relationship he had now with his parents. His sister said the only response she'd ever received to questions had been blank stares or reprimands about fishing for information that was none of her business.

"Are you sure you don't want your old room?" Jonny asked—mainly as an effort to help ease the tension in the room.

"More than sure. Don't worry about me."

Jonny felt bad, even though he knew there wasn't anything to feel badly about. Unless it was that he was reminded that he hadn't actually worried about his father for most of his life. For better or worse, he'd always viewed his dad as a man who could handle anything.

He was only now realizing that was hardly fair.

"Well, um . . . let me know if you change your mind." Yes, his words were stilted. Just as awkward as he was feeling.

"I will, son. But I won't change my mind."

"Now that that everything is finally arranged, it's time to get to work," Jonny's *mommi* said in a brusque tone. "Matthew, you go upstairs and get settled. Jonny, come with me and help in the kitchen. Kelsey and Richard will be here soon."

"They're coming for supper?"

"Oh yes. And we're having your favorite supper, too." Treating him to a sly wink, she said, "Roast chicken."

Jonny grinned. Until recently, his grandmother's fried chicken was his favorite. Maybe she really had been listening after all. "Mommi, you're amazing."

Wrapping a slim arm around his back, she guided him into the kitchen. "I'm hardly amazing, child, but I do want you healthy. I'm going to try to be better about planning meals that are lower in fat and calories. At least most of the time."

"I can work with 'most of the time.' *Danke*."

"No reason to thank me for that. I am pleased about having you here. And that Matt has come down, too."

"I hope everything will go okay."

"Everything will be fine." Lowering her voice, she added, "As much as you *kinner* like to believe that your parents don't care about each of you, I know differently. They just let life get in the way. Don't fret, child."

"I love you, Mommi."

"I love you back. Now, I'm no spring chicken. I'm gonna need some help to put this meal together. Roll up your sleeves and grab a knife. We have much to do . . . and much to be grateful for."

"Always," he whispered as he picked up a knife and reached for the cutting board.

He'd do whatever he needed to do in order for the upcoming supper to go well. All of them needed for it to.

CHAPTER 10

She'd just finished putting the last of the four dozen blueberry muffins into the bakery case when her first customer of the morning arrived.

Unable to help herself, she glanced at the clock on the wall. Hmm. He was earlier than normal. It was only half past six.

She'd only been ten minutes off.

Treva had begun to play a mental game with herself regarding Jonny Schrock's morning visits. She liked to try to guess the exact time he'd stride through her shop's front door. It gave her something to think about besides the way the sight of him made her feel—like she'd finally woken up after living in a fog of grief and disappointment during the last couple of years.

Today was the closest she'd come to guessing his entrance yet. As far as she was concerned, it was a cause for a celebration.

"Tell me congratulations, Jonny," she called out.

His serious expression brightened at her words. "For what?"

"For making such a good guess about what time you'd walk in through these doors." Only after her words flew out of her mouth did she realize that she sounded way too interested in him.

Perhaps even stalker-like?

"I didn't know you noticed things like that."

Of course he didn't. Because he probably didn't think of her at all until he wanted a good cup of coffee. It was time to backpedal—and fast. "You know what? Please forget—"

He laughed, interrupting. "No way. Am I really that predictable?"

"Only a little bit." Of course, it was more likely that she was the predictable one. She was the one who stood behind the coffee counter and looked for Jonny Schrock to arrive sometime between half past six and half past seven.

"You better be careful, son. It sounds like she's got your number," the man standing next to Jonny said.

Startling her. She hadn't even noticed that Jonny wasn't alone.

Jonny noticed. "Treva, this is my father. He's in town for a few days."

Even if they both hadn't referred to their relationship, it was obvious that the two of them were related. The older man—who really wasn't all that old—had the same dark-blond hair, piercing blue eyes, and lanky build as Jonny. He also had that same aura of confidence floating around him. "It's nice to meet you, Mr. Schrock," she said.

He grinned as he strode forward. "Call me Matt. And it's nice to meet you, too. Especially since Jonny told me that your coffee is amazing."

"*Danke*. What would you like?"

"I'll take my usual," Jonny said.

"One large latte with almond milk coming up. Matt, what about you?"

"I'll have a large latte and a blueberry muffin. Did you make them?"

"I did, just a couple of hours ago."

Matt grinned. "I'll take two, then."

Hoping that he would finally give one of her treats a try, she smiled at Jonny. "Do you want anything to eat?"

"*Nee*. The coffee will do me fine."

"All right." She knew that food wasn't love and a person's preference for food was a personal choice. But she was starting to feel a little hurt that he always looked as if taking one of the muffins, donuts, or scones was a terrible idea. "Everything will be ready in a couple of minutes."

She turned to begin the process of heating the water and tamping the espresso grounds when her door opened again. "I'll be right with you," she called out.

"*Danke*, Treva," a familiar voice replied.

She turned and smiled. "Hiya, Preacher Richard."

"*Gut matin*. Have you met *mei frau* yet?"

"I'm sorry, *nee*." They were in different church districts.

"This is Kelsey. Kels, this is Treva. Not only does she make the best coffee and apricot bars in town, but she's genuinely nice."

"It's nice to meet you," the blonde said.

"Likewise. I'll take your orders in just a moment," she replied before turning back to the espresso machine.

When she turned around with two drinks in her hands, she noticed that Kelsey and Jonny were in some kind of quiet argument off to the side. Matt and Richard were standing in front of the counter in silence.

"Here's your two drinks," she said, "and here's your two blueberry muffins," she added as she handed the paper sack to Matt.

"Thanks. How much do I owe you?"

After she told him the price, she glanced toward Jonny

and Richard's wife again. The woman was shaking a finger in Jonny's face, and Jonny looked like he was mere seconds from grabbing her hand and putting a stop to it.

Richard Miller noticed her worry. "Don't mind them," he said in an easy, reassuring tone. "They look like they're coming to blows, but they won't."

"Are you sure about that?"

"Very. It's a sibling thing."

"Ah, yes. " She glanced at both of them, looking for similarities. Immediately, she noticed that their stances were exactly the same. And . . . very similar to the older man standing nearby.

"They're my two youngest," Matt added. "They're close in age and have no problem sparring about everything."

"I see."

He smiled at her. "It's okay if you don't. I barely understand what's going on in our family half the time," he added, as he put most of the change in her empty tip jar.

Treva didn't know how to respond, so she was very grateful when the door to the shop opened and another customer entered. "Preacher Richard, what may I get for you?"

Looking at his wife, he murmured, "Kelsey, love, leave your poor brother alone and come tell me what you want."

Immediately, Kelsey broke away from Jonny and moved to her husband's side. "A vanilla latte. And . . . maybe one of those chocolate scones?"

"And for you, Richard?"

"A plain coffee and an apricot bar, Treva."

"Coming right up." By the time she handed the couple their order and gave Richard his change, three more people were in line. "Thank you for coming in," she said.

"I'll be back," Kelsey said with a sweet smile. "This drink is so good."

"I'm glad you like it." Looking at the next customer, an

older man obviously just done with a run, she said, "May I help you?"

"Coffee, water, and a scone, doll."

"Coming right up." Just as she turned around, Jonny walked up to the counter. "Do you need something else?"

"Yeah. I need to make an apology."

"For what?"

"For having an argument in here."

Pouring the runner's coffee into a large cup, she shrugged. "It didn't bother me none."

"Still, I'm sorry."

"You're forgiven." She smiled at him, then waved goodbye to his father as she picked up a pair of tongs to retrieve the scone. "Here you go," she told her customer.

"Thanks." The runner slid a ten toward her. "Keep the change."

"Thank you," she said with a smile.

Though she couldn't help but give half her attention to the four people who were now standing in the middle of the sidewalk outside. Each one of them looked uncomfortable.

"Lord," she silently prayed. "Please be with them today. I think each is going to be needing a little bit of extra attention."

Then she smiled at the pair of Mennonite women who'd moved forward.

"Tell me about those muffins. Are they vegan?" one of the women asked.

"*Nee*," she said as she attempted to focus on her job again. She had enough on her plate without borrowing anyone else's problems.

She and Jonny might be forming a special friendship, but he wasn't hers. That meant she didn't need to load his burden onto her shoulders.

She'd learned the hard way that never helped too much. All it seemed to do was give her a backache.

Two hours later, she was still thinking about Jonny, his sister, and their father. Maybe it was because she was an only child, but she had felt like something had been "off" with them. She wondered what it was.

Unable to help herself, she wondered about their father, too. Even though he'd been wearing jeans and a flannel, he looked anything but casual. Actually, he looked as fancy as any city dweller who came to Walden during the holidays in order to visit the Christmas tree maze and load up on quaint crafts to give to friends.

But that said, he didn't exactly look out of place. And she could be wrong, but she was pretty sure she'd heard him speak Pennsylvania Dutch to Preacher Richard.

When Aunt Ruth came in to take over for the last two hours of the day, Treva took advantage of the momentary lull to get some information.

"Hey, Aunt Ruth?"

"*Jah*, dear?"

"I met Jonny Schrock's *daed* this morning. His name is Matt."

"Yes?"

"Um, well, it occurred to me that he must have been raised Amish since Jonny's grandparents are. Did you happen to know him?"

"Matt . . . Oh, my. You met Matthew." Sounding stunned, she murmured, "Boy, I haven't thought about Matthew Schrock in years."

"You know him?"

"Well, yes. I mean, I knew him slightly years ago."

"Really? So, he did grow up Amish?"

"He did." Looking wistful, she smiled. "All of us girls had crushes on him. He was handsome and charming." She chuckled. "I guess you would call him a catch."

"What happened to him?"

Stepping behind the counter, Aunt Ruth pulled on an apron and smoothed it over the front of her dress. "Well, he jumped the fence in the middle of the night."

"What? Really?"

Aunt Ruth nodded. "Really. I wouldn't lie about something like that." Looking more pensive, she added, "It caused quite the commotion, I'll tell you what. Everyone said his parents were surprised and devastated. All at the same time!"

"Goodness." Aunt Ruth sure had a way of telling a story, but it wasn't boring, she'd give her that.

"*Jah.* I do remember hearing that he married an Englisher and he became successful in business or some such. He's rich," she whispered.

Treva couldn't help but be surprised. Some of the kids she'd gone to school with used to share stories they'd heard from various relatives about how hard it was for teenagers who jumped the fence. Of course, some had elected not to be baptized Amish with their parents' understanding. It might not have been the parents' choice, but they didn't fight them—especially if the son or daughter had a wish to go to college or be a doctor or dentist.

But for the *kinner* who left in the middle of the night with nothing but a few dollars in their pockets and fear in their hearts? Well, rumors abounded about the trouble that befell them and the things that could happen. For a boy to leave with so little and become so successful was impressive. "I wonder what he does."

"I couldn't guess. You'll have to ask Jonny if you want to know more, dear."

"I couldn't." He already knew she was watching for him every morning. What would he do if she started asking him personal questions about his father?

Aunt Ruth studied her for a moment. "Maybe you could,

maybe you couldn't. But if Matthew was here with Jonny, then they must be close, *jah*? There's nothing wrong with being interested in one's family. One can't escape one's roots, you know."

"You might have a point."

"Ack, Treva. Relax and try not to worry so much. Whatever the Lord means to happen will happen."

"That's easy for you to say."

Looking pleased, she nodded. "It is easy. I've been having a good life. The Lord has been good to me." Reaching for Treva's hand, she squeezed. "He's been good to you, too, love. Keep the faith, all right?"

"All right."

"*Gut*. Now, get on out of here and enjoy the day."

Taking off her own apron, Treva decided to do just that. She needed to take a long walk and maybe curl up for an hour or two with a good book.

Anything to get her mind to take a break.

Anything to stop thinking about Jonny Schrock.

CHAPTER 11

There was nothing like being home to humble a man's pride, Matt mused. So far, his visit to his parents' house had been anything but smooth sailing. Very quickly, he'd learned that sleeping on either a hard twin bed or a lumpy foldout couch was not for him. He'd spent a restless and painful night in hopes of a comfortable position. To make matters worse, he'd even managed to stub his toe on the corner of a dresser and then had overslept. Jonny had had to wake him up!

After suffering through that embarrassment, he'd moved to a nearby new hotel. There, he had a king-sized bed, four pillows, a roomy walk-in shower, and his own coffee maker. He also had a way to charge his phone and connect to the internet—two things that he'd begun to take for granted. His younger self might have been embarrassed by his new needs for modern comforts, but his current back was thanking him.

He'd woken up early and had arrived at the farm in time for breakfast. The meal had gone well. Jonny had seemed to thaw a bit, and his parents were their usual giving selves. After his mother had refused his offer to help with the dishes, he'd turned to his father and asked how he could help.

Which led the two of them to their current spot.

His usually implacable father seemed to be at a loss for words.

Or maybe it was more a matter of him worrying about the state of his beloved barn.

"Are you sure you want to help me in here, son?" his *daed* asked. "It's a dirty job for someone used to working in an office."

"I'm sure," Matt replied. "There's nothing I have on that can't handle a little dirt."

"We'll see." He cleared his throat. "At least you're wearing sturdy gloves."

"*Jah*. I bought them at Lehman's. I might not be as fit as I used to be, but I can muck out stalls and tend to horses well enough." He hoped so, at least. It had been decades since he'd done such things.

If his father heard the touch of hesitation in his tone, he didn't show it. Instead, he continued to look at Matt in his usual, steady way. "I'm not saying you can't. Only that it was never your favorite type of work. I don't suppose that's changed none."

His father was right. He'd never been afraid to work hard on the farm, but he'd always preferred working in the fields. He'd used to say that working for hours in a dark, dusty barn made him feel trapped and stifled. Ironically, he'd spent most of his life in a small room hunched over a computer ever since he'd jumped the fence.

"It hasn't." Sharing a smile with him, he added, "I've gotten a lot more used to being indoors, but I don't sit on my rear end all day long. I do try to get some exercise." Sure, it was in an air-conditioned gym with trained associates super-vising his workouts and handing him towels and water bot-tles after every session. But, it still counted. "I'll be fine."

His father's expression eased. "All right then."

When he paused, Matt wondered if his *daed* was finally going to ask him about his job and his life. Though Matt didn't visit very often, he did call every now and then. What's more, Matt knew his success was no secret. He'd be-come very wealthy and influential in the finance world, which was no easy feat for anyone, but almost unheard of, given that he'd left home with only an eighth-grade educa-tion.

But so far, even though his father had always asked him if he was happy, he never seemed to want to talk about Matt's life in the outside world.

It was a small reminder that Matt's departure hadn't been what his father had wanted and that it still remained a sore subject between the two of them.

"Well now, let me tell you a bit about Ribbon." Moving to stand beside the mare, his *daed* ran a hand along her dark brown forelock. The horse nudged against him, obviously enjoying the attention. After rubbing her nose and murmur-ing something to her, his *daed* straightened. "Matt, mind yourself around Ribbon. She looks sweet as can be, but she's full of attitude. She'll have you wrapped around her hoof if she thinks you're a pushover."

"Will do."

"And don't forget to put the old straw in the barrow and then wheel it out to the compost pile."

"I won't."

After another nod of his head, his father walked away.

Watching him head out to one of the fields, Matt felt a burst of affection for his father. Though he'd shrunk an inch or two over the years, he was still fit. From the back, he looked exactly like Matt remembered him looking when he was a boy. Loose dark blue trousers, loose blue shirt, suspenders, a canvas barn coat over the shirt, and muddy, well-worn boots on his feet.

His gait was the same, as well. His father had always walked with a purpose on the land. It was in other areas that he wasn't as confident.

When they were all alone, Ribbon swung her head in his direction, giving him a curious look. She was a pretty thing, and that was a fact. "A lot of women would pay big bucks for eyelashes like yours, Ribbon."

She blew out a burst of air, making him grin.

Unable to resist, he walked over and rubbed his hand over her soft muzzle. When she pressed against him, he petted her cheek and neck. "You're a *gut gaul*, ain't so?" he whispered.

She scraped the dirt floor with a hoof.

He laughed, wondering if she was pleased that he'd noticed.

"All right then, let's see if I can remember how to get you out and clean out a stall good enough for my father."

Hooking up the lead to her bridle, he led Ribbon out of her stall and down a couple of feet. To his relief, she seemed agreeable enough around him.

Hooking her lead to the post, he patted her side. "I'll spruce you up in a little bit, Ribbon. Until then, feel free to watch me make a fool of myself."

And then he got to work.

Fifteen minutes in, Matt was feeling very glad that his father hadn't stayed in the barn. If he had, there was a good chance that he wouldn't have been able to stay quiet while Matt did everything a little bit backward.

His muscles were also letting him know that his hours in an air-conditioned gym were no match for raking up old, soiled straw and tossing it into a wheelbarrow. Even though it was fall and the air was far from stifling, he soaked his shirt in no time. "I should've brought an extra shirt."

Ribbon whickered.

"Laugh all you want. I won't be offended. It's shameful how out of shape I am. Looks like my thirty-minute workout in an air-conditioned gym doesn't exactly pack the same punch."

He couldn't deny that the hard work was doing him good, however. His mind felt clearer, and his sense of peace became more pronounced.

Even more surprising was the sense of accomplishment he was feeling. A different mindset was involved when it came to doing a task for someone else's benefit. Even if it was a pretty, flirty Tennessee Walker.

An hour later, he had swept out the last of the dirt, had allowed Ribbon to graze a bit in the small field, and had put her back inside her stall.

Deciding to take a break, he filled a cup from the spigot like he used to as a boy and sat back behind the barn under the shade of an oak tree. He felt good. He had serious doubts about whether he was ever going to be able to stand up again, but he felt good.

"Hi, Dad."

The sweet voice startled him enough to jump to his feet. His muscles protested, but they couldn't compete with his happiness. "Kelsey."

It was obvious that his unkempt appearance shocked her. "You're all sweaty."

"Indeed, I am."

Looking confused, she asked, "What have you been doing?"

"Mucking out stalls and tending to Ribbon."

"You've been taking care of Dawdi's horse?"

"None other."

Looking even more puzzled, Kelsey walked toward him.

Matt took a minute to appreciate how pretty—and how perfectly Amish—she looked. Today she had on a light-blue dress, plain black tennis shoes, and her white *kapp*. The sleeves on her dress were pushed up a bit.

She also looked happy. Very happy. He said, "I'm glad to see you, honey."

Her eyes softened, but she still couldn't seem to get her head around him being in the barn. "How come you were doing all that?"

"I asked your grandfather how I could help him. After he hemmed and hawed, I volunteered to work in the barn."

"Jonny should've been doing that."

"There was no need. I still remembered what to do." Rubbing a spot on his neck, he added, "Though I have to admit that the rest of my body isn't too thrilled with the chore." Grinning, he added, "I'm fairly sure I'm going to be hobbling around like an old man tomorrow."

Her lips twitched in amusement. "This is going to sound dumb, but sometimes I completely forget that you ever lived this way."

"It doesn't sound dumb at all. Sometimes I forget it, too." Realizing that they were standing in the sun and that Kelsey had likely come over for a reason, he asked, "Is everything okay?"

"Yeah."

Something was up. She either looked embarrassed or . . . shy? Was she sick? "Did you, ah, come to see your grandma? And where's Richard?"

"Richard wanted to visit with Martin for a moment. He's in town again seeing Patti. You know she's our closest neighbor."

"Ah." He wanted to say that Richard's errand had become his blessing, but it would no doubt sound too stilted. Kelsey might not believe him, either. He really did want to

have a better, easier relationship with her. With all his children.

"Dad, I came over to talk to you."

"Well now. That's . . . great." He flashed a smile. "I'm
glad." He just hoped she wasn't gearing up to tell him that
she didn't want to see him again.

"You do have time, don't you?"

"Kelsey, I always have time for you. For all four of you."
He paused. Letting that sink in for a moment. "Now, where
would you like to chat?"

She pointed to a couple of turned-over barrels. "We could
sit here, if you'd like. It won't take long."

"Honey, no offense, but I smell to high heaven. Would
you mind sitting on the front porch or in the house with
your grandma while I take a quick shower?"

"I wouldn't mind." Giggling softly, she added, "You do
smell like a dusty barn."

"Come on, then." He walked her to the main house. "Do
you want to come in?"

"*Nee*. I mean, no. I'll stay out here, if you don't mind."

She was being so polite. So tentative. Something was going on. "Do you want me to tell Grandma to come out or
give you some space?"

She scrunched up her nose. "Is there a way to ask her not
to come out without hurting her feelings?"

He nodded. "I'll find a way. And I'll be back down in ten
minutes." *Please don't leave before I return*, he silently
added.

She looked relieved. "Thanks, Dad."

Taking off his boots, he left them on the bottom of the
porch steps and hurried inside.

"Matt?"

"Hey, Mamm."

"Is someone outside?"

"Yeah. Kelsey's here. She came over to talk to me. I've been cleaning the barn, so she's going to wait for me on the porch."

"There's no need for that. She should come in the kitchen."

"Mamm, she asked not to see you just yet."

She stiffened. "Why?"

"I don't know, but I guess it's probably because she's got something to say to me." He shrugged. "You know how many mistakes I've made. Maybe it's something about that. Or she might have something to ask about her mom." He steeled himself, ready to push back if she argued.

Luckily, although a line formed between her brows, she didn't put up a fight. "All right. I'll give her space. But, I'll make you two some glasses of lemonade."

"*Danke*, Mamm."

She smiled up at him. "You'd best hurry."

Sore muscles forgotten, he trotted up the stairs, took one of the fastest showers of his life, and was in the kitchen picking up the glasses in less than eight minutes.

"I'm back," he said as he joined Kelsey on the porch. "And I brought lemonade."

"Mommi made us glasses of lemonade?"

"Yep."

"So she knew I was here." Looking more agitated, Kelsey added, "Was Grandma upset that I didn't want to see her yet?"

"Honey, you know your grandmother. She understands that sometimes everyone needs space. Even granddaughters."

"I hope so."

"I promise, Mommi wasn't upset at all." Perching on the edge of the rocking chair next to her, he said, "What's on your mind?"

As Kelsey visibly pulled herself together, Matt cautioned himself to remain calm and listen to whatever she had to say.

Please God, he prayed. Give me the strength to be what she needs. Help me listen to her needs before spouting off excuses for whatever problem she has with me.

Kelsey looked down at her lap. Fiddled with the fabric of her dress. "I . . . I'm not sure how to tell you this."

Was it Richard? Had that husband of hers been making her cry? He had better hope not. "Whatever it is, we can figure it out. And I won't be mad."

A line formed between her eyebrows before it vanished in the midst of a beautiful smile. "Oh, Dad. It's nothing bad. It's the best news ever. I'm pregnant."

He gaped at her. "What?"

She giggled. "Dad, I'm going to have a baby. Richard and I went to the doctor yesterday." She laughed again. "She said I'm ten weeks along."

"You're ten weeks," he parroted.

Reaching out for his hands, she gripped both. "Dad, you're going to be a grandfather!"

Finally, finally . . . her words sank in. His darling daughter wasn't upset with him. Instead, she'd come to find him to tell him the news.

Before his parents.

"Dad?" she said in a soft voice. "Um . . . are you upset?"

Jumping to his feet, he wrapped his arms around her and hugged her. When she gazed up at him, her pretty face surrounded by the white *kapp*, he'd never thought she'd looked more beautiful.

Kissing her cheek, he said, "I'm not upset at all. I . . . you just gave me the best news I've received . . . since the moment the doctor told me that Jonny was a healthy eight-pound boy. I'm very happy for you. For both you and Richard. Congratulations, sweetheart. You're going to be a wonderful mother."

Tears filled her eyes. "You really think so?"

"I know so."

When he released her, she did a little hop. "I'm so excited, Dad. So excited and happy. And Richard . . . well, I don't think he's stopped smiling . . . or fussing over me."

"That's how it should be, I think. Now sit down, sip some lemonade, and tell me all about what the doctor said."

When she did, he realized that he had tears in his eyes, too. Happy tears. The first ones in ages.

They felt good.

CHAPTER 12

There was nothing worse than a slow day at the café, Treva decided, as she glanced at the large clock mounted on the wall for at least the fourth time in the last hour. Okay, that was a bit of an exaggeration. Of course, there were a lot of things worse than a lagging afternoon, but she did find a very slow clock difficult to bear.

Frowning at the thing, she remembered when she'd bought it. She'd been in Medina on a shopping trip with her mother, aunt, and Emma Jane. Once a year they joined a shopping expedition put on by a local bus company and spent the day exploring the Cleveland area. First they'd gone to Edgewater Park in Cleveland for brunch, then to the mall in Strongsville. Their last stop was for snacks and shopping in Medina before they returned home to Walden. After enjoying coffee and fresh donuts, they wandered around the town's square. And then she'd seen it. A beautiful clock housed in a black metal framework. The face was a pale gold, and the clock's black hands were intricately designed. It was the most beautiful clock she'd ever seen. It had almost been the most expensive one.

But something about it had spoken to her, and she'd known that she had to have it. Her mother, aunt and even Emma Jane had tried to talk her out of the purchase, but Treva had refused to listen to their practical and well-meaning arguments. All she had been able to think about was how perfect it would look in her otherwise rather sparse coffee shop. So she'd bought it. Lugged it home. Begged her father and one of his friends to hang it up on special black iron hooks.

And now it stared back at her in all its perfect glory.

Taunting her.

If she had a full kitchen in the back, the lack of customers would be easier. Then, at the very least, she could be making dough and refrigerating it. It would be so nice to only have to bake her scones, muffins, and bars in the evening.

Because she didn't, Treva was occupying herself by cleaning the baseboards. That task was almost as bad as watching the beautiful clock stare back at her.

Maybe even worse, because she was continually resting on her knees.

Aunt Ruth had stopped by, eager to help her wait on customers. She'd stayed to supposedly keep Treva company, but their conversation was long gone.

For the last hour, her aunt had sat in a chair and watched Treva clean. And that, of course, was worse than being alone.

"It's slow as molasses in here," Aunt Ruth said. "How often is it like this?"

"Not often, praise the Lord. I haven't had a day so slow since the first week I opened."

Her aunt frowned, making her rather thick salt-and-pepper eyebrows almost meet. "I wonder what's keeping everyone away?"

"No telling."

"Hmmph." She folded her arms across the front of her cranberry-colored dress.

"Aunt Ruth, I told ya that you should go on home. There's no need to stay here."

"I know you don't need me, but I hate to leave you all alone."

"I'm alone here a lot. I'll be fine." Hoping to convince her, she added, "You could work on that quilt you started for Dora." Her cousin's youngest.

"I suppose I could. Dora ain't getting any younger, you know."

"I didn't think she was," Treva joked.

Either Aunt Ruth didn't catch her humor, or she was already thinking of her quilting plans. Whatever the reason, she looked serious as she stood up. "All right then, dear girl. I'll be on my way."

"Thank you for coming over, anyway."

"Of course. Oh! Looks like you've finally got a customer." She turned to the newcomer. "*Wilcom!* It's a fine day for a cup of coffee, ain't so?"

"I couldn't agree more," the man said.

Making Treva freeze in her tracks.

She knew that voice. At one time, she even knew it better than her own.

Turning around, she gaped. It was Reuben Holst. There was no doubt about that. He had the same eyes, same square jaw, same broad shoulders and solid build.

What was different was that he was now looking as English as if he'd been born in an apartment in the city. Who would've ever imagined Reuben would be wearing jeans with brown loafers and a green sweater?

Or that she would think that such clothes suited him?

"Hi, Treva."

Reuben was looking at her in a way that he never had when they were courting as teenagers. Like she was something special.

It made her pulse race and her breath hitch, despite a dozen warnings going off in her brain.

"Reuben, is it really you?" she asked. It was a silly question, but she needed time to pull herself together.

Aunt Ruth blatantly scanned him from head to toe. "It's almost hard to recognize ya, dressed the way you are."

"It's been a long time, but I haven't changed that much," he said. "And neither have you." Completely ignoring her aunt, Reuben stepped closer. "I couldn't believe it when I heard you converted your family's old barn and opened up a coffee shop."

"Actually, her father and uncles did most of that," Ruth said.

Again, he didn't spare her aunt a second's glance. Looking around the place, he smiled. "It's really cool, Treva."

"*Danke.*" Looking into his blue eyes, she tried to convince herself to harden her heart or turn him away, and to feel a little of all the hurt feelings she'd been trying to get rid of for years.

That would be the smart thing to do. Yes. She should keep everything businesslike. "Would you like a cup of coffee? Or a latte or something? It's on the house."

Continuing to look at her intently, he murmured, "I'd like that a lot."

Goosebumps formed on her arms. Unbelievably, her body was responding to him again. And—the fierce traitor that it was—it had her suddenly forgetting all of the ways he'd hurt her.

No doubt about it, Reuben Holst was still dangerous.

Moving around the counter, she breathed a little easier. The space gave her at least a feeling of control. "What would you like?"

"How about a medium latte?"

"Would you like any flavoring?"

"Nope." He looked in the case. "But I would like something from there." He smiled at her. "You made them all, didn't you?"

"Guilty." Ugh. Her cheeks were heating up! What was wrong with her?

"I'm so proud of you, Trev."

Treva wasn't sure if Reuben was being completely sincere, but she wasn't going to complain.

Ruth hurried to her side like a nervous sparrow. "What are you doing, Treva?" she whispered. "You need to tell him to leave."

Her aunt was right. But wrong, too. Treva needed to hear what Reuben had to say. "Stay out of this, Aunt Ruth."

She puffed up like pigeon. "Excuse me?"

"I love you, but I'd like you to leave."

Looking scandalized, she shook her head. "You canna be alone with him."

"I'm not a young miss, Aunt. We both know that."

"But still."

"I won't hurt her, Ruth," Reuben said.

The air practically crackled as her aunt turned to face her ex-boyfriend. "You already have," she said.

Reuben looked ashamed but didn't turn away.

"Aunt Ruth, please. I know you mean well, but I need to do this. On my own."

"All right, fine. I don't understand, but you are a grown woman." She looked Reuben over, practically bit her lip from trying not to say anything, then grabbed her canvas tote bag and walked out the door.

Treva tried to pretend that the espresso machine needed a hundred percent of her attention as she prepared two lattes. One for him and one for herself. "Here you go."

"Thanks. Can we sit down?"

"*Jah.* I mean, yes. What pastry would you like?"

"Whichever one you think I'll like best."

His wording irritated her, but she tried to pretend it didn't. Just as she tried to pretend that she wasn't remembering all of his likes and thinking that the chocolate and orange scone would be his favorite choice.

Setting it on a plate, she walked around the counter and met him at a table.

"It's not usually this empty."

"I heard that it's usually packed and that sometimes the wait is as long as ten minutes."

She wasn't sure if his statement was criticism or some sort of backhanded compliment. That was why when she spoke, she weighed each word with care. "We're trying our best. Customers don't have to wait that long all the time."

Reuben shook his head. "Don't you apologize. I'm only sharing what I've heard."

"Ah."

"It's selfish, but I'm glad that I got here in the middle of a slow spot. I thought I might have to ask you to meet with me another time, and I was worried about what you would say about that."

"I would've told you no."

"I thought you probably would." He took a sip from his drink. "This is really good. Fantastic."

"I'm glad you like it." She was pleased he liked it. But she hadn't done anything amazing. She'd made a good cup of coffee.

"What kind of scone is this?"

"Chocolate and orange." She could feel her cheeks heat. She was blushing. What was happening to her?

His eyes warmed. "Like I said, I'm selfishly glad that isn't what happened."

"Why are you here?"

"I know I have a lot to tell you, but give me a second, okay? Can you tell me a little bit about how this came to be?"

"All right. Fine." Little by little, she told Reuben about her dream to own a coffee shop of her own and how she'd cleaned houses and done all kinds of jobs at night while she worked at a coffee shop in Berlin to learn all about running one of her own.

Then she'd sat down her parents and two uncles and proposed a business plan. She'd discussed the prices of an espresso maker, her vision for the barn, and her long-term goals, which ended with her being able to open her shop after two more years of hard work and penny-pinching.

To her surprise and delight, all of the men shook their heads and presented a business plan of their own. That one included them buying the machine and converting the barn right away. Then she would pay them back a little bit at a time in installments.

While she talked, Reuben ate his treat and sipped the coffee. He listened intently and didn't interrupt her once.

That was a surprise. The Reuben she'd known had always been about himself and his wants. Never listening to hers.

When she finally finished her story, he was done with his scone, as well. He grinned.

"That was quite the tale. It's impressive."

"It's a tale of a woman with many blessings. My family is wonderful."

"They are. They're the best."

"Are you finally going to tell me why you're here?"

"I guess I should." Taking a deep breath, he said, "Treva, I want you back."

And . . . that's when Treva knew that she really should've made her aunt stay. She was in way over her head.

CHAPTER 13

Reuben wanted her back. While she gaped at him, the shop's front door opened wide and no less than three different groups of people wandered in. Worse, half of them she knew.

Which meant that half of the people knew whom she was sitting down with—and that they were finding it shocking.

She did, too.

"I've got to go. I have customers to see to."

He stopped her before she could completely get to her feet. "Treva, don't leave me hanging. What do you think?"

What did she think?

"I don't know what to think." After all, it wasn't every day a girl got a bombshell like that plopped in her lap. It currently felt far too heavy. She wished she could toss his declaration out of her life and hurry home. Hide under the covers for a couple of hours.

But because that wasn't possible, she simply hurried behind the counter, took a customer's order, and breathed a sigh of relief when all he wanted was to buy a bottle of water. The next two only wanted plain coffees and baked goods. She smiled at them gratefully, hoping the easy tasks would give her the boost she needed to do her job while Reuben continued to stare at her.

"May I help ya, Mary?" she asked a woman from her church district.

"We want three coffees and three scones, please."

"Coming right up." She flashed what she hoped was a smile before she turned around to fill the cups.

It was too bad that she could barely remember what they asked for when she stared at the stack of paper cups. Yep, her mind had almost gone completely blank.

But how could it not? Reuben had just said the words she used to pray she would hear. To make matters worse, he'd looked so sincere that she was sure he'd meant every word.

At least, she wanted to believe he did.

But what did that mean to her? She just wasn't sure.

"Treva? The coffee and scones, please."

"Oh! Of course." Like a robot, she filled the cups, secured the lids, bagged the scones, and handled the payments. And then she waited on the next set of customers. And the next.

Reuben leaned on the side of the counter. "Should we discuss this later?"

"*Jah.* I mean, I don't know." Honestly, why was he asking? She had coffee drinks to make!

He laughed softly. "Do you really not have anything to say?"

"I don't know if I do or not."

"I think I'll wait another few minutes, then."

She gritted her teeth. She did not appreciate him pressing her for words. By the looks of things, a couple of the remaining customers—some of whom she'd never met before in her life—didn't seem too impressed by his pushiness, either.

"You okay?" an elderly man asked, when she handed him a cappuccino.

"Yes."

"Don't let him push you around."

His advice made her smile. "I won't. Thanks."

And then, there was another lull. Walking out from behind the counter, Treva said, "Reuben, I'm not sure what you're thinking, but I'm in shock. I . . . well, I never thought I'd see you again."

"Never's a long time."

Yes, that was true, but it didn't give her a bit of explanation about why he'd returned or what had happened in his life to bring forward such a declaration.

When someone behind her cleared their throat, her head finally cleared. "We can't do this here."

His gaze warmed. "You're right. We should go speak somewhere privately. Where do you want to go? I have my car."

There it was again. Statements that were so confusing and contradictory that she wasn't sure how to respond. Here, he'd just commented about how he knew her shop was busy, but he was acting as if she could simply walk out because he'd walked through the door. Then there was this car of his. Had he forgotten that the last time she'd seen him he'd been Amish?

She needed time to think about this. About him.

"I can't just leave."

"Why not? It's your place."

"I can't leave because it is my place."

"Okay. When, then?"

"I don't know." Next week? Next month? Tomorrow?

"Trev, you don't have a single hour to spare for me today?" Reuben smiled at her in that boyish way she used to find so adorable. "What if I came back here early this afternoon?"

And there it went again. Her traitorous insides did a little excited lurch, letting her know that Reuben might have broken her heart, but it was still intact and working. This heart of hers might be bandaged and bruised, but it was still beating and there was something about Reuben that still made her excited.

Was it love? She doubted it, but she knew she couldn't ignore her body's response. Plus, perhaps it would be best to get this meeting over with. "Four is good. Do you want to come to the house?"

He glanced behind her. A muscle in his jaw tightened before he shook his head. "I'm not sure if that's a good idea," he said quietly. "I'd rather face you instead of your entire family."

That was probably for the best. Her aunt Ruth and mother were likely shooting daggers at him from across the shop. "Where should we meet, then?"

"May I pick you up here? We can go get a sandwich together. Or, if you'd rather, head over to Charm to visit the animals at Hershberger's."

"Would you really do that?"

"I just offered, didn't I?"

"But you hate all that touristy stuff."

"It's not my favorite, but I'm feeling a little touristy myself. I'm almost missing everything in Holmes County. Besides, I'd do just about anything to make you smile like that. Even be around a herd of goats."

"All right, then. I'd like that."

"See you then." He leaned a little closer. "Don't change your mind, okay? Give me a chance."

Give him a chance after he'd broken up with her and jumped the fence? After he'd stomped on her heart and made her feel like she wasn't worthy? It was unlikely that she'd ever return to his side.

But if she refused to take the time to hear what he had to say, she worried that she'd always regret it. "I already made too many mistakes with you," she said slowly. "I'm not going to do that again. I'll be there."

"*Danke*, Treva."

She stood still as he turned and walked out the door.

When the door closed behind him, a collective sigh echoed through the space.

Emma Jane hurried over to her side and curved an arm around Treva's shoulders. "Treva, I walked in just as he was begging you to see him again. Are you all right?"

"I don't know."

"I can't believe he came back." Her voice was the perfect combination of shock and incredulousness.

Leaning into her friend for support, she whispered, "I can't believe it, either."

"Did you really say you'd see him again?"

"*Jah*."

"Treva, he broke your heart."

"That's what I'd thought. But it seems to still be beating. Now lower your voice, Emma Jane. And, please, try not to gossip about this. If my family finds out, it's going to be horrible." Of course, the way news spreads through their community, someone was probably already sitting in her parents' living room.

"What about Jonny Schrock? I could've sworn there was something brewing between the two of you."

"There might be, I don't know. I . . . I need to do this, Emma Jane. I was so hurt when he left I prayed and prayed for a moment like this. I need to listen to what he has to say."

"But he was so bad." Giving her shoulder a squeeze, Emma Jane added, "You were upset for months, Treva."

"I know. He did things that weren't right, but that doesn't

mean I can't forgive him. Plus, he might have had a good reason for his actions." She was trying really hard to act like it was a possibility, but she knew she was failing given the way Emma Jane was staring at her.

"Come now, Treva, you know that is doubtful."

"One never knows the miles the other has walked."

She rolled her eyes. "First, I don't think that's quite how the saying goes. Secondly, I can't think of anything that Reuben could say that would excuse his actions toward you."

It made no sense, but she was a little hurt that Emma Jane was making no effort to temper even a little bit of her opinions. "I guess it's good he didn't come to see you, then," she joked as she approached the counter.

"Treva, wait." She tugged on her sleeve.

"What?"

"Trev, just please remember what he did. He knew you loved him. He knew you were planning to marry him. He'd told you he was going to get baptized. He'd promised." She lowered her voice. "But while he was saying all those things to you, he was learning how to drive, dating an English woman, and making plans for a future. He didn't make a mistake, Treva. He played you for a fool."

"I think you should go. More customers are here."

Without waiting for Emma Jane to say another word, Treva washed her hands and stood in front of the expresso machine. "May I help who's next?"

"I'd like a vanilla latte."

"Great. I'll take care of it." Turning to the espresso machine, she measured out the grounds, tamped them twice, and set the cup underneath. As a slow, thin stream of espresso made its way into the cup, she watched it intently.

Pretending such a thing needed her full and undivided attention.

After topping off the milk and giving the drink a stir, she

turned to the customer at the counter. "Here is your latte. Would you like anything else?"

"An apricot bar. I'd love one."

"You got it." Sure, both she and the customer knew she was putting on a show. But there was nothing wrong with that, was there? After all, sometimes putting on a show was all that one could do.

Especially because it was either put on a show or cry.

CHAPTER 14

"It's been a while since the two of us have gone out together," Kelsey said.

Glancing to his right, Jonny smiled. His sister had stopped by their grandparents' house the night before to ask if he'd like to get together soon. He'd jumped at the chance and invited her for an afternoon walk on the bike trail. They'd quickly made meeting plans and agreed to end their walk at the Trailside Café so they could get a cup of coffee when they finished.

Now that they were on their way in the waning afternoon sunshine, he couldn't resist teasing his sister a bit. After all, she was looking so prim and proper in her pink dress and matching apron. A pristine white *kapp* covered her blond curls, and not a smidge of makeup decorated her face. She looked every bit the perfect preacher's wife. No one would ever know she'd been a college coed just a few years ago.

"It's not my fault that you only have eyes for your husband," he said, teasing her.

"Come now. You know that's not true."

"Kelsey, you hardly go anywhere without him."

Her cheeks turned pink. "Sometimes we're apart. He still has his construction job, you know."

"I've heard through the grapevine that you often join Richard on his calls to people's homes."

"He is a preacher and I am his wife. It's expected. And I don't go on every call with him. Just some."

"Oh, I know." When his sister looked ready to explain herself yet again, Jonny knew it was time to give her a break. "Kelsey, you know I'm just teasing ya. I'm glad you and your man enjoy being together."

"We are still newlyweds."

"That you are." He bit his lip to keep from bursting into laughter, but he was only halfway successful.

Kelsey looked about to protest, then chuckled when she got a good look at his eyes. "Ack. You're getting me riled up on purpose, aren't you?"

"Maybe a little bit. You are my sister, after all."

"Always." She smiled at him.

Unable to help himself, he flung an arm over her shoulders. Jonny liked that thought. Liked that no matter if they both were Amish or not, they'd always be brother and sister. There was a special bond between them—between all four of them—that was stronger than their chosen lifestyles.

They continued to walk the last few yards to the Trailside Café. Kelsey had refused to borrow one of the shop's bicycles, claiming that she wanted to talk to him, not go for a bike ride. Jonny figured she had a point. As much fun as bike riding was, it didn't allow for easy conversations. Especially not private ones.

"Is there anything in particular that you wanted to chat about?"

"Uh, Dad?"

"Oh."

Kelsey's voice—and expression—hardened. "Why do you look so surprised? Don't you think that it's odd that he's here?"

"Yes." But also maybe not. When he'd sat at his grand-parents' table the other night, their father had looked happier than Jonny had seen him in years. At first, he'd figured it was because he was around his parents, but after he'd talked about Ribbon and mucking out stalls, Jonny realized that he'd enjoyed himself. He was finding peace in his childhood roots.

Was he suddenly starting to miss living Amish? The thought struck Jonny as odd . . . but maybe it wasn't.

"What do you think he wants?" Kelsey asked. "And don't you start acting like his living in an inn in Walden is normal. He never stayed more than an hour when he used to drop the four of us off in the summers."

"You're right. His actions are surprising. I'm not sure what's going on." He chose his words with care. "Maybe he wants to reconnect with his family."

"Here?"

Jonny was starting to get annoyed about how judgmental she was sounding. "I know you're finding it hard to believe, but you should've seen him the other night, Kels. Dad was all smiles. He really loved being in the barn all day. He's happy."

"Have you ever seen him act so happy to be around all of us?"

Stopping in the middle of the bike trail, he frowned at her. "Whoa. I didn't know you resented him so much."

"I didn't know you didn't. And, speaking of that, why don't you? He was never around."

"He shared custody with Mom, remember?"

"Yes, but he was still always working." She waved a hand. "Plus, you know how Martin and Beth feel."

"I do. But . . ."

"But what?"

He shrugged. "I guess I feel a little bit differently about Mom and Dad living apart. I know you wish they hadn't gotten divorced, but I don't remember them being all that happy together."

"Come on. Don't you think they should've tried harder to stay together?"

"Fine. You tell me a story about when they were happily married."

"Don't you remember how Martin said they used to—"

"No, Kels. Don't tell me something that Martin or Beth told us. Tell me something that *you* remember."

She blinked. With a little sigh, she slumped. "You might have a good point."

"Look, I don't want to give Dad a break for all the times he wasn't around, but I'm not going to hold onto a bunch of hurts that may or may not have come from my own experiences. Not when I realize now that he was doing the best he could."

"I don't think he was doing the best. I think he could've tried harder with all of us. He could've been better."

"Then I guess you'll have to figure out a way to talk to him about that."

"I couldn't ask Dad that!"

Now that they were almost to the café's entrance, he pulled her to one side. "Kelsey, do you hear yourself? I might not know a lot of Pennsylvania Dutch words yet, but I sure know about how important forgiveness is. Maybe you need to think about that."

"Are you saying I'm not acting Amish enough?"

"Of course not. But I am saying that forgiving our parents for being imperfect might make you feel better—and might make having a good relationship in the future with them a lot easier."

Her eyes widened. "Jonny, when did you get so wise?"

He lifted his chin as they stopped just short of the coffee shop. "Your problem, Kelsey Miller, is that you continually underestimate me. I'll have you know that a lot of people seem to think I've got my act together."

"Is that right?"

"I wouldn't lie about that."

"Well, in that case, I guess they'd be right." After giving him a hug, she said, "Are you still going to buy me a cup of coffee?"

"I am. And, because I'm feeling generous, I might even buy you a cookie or something, too," he said as he opened the door.

She was smiling at him as they walked inside. But right away his sister's happy expression faded.

Confused, Jonny glanced toward the front of the shop . . . and then saw what had caught his sister's attention. Treva was glaring at the man standing in front of her on the other side of the counter. The guy seemed to be whispering something that definitely wasn't settling easy with her.

Before he could stop himself, he was striding forward. "Hey, Treva. You got any of those apricot bars left?"

Okay, it was a pretty dumb thing to call out, but it served his purpose. The guy stopped talking and turned to him . . . and Treva's expression could only be described as relieved.

It was a fact—she had not liked whatever he'd been saying to her.

Taking another look at the guy, Jonny decided that he didn't like a thing about him. He was dressed English, but nothing about his clothes said that he was comfortable. Instead, it was like he was trying on a costume. Or at least pretending to be someone he wasn't.

Jonny walked closer. "Treva, did you hear me?"

"*Jah.* Um . . ."

"Excuse me," the guy said. "You were being rude. Wait your turn."

"My turn?" He looked pointedly at the counter. "It doesn't look like you're ordering. Or are you?"

"What I'm doing is none of your business."

"Sorry, but I disagree." Returning his attention to Treva, he decided to stop playing games and lay it all out there. "What do you want me to do?"

She bit her lip.

Kelsey put her hand on his arm. "Careful, Jon."

"I know," he murmured, still not taking his attention from Treva.

The guy tapped his foot. "Treva, are you going to say something to this couple or should I?"

Kelsey shot him a dark look. "We're not a couple. He's my brother."

"Then tell your brother to mind his own business."

"We do have apricot bars," Treva said suddenly. "Would you like one, Jonny?"

"I would."

She darted a look at the man but seemed to collect herself a little bit more. "How many?"

"Six?"

"Six?" Kelsey said.

"Richard's going to love them. So will you."

"Um, I don't know . . ."

"Put one on a plate, would you, Trev? And we'll take two lattes."

"Flavoring?"

Kelsey stepped forward so that she was now closest to Treva. "What do you have?" she asked with a smile.

"Well, um, chocolate, hazelnut, vanilla, caramel . . ."

"I'll have vanilla. Decaf, please." Then his sister had the gall to give the guy an annoyed look. "Oh, did you still have to pay for your order?"

"No. I . . . I decided not to buy anything right now."

Kelsey smiled at him again, but it was a mean girl smile.

The same attitude his sister adopted when she was in middle school and had used on him and his friends whenever they bugged her and her friends too much.

And just like it had done to him all those years ago, it seemed to neatly put Treva's intruder in his place. He stared hard at Kelsey, glanced back at Treva, then turned and walked out the door.

The wood seemed to clank as it shut.

But the air felt fresher.

Or maybe it just felt that way to Jonny.

Noticing that Treva still had her back to them, he said, "Hey, are you okay? Are you mad at us for getting into your business?"

At last she turned around, each of her hands holding a paper cup. "I'm not mad. Honestly, I'm not even sure what to think."

"Who was that?" Kelsey asked. "I mean, if you don't mind my asking."

"That was my ex-boyfriend. A couple of years ago, just when I thought he was about to propose, he jumped the fence for an English girl."

"Why was he here?"

"I have no idea, but I think he came to see what I was like after all these years. I agreed to meet with him and catch up, but when it became apparent that he expected me to change, I came inside. He didn't care for that."

"I'm so sorry," Kelsey said.

"I am, too. I think he thought I was still going to be the same, but obviously I've changed."

Kelsey chuckled. "For better or worse?"

"I think I'm better. And I could be wrong, but I have a feeling Reuben has decided that I'm much worse."

Jonny looked out the door, half expecting Reuben to be lurking around the sidewalk in front of the shop, but he didn't see a thing. "Do you think he'll be back?"

"I couldn't tell you. But I really couldn't care less." After placing one on a plate for Kelsey, she asked, "Do you really want six apricot squares?"

"Yep. Throw in six cookies, too."

"You've decided to eat treats after all?"

"No." Lowering his voice, he said, "I'm trying to lower my cholesterol, but I'll be happy to send my sister home with lots of treats for her husband."

As she did as he asked, she smiled at him. "Your sale has emptied my bakery counter. I'm mighty pleased about that."

"If that's the case, then I'm pleased, too." Realizing how good making her happy made him feel, he said, "Obviously, I need to help you out more often."

CHAPTER 15

Agreeing to meet with Reuben a second time had been a bad idea. Thinking about the way he'd acted, the way he'd presumed she'd simply drop everything for him . . . well, it made her boiling mad.

Their conversation had been so bad that it was right up there with the moment she'd discovered that Reuben had been stepping out on her. That he'd been meaning to break up with her but hadn't been in any hurry to do it properly.

Having a boyfriend not feel that you were worth even ten minutes face-to-face to break up with had been a blow to her ego. Especially because everyone knew he'd felt that way.

But today had come close.

As that sinking feeling settled in like a bag of rocks, she grimaced.

"This is why you are such a mess, Treva," she told herself, as she locked the front door of the café a little after five o'clock. "You need to simply put that man out of your mind. Forget about him and move on. Instead, you over-think everything."

She was pretty sure that was no lie, too.

What she would give to have been able to have known exactly what to say to Reuben when he'd shown up out of nowhere. Instead, she'd felt as if she'd been in slow motion. She could barely do more than stare at him . . . all while her mind had been spinning as she'd tried to figure out why he'd sought her out.

Which she still had no idea.

Walking inside the house, she saw a pot of soup on the stove, but otherwise it was quiet. Pleased to have some time to herself, she trotted upstairs to her room and changed into one of her oldest and most comfortable dresses.

Then, instead of sitting on the downstairs couch and reading or working on a puzzle, her mind started spinning again.

Just like that, she remembered how awkward everything with Reuben had gotten when Jonny and his sister had come into the café. And how Jonny had decided that she'd needed saving. Then his sister had gotten into the act! And she'd let them!

There was no way she was going to be able to simply sit around, so she pulled out all the cleaning materials, filled up the bucket with hot, soapy water, and got down on her hands and knees.

Feverishly scrubbing the bathroom floor, she attacked the tile as if it had personally affronted her.

And wondered yet again why she'd ever wanted to give Reuben even a moment of her time. Why had she?

Honestly, why was everything in her love life so difficult? Did she make it so, or did she, for some reason, create chaos? Why couldn't she have fallen in love with a steady sort of man like Paul Troyer? Thinking of Paul, she felt a burst of melancholy. Paul had tried to court her when they'd just graduated middle school. She hadn't given him the time of day, though. Instead of longing for quiet, steady, boring Paul, her eyes had followed Reuben.

But then, after she'd spent years by Reuben's side, silently pining for a proposal, Reuben had up and left her for an English girl.

And Paul? Paul had turned his attention to Jenna Weaver. Now Paul owned a large farm and had two children with Jenna.

She? She had a busy coffee shop.

After dipping the sponge into the hot, soapy water again, she scooted back toward the wall and continued her washing tirade.

Why had she never actually answered Reuben? Why had she hesitated? Was it because she'd never gotten over him? And if it was, what did that say about her?

"Treva!" her mother called out. "What are you doing?"

"Cleaning the bathroom floor, Mamm!"

Two seconds later, she heard her mother trot up the stairs. When she appeared in the bathroom's doorway, so pretty in an eggplant-colored dress, she frowned. "Why in the world are you cleaning the floor? I washed it just a few days ago."

Surprised, she sat back on her knees. "But this is my job."

"Darling, you have a business to run now. You're cleaning the bathroom there. I washed this floor before you got old enough to walk on it. I'm not so old that I canna do it now."

Her mother was in good shape. There was no denying that. But that didn't mean her mom had to take over her chores. That wasn't fair at all. "I feel bad about that, though." Pulling the wash bucket closer, she rinsed the sponge.

"I disagree."

She tried one more time. "Mamm, I might clean bathrooms at the café, but that's to be expected. When I asked you and Daed if I could open my café in our old barn, I never intended to stop doing my part around here."

Her mother propped a hand on one of her hips. "I think it's time we talked."

"Okay. I'm listening."

"Not here, child. Downstairs. At the kitchen table. Over a glass of lemonade."

"Oh."

"Now."

Her *mamm's* tone left no room for argument. "Yes, Mamm. I'll be right there."

Her mother didn't budge. "Hand me the sponge."

"I was just going to finish the floor."

She wiggled her fingers. "Exactly. Hand it over, dear."

"Fine. Here." Handing her the soapy sponge, Treva felt like laughing. Who would've ever thought that her *mamm* would have to practically use force to get her to stop cleaning a bathroom floor?

"Thank you. Come along." After taking two steps, she paused and looked back over her shoulder. "If I have to come back for you, I'm not going to be pleased, Treva," she warned.

"I know."

"Hmmph."

Memories of being fourteen and obstinate came running back. Her mother was the sweetest, most kind-hearted woman in the world. But when she wanted Treva to do something, she expected it to be done right away. If that didn't happen, she'd deliver the longest lecture, bringing up every supposed infraction Treva had done in her entire life.

She'd often wished her mother would have been like her friend Beth's *mamm*, who'd rapped Beth's knuckles with a wooden spoon. Beth had said the sting would only last a minute or so. Here Treva was, all these years later, still remembering portions of those lectures.

"You won't have to come get me."

"Umph. We shall see."

Treva mentally rolled her eyes. Of course, her *mamm* had to get in the last word.

She carried the bucket downstairs, poured its contents outside on the gravel near the driveway, then walked back in and washed her hands in the stationary tub's faucet.

When she sat down at the table, only five minutes had passed. Not even her mother could find fault with that.

Her *mamm* brought her a glass of lemonade. "Have a sip of your drink, child."

As always, the liquid was slightly tart, icy cold, and very delicious. "*Danke.*"

"You are welcome."

Perching on the edge of her chair, her *mamm* exhaled. "Treva, dear, I think we should talk about Reuben."

"I'd rather not."

"That's the problem. You're keeping all your feelings inside. That ain't good."

"I agree, but I don't know if there's much to say. Reuben came back to Walden for a visit and just happened to stop into the café."

"Just like that?"

"I think so."

"Your Aunt Ruth seems to believe that he came for a special reason, and it wasn't to see his parents."

"You two are talking about him?"

"Reuben's return is noteworthy, child. Now, what did he say when the two of you went out early this afternoon?"

"Well, first of all, we didn't go very far. I refused to take a ride in his vehicle, so we walked to the park."

"Why did he visit you, Treva?"

There was no delicate way to say it. "He paid me a visit because he wants me back." She steeled herself for either a lecture or a tirade. She got neither. Instead, her mother appeared to be intrigued.

"Hmm."

"Hmm? What does that mean?"

"It doesn't matter what I think, does it? You're an adult and this is your life."

"That's what you have to say?"

She blinked. "Were you hoping I would say something else?"

"I was expecting you to offer your opinion."

"I don't know if I have one."

"You don't have any feelings about Reuben?"

"I'm not sure." She shook her head. "No, that's not right. I don't want to have feelings for him, but I'm afraid I might."

After taking another sip of lemonade, she set the glass down with care. "Here's what I think, Treva. You loved him once. He left our community and became English. He also started dating another woman."

"Janet."

"Hmm. Well, ah, yes."

"So I shouldn't want anything to do with him, should I?"

"I don't know. You see, I am feeling like the Lord had a plan in all of this. If Reuben hadn't made those choices, you two might have already been married."

She knew they would have. "*Jah.*"

"So you would've never opened your coffee café."

To her surprise, the idea of not having her little coffee shop made her insides clench. "I might have."

"Perhaps the Lord would have guided you there, but I don't know. You seemed certain that you would marry and have children right away." She hesitated. "And then there are Reuben's parents."

"Sally and Neal." Thinking about how both of his parents had never had an opinion they didn't share, she winced. "They would've never allowed me to open a coffee shop."

"What if you had really wanted that? Would Reuben have stood up to them?"

She didn't need to think about that even for a second. "*Nee.*"

"Now, I didn't see Reuben, and you've yet to tell me your impression of him. But your aunt seemed to think that he didn't seem all that bad. Was he?"

"No. At first, he caught me off guard, because he walked into Trailside like he wasn't surprised I had the shop. Then he ordered a drink and a scone."

"And then?"

"And then he was full of compliments. About the store and me." She swallowed. "And then he said he wanted me back."

"Well now, isn't that something?"

"It's something, all right."

Looking thoughtful, Treva's mother took a sip of lemonade. "I could be wrong, but it sounds to me like this new Reuben is a far different man than the boy you fell in love with."

"He is."

"Worse?"

"I . . . I couldn't say. Maybe not." She couldn't lie about that.

"Treva, are you the same person who Reuben courted?"

"No. I'm a lot more confident. And . . . and I expect more. I expect more out of a relationship." And of herself. And of whoever she was going to share her heart with.

"Aunt Ruth also shared that she got a good eyeful of Jonny Schrock."

Treva squirmed. She'd been kind of hoping her aunt

wouldn't have shared the whole soap opera. "He was there. He'd come in with his sister Kelsey, who is now married to Richard Miller."

Her mother didn't crack a smile, but her dancing eyes made it perfectly obvious that she didn't need to.

"Mother, my life is a mess, isn't it?"

Though it was obvious she was attempting not to laugh, her *mamm* continued her pep talk. "On the contrary, it sounds like you're having a mighty full life right now. You have two men interested in you and a busy café to run."

"What do you think I should do? Part of me doesn't want to see Reuben ever again, but part of me thinks I do. And I don't know what I should do about Jonny Schrock. He's not the type of man I thought I'd ever want, but I seem to think about him all the time."

"Perhaps you need to give them both a chance."

"Really?" Wasn't her mother supposed to be guiding her to be more circumspect and cautious?

"One day, all of this will be over. You'll have either chosen one of those men or someone else. But no matter what happens, you'll have lots of time to reflect on this moment that the Lord has brought you." Softening her voice, she added, "I would hate for you to look back upon this time and wish that you hadn't rushed through it."

"Or made the wrong decision."

"I think if you open your heart, pray, and don't hide out in our bathroom scrubbing the floor, you won't make the wrong decision, dear. The Lord has a plan."

The Lord has a plan. The words echoed through her heart and seemed to settle in. "I just have to listen."

"Yes. And maybe . . . be a little selfish, too. There's nothing wrong with asking the Lord to remind you about what makes you happy."

"How did you get so smart, Mamm?"

"The Lord gave me a daughter. Raising her has taught me a lot about love and trust and happiness." Standing up, her mother walked to Treva's side, bent down, and kissed her temple. "Everything is going to be just fine, dear." She chuckled. "Eventually."

Sitting there stunned, Treva allowed her mother's words to float into her heart.

And then, at long last she closed her eyes and spoke to the Lord.

And asked Him to help her find her happiness.

When a sense of peace settled into her heart, she knew that He'd heard her.

Or that He'd simply been waiting for her to reach out to Him.

Finally.

CHAPTER 16

Matt knew that there was no getting around the obvious. He'd had a very tough day. He'd pulled a muscle while cleaning out the tack room in the back of the barn but had been too full of pride to admit to his father that he'd hurt himself. To make things worse, his accident had been because of a stupid mistake that was completely his fault.

He'd been distracted because he'd been going over the last conversation he'd had with Kelsey. She'd been polite but distant. Again.

Making him realize that he'd been naïve to imagine that he could close the gap in their relationship in just a couple of days. Even though he'd known that he shouldn't imagine it was possible to mend their relationship so quickly, there had been a big part of him that had believed it would be possible.

It absolutely wasn't.

Worse, because he knew he was going to have to go back to the office soon and would likely not return to Walden for several weeks, he was beginning to wonder if he and Kelsey would ever get to the place where things between them would be good again. How was he ever going to build a healthy relationship with each of his four grown children if his job kept getting in the way? Remembering that they, too, had other obligations besides reconnecting with their dear old dad didn't help that much.

Finally, after finishing another supper filled with a nearby restaurant's tasty but too heavy food, he was sitting in his room at the Walden Inn wishing for a salad, a piece of grilled fish, and a couple of hours of mindless TV.

Since that wasn't going to happen, he'd read a couple of pages of a book and thumbed through a magazine.

Finally, he'd picked up his phone, intending to skim through his e-mails. But he'd had something better—a text from Kennedy.

How are you? Hoping you're having a good time!

Immediately his mood had lifted. Anxious to hear her voice, and realizing that she would be the perfect person to talk about everything with, he'd given her a call . . . and then had probably said too much.

"Sorry. I didn't mean to bore you," Matt finished, after giving Kennedy a summary of his visit.

"You didn't bore me, but are you sure that's all that's happened?"

He opened his mouth to reply, then realized that she'd been sarcastic. "Pretty much," he ended up saying with a laugh.

"How are you doing?"

"What?"

"Matt. It sounds like you've been through the wringer. Are you hanging in there?"

Kennedy had hit the nail on the head. He actually had been feeling like he'd been through the emotional wringer. He should have thought things through before making the impulsive choice to see his parents and try to mend his relationships with his grown children. "I'm fine. Nothing's been easy, but I shouldn't have thought it would be. I made a lot of choices, and now I'm reaping the consequences."

"You know what? I think you need to consider not thinking of your future with them in such a bleak way. Maybe all the consequences won't be negative ones."

"That's a sweet thought, but I don't know how that would be possible."

"Sorry if I'm making everything sound too easy, but it's been my experience that good things happen when everything is out in the open."

"I'm glad that's been your experience, but I'm afraid that end result might not be the same for me." Of course, he could privately admit that he wasn't all that used to being completely open with anyone. Even with Helen, he'd kept a lot of his feelings to himself.

Of course, that had obviously been the wrong thing to do.

"I guess we'll see what happens, hmm? The Lord will work through all of you, and time will take care of the rest."

He smiled. "I reckon you're right. Listen, I'm tired of talking about myself. What's been going on with you?"

"Nothing very noteworthy, though I did get a new client."

He smiled. "House-sitting or pet-sitting?"

"Pet." She paused. "Matt, get this. A woman reached out to me about taking care of her old turtle."

"I didn't know turtles needed to be taken of care of. Don't they, um, just sit in one place most of the time?"

"Matt, turtles do a lot! They take walks, eat, drink, and sometimes even like to swim." She chuckled. "But not this turtle. It's lived most of its life as a pet, and it kind of has a fancy life. He has special food and everything." She giggled again. "And he likes to be entertained."

He laughed, loving every bit of their conversation. "I

don't even want to think about what entertaining a turtle entails."

"Music, a cool bath, time to wander in its pen."

"It has its own pen?" He thought they lived in glass aquariums.

"Oh, Matt. You don't even know. This is a big guy."

"How big are we talking about?"

"Hmm . . . its shell is about the size of a dinner plate?"

He wrinkled his nose. He wasn't sure why the thought of having a turtle that big as a house pet sounded strange, but it did. Plus, didn't turtles carry salmonella or something? "You didn't accept the job, did you?"

"Of course I did. Turtles need love, too, Matt."

Well, that put everything he'd been about to say in its place. Because he'd been spending so much time alone lately, he'd been thinking the same thing. And then, of course, there was the way he'd been fussing over Ribbon. Sure, the horse was beautiful, smart, and affectionate. Everything a turtle was not. But that didn't mean his feelings for the old mare—or the turtle owner's feelings for her pet—weren't justified.

"I hope he is easy. And, um, doesn't snap your finger off."

Her laughter was so filled with joy it made him smile. "I'll let you know if he gets violent."

"Thanks for that." He mentally groaned.

"So, when are you coming home? Anytime soon?"

"I was planning on returning this week, but now I'm not quite so sure. I think I'm finally connecting with everyone. My *daed* and I are having conversations that don't have anything to do with the weather, and my mother seems more relaxed around me each morning. I don't want to go backwards."

"What about your kids?"

"I've only gotten to spend much time with Jonny. He's been all right. I've only seen Martin once, and it was in the middle of a family dinner. I haven't seen Beth at all, though she is in Cleveland, not here."

"Let's see . . . that leaves Kelsey, right?"

"Right."

"How are things with her?"

"Well . . . that's a different story." Searching for the right word, he added, "I guess you could say that things between us have been civil."

"Civil?"

"Yeah. Polite. Respectful. Nothing like I'd hoped." Alone in his hotel room, he frowned again.

"I'm so sorry."

"I am too, but it's my fault, Kennedy. I was a fool to think that the bridges I've broken could be mended with just a couple of conversations."

"Maybe you're being too hard on yourself?"

"I'm not. The only good thing I can say about our conversations is that we're talking."

"And neither Kelsey nor Jonny are yelling at you?"

Her quip startled a bark of laughter from him. "I guess there is that," he acknowledged. He was smiling because Kennedy had not only reached out to him but also remembered his kids' names. "You're right," he said at last. "That is something to be grateful for."

"This is none of my business, but how do the kids get along with your ex?"

"With Helen? Honestly, I don't think things are much better."

"Really?"

"Yeah, neither of us acted like great parents for a while after we divorced." Hearing his words out loud made him wince. Realizing he was probably making himself sound better than he'd been made him feel ashamed. He cleared his throat. "To be honest, there were times when I was a pretty bad dad."

"There's still time to fix things, Matt."

"Do you think it's that easy?"

"No. I don't think it's going to be easy at all. But you aren't looking for easy, are you?"

That question brought him up short. "No, I'm not."

"Well, there you go."

Hating that so far all he'd done was complain about his faults, he said, "Are you okay? Do you need anything?"

"What if I said I did?" she asked in a warm tone.

He knew she was teasing, but at least he had an answer. "If you did, then I would make sure you got what you needed."

"Just like that?"

"Exactly like that."

"You're being completely honest, aren't you?"

She sounded incredulous, which made him start to wonder just how badly she'd been treated in past relationships. "I am. Listen, I still have a lot to learn about being a parent and a son, but I do know a lot about getting things done or helping out someone in need."

"I don't need a thing. I'm good."

"I hear you. But if you do need something . . . a break, a hand, someone to bring you dinner, let me know."

"And you'll make sure that happens."

"I would. I'd also consider it my honor to help you." Sure, that sounded a little over-the-top, but he wasn't going to back down. Besides, hadn't he just been wishing that he'd been more open with Helen?

After speaking for a few more minutes, mainly about the weather, he hung up and lay down on the inn's surprisingly comfortable king-sized bed.

And decided that he was going to do whatever it took to keep Kennedy in his life. He loved talking to her on the phone. He loved seeing her in person.

And, at moments like this, he liked how Kennedy made him feel—like he was worth something.

He wanted to be the type of man to make her feel the same way.

CHAPTER 17

"These new bicycles from Harley-Davidson are beauties," Jonny's new friend Ben said as he ran a hand along the aluminum frame. "And you said the throttle is easy to work?"

"Easy as pie."

"Hmm." Wearing old-looking faded overalls, he squatted down to look at the motor. "How does it compare to those Stromer bikes from Switzerland?"

"I think they're comparable. Other people have told me they felt the Swiss brand was better."

After standing up, Ben glanced at the price. Then whistled low. "Man, but that's a pretty penny."

Glancing at the three-thousand-dollar price tag, Jonny nodded. "It is. They all are, though." He smiled. "I could tell you all about the bells, whistles, and engineering, but it might be simpler just to concentrate on what your grandfather says."

"It's all less than feeding a horse," Ben said with a laugh. "I canna believe that my old grandpa was the first one in my family to take up electric bike riding. He used to tell me that old ways were the best. Now he's zipping along the farm roads like he's on a racetrack."

"It is a surprise, but I'm glad your Grandpa Bill did. If Bill wasn't such a fan of these bikes, I don't think half the community would be trying them out." Thinking of the number of people who'd come into the store spouting off some bit of information Bill had told them, Jonny added, "Alan should be giving your grandpa a bonus for every bike sold."

Ben grinned. "It's *gut* you didn't, then. *Mei dawdi* wouldn't make you offer twice. In no time, he'd take you up on the offer and never look back."

"I wouldn't blame him a bit."

Folding his arms across his chest, Ben grinned. "Bill is quite the leader. Always has been."

"So, do you want to take one of them out for a spin?"

After examining the bikes one more time, he nodded. "I do."

"Which one?"

Ben grinned. "This one. I like that the Serial 1 is made by Harley-Davidson. Even though we're talking bicycles and not motorcycles, there's something about owning a Harley that makes me grin."

Jonny grinned, too. "I think you'll be pleased. And if you're not, you can try some of our other models."

"And the payment plan is still in effect?"

"Yep. Half down, then the rest divided into six payments. Or we even offer zero percent financing."

"That helps."

"Sure it does."

"At first I thought that not making everyone pay the full price was a strange way of doing things, but it seems to be working for you."

"It is. Alan says that these bikes are an investment, and I agree with him. But it doesn't just work well for our store.

It's helping out a lot of our customers, too. That's what's important." He paused. "Go take a test ride. See what you think. If you aren't sure and want to test some other bikes, that's no problem."

Fifteen minutes later, Jonny was standing in the parking lot and watching Ben pedal down the bike path. Pleased that he seemed to be handling the bicycle well, Jonny watched until his friend pedaled out of sight. Ben didn't look as if he was going to have any trouble getting used to having a motorized bicycle.

When he went back inside, Jonny glanced at the clock. Three more hours to go.

Grabbing his water bottle, Jonny took a long pull and hopped on a stool. He really did need to start thinking about his schedule more. The afternoons lagged too long, especially because he seemed to be opening up the shop earlier and earlier every week.

He was also starting to feel torn, and for the first time was beginning to doubt his ability to change his life. He loved a lot of things about living Plain. He liked not worrying about too many possessions and feeling less of a need to be constantly running around and busy.

But he also missed his friends. And, if he was honest, he missed his phone. He'd done everything on it. E-mails, texts, read the news, played games, scanned social media. Now that he barely used it, he felt as if he was missing out and was out of the loop.

Maybe Beth had been right when she'd said that she wasn't sure if living Plain was the right path for her to follow.

Before he'd moved in with his grandparents, he'd simply assumed that Martin hadn't given their experiment a good try. After all, if Kelsey could adapt so easily, why couldn't the rest of them?

But maybe he wasn't as committed to being Amish as he thought he was.

When the shop's door opened again, he glanced toward it with relief.

And then shock.

Because there were Martin and Patti. And Treva?

"Is this how you greet all your customers, little brother?" Martin asked.

"Stop. I didn't know you were coming in town." Smiling at the women, he added, "All three of you are a sight for sore eyes, though."

"Ignore Martin," Patti said. "He's just giving you a hard time. We know we caught you off guard."

"You did catch me by surprise, but in the best way possible. Believe it or not, I was just thinking about Martin. That's why I was gaping at you all." Remembering his manners, he reached for Patti's hand. "It's been too long since our paths crossed. I'm glad to see ya, Patti."

To his surprise, she rose up and kissed his cheek. "I'm glad to see you, too. I must say that this shop is impressive."

"Alan did a fine job setting it all up."

"I heard differently," Martin said. "I heard that your work managing it has made a world of difference."

"I don't know about that. I do know that it's good to see you."

"I feel the same way." He clapped him on the back. When they parted, Martin smiled at Treva. "I have to be honest. Patti and I were going to surprise you at supper, but then we got to talking to Treva here and discovered that you two know each other."

"I just happened to mention you in passing," Treva said, her cheeks turning pink.

"Of course we know each other," he said with a laugh. "I'm in your shop bright and early every morning."

"Just like the sun."

As they shared a smile, he realized that his exchange with Treva had definitely taken both Patti's and Martin's notice.

They were exchanging looks. Martin had the gall to actually look a little smug.

About what, Jonny had no idea.

"When do you get off work?" Martin asked. "Patti and I thought the four of us could go sit down somewhere and visit."

"*Jah.* There's a cute restaurant nearby that has really good half-and-halfs."

He knew she was referring to the half-lemonade half-iced tea drink. He'd always called it an Arnold Palmer. Whatever the name, it was his favorite. "That sounds great, but I can't leave just yet. I've got a guy out on the trail test riding a bike."

And then, just as if he'd planned it, the door flew open and Ben strode in, rolling the bicycle by his side. He was grinning broadly and his eyes were bright.

"Jonny, by golly, but you were right! Riding that bicycle there was fantastic."

"I'm glad you enjoyed it. Do you have any questions? Or would you like to try out another?" Sure, he'd like nothing better than to go spend time with his brother, Patti, and Treva, but work came first—especially when it involved the possibility of a new sale.

Ben shook his head. "No way. I've made up my mind. I've got to get me a Harley."

Martin's laughter lit up the room. When Ben looked at Martin in confusion, his brother attempted to settle down. "Sorry. Didn't mean to be rude, but there's just something about an Amish man saying he wanted a Harley that struck me as funny."

"No offense taken," Ben said. "I daresay you have a point." Turning to Jonny, he said, "I'm going to need the paperwork in order to get that zero percent financing."

"No problem." Handing him a packet, he said, "I can scan

all your information, send it off, and get an answer for you in about fifteen minutes."

"Would you mind if I took it home? I want to talk to *mei daed.*" He lifted a shoulder. "He might be willing to give me the loan. That's worth a try, right?"

"Whatever way you want to pay works for me."

"Are you working tomorrow?"

"I am."

"I'll be back before ten."

"I'll be here by eight."

Jonny held out his hand, and Ben shook it. "*Danke,* Jonny."

After Ben walked out the door, Martin, Patti, and even Treva clapped.

"What's the applause for?"

"We all peeked at the price on that fancy bicycle," Treva said. "Selling one is something to celebrate."

He chuckled. "It's not sold yet, but Ben has been in here a couple of times. He sounds sure."

"Do you still want to get out of here?"

"Yep, give me ten minutes to straighten up and give Alan a call."

"We'll straighten up. You call," Martin said.

Fifteen minutes later, the four of them were sitting in Andre's Taco Shack sipping Arnold Palmers and munching on warm tortilla chips. They'd also ordered a flight of appetizer-sized tacos to share.

Because Martin and Patti were sitting on one side of the booth, he was sharing his side with Treva. She smelled faintly like pumpkin and cinnamon. It was obvious that she'd been baking earlier that day.

When Martin leaned down to whisper something in Patti's ear, he said, "You smell good, Treva. Like pumpkin pie."

She laughed. "I bet I do. I made five dozen pumpkin pie muffins this morning."

"Five dozen? You'll sell five dozen at the shop?"

"Oh, *nee*. I'll sell about two dozen. The other three are a special order for the Methodist church downtown."

"I didn't know you baked special orders. That's great."

She smiled back at him, obviously pleased by his compliment. "*Danke*."

"We've been learning all kinds of things about Treva's business," Patti said. "I'm mighty impressed."

"You shouldn't be, but I am pleased. When I first dreamed of opening the Trailside Café, I asked God to help me believe in myself. I never expected to have so many customers."

"I think you might have to start dreaming bigger, Treva," Martin said.

"Perhaps I should," she murmured, as she stole a glance his way.

Jonny caught it, though. He realized then that it was time to step things up. Not just for the two of them to spend time together but also for him to share some of his feelings more openly. "Treva, maybe I could come over one evening and we could visit for a spell."

Her eyes widened. "You want to come over in the evening?"

"Uh, yeah." Wasn't that what he'd just said? Why was she looking so surprised?

"All right. Um, I think that would be agreeable to my parents."

"Great." Still feeling like he was missing something, he nodded. "Is tonight okay? Say, about seven?"

"Seven will be fine. I'll let my parents know."

"*Danke*, Treva."

Her cheeks pinkened just as the server brought their taco flight.

They each grabbed a taco and said a quiet prayer. Then

dug in. As the girls started eating, Patti started talking to Treva about a mutual friend.

Pleased that their impromptu get-together was going so well, Jonny added some fresh lettuce to his grilled chicken taco and took a bite.

Only then did he notice that Martin was looking at him in a bemused way. "What?" he asked.

After glancing at the women, Martin leaned forward. "You do know that you just asked Treva if you could come calling, right?"

"No, I didn't. All I asked was . . ." His voice drifted off. "Wow, you're right." A knot formed in the pit of his stomach before his brain kicked in and reminded him of one thing—he liked Treva. He liked her a lot.

If he didn't start calling on her, either that putz Reuben would or some other guy whom she met at her café would probably start getting ideas. He didn't want either to happen.

Looking a little concerned, Martin added, "Are you okay with that?"

"Yeah," he said. "I'm good with it."

"Good with what?" Treva asked.

"Just having one taco," he improvised quickly. "I had thought I might want more, but it's plenty."

"Oh. Well, that's good."

He smiled at her. "It sure is."

CHAPTER 18

"Treva, you certainly have a way of turning this house upside down," Aunt Ruth announced as she ran a cloth along the window frame in their already-clean living room. "I thought we were going to enjoy a relaxing afternoon. Instead, your mother has us cleaning this house top to bottom."

Even though she had her hands full of flowers, Treva stopped in her tracks. Her aunt's statement wasn't wrong, but she certainly wasn't going to take all the blame! "Aunt, all I did was tell Mamm and Daed that Jonny asked to come over this evening at seven o'clock. I didn't add that he expected to see the entire *haus*—or that he was the sort of man who cared about dirt or dust."

"That's not how your mother took the news."

"Well, she should have. Plus, we both know she wants this house to be perfect for her, not Jonny. After all, he runs a bicycle shop! He's not going to care one lick about a dust bunny in the corner," she added, as she finished arranging the bouquet of hydrangeas in a wooden vase on the table in the entryway.

"Hmmph."

Ignoring her aunt's complaining, Treva said, "Aunt Ruth, what do you think? Should I cut one or two more flowers for the vase?"

Aunt Ruth walked over to the hand-carved wooden vase, which Treva's grandfather had made when he was just a newlywed. After fussing with the blooms a bit, she shook her head. "I don't think we need to add a thing. These blooms are so beautiful, adding another stem won't make any difference."

"They are pretty. Maybe even more beautiful than last year's blossoms." Her mother's prized hydrangea blooms were a dark, vibrant, violet purple. She said that the coffee grounds she spread around the plant's base every August were what made them so vibrant, but Treva believed it was more likely her mother's green thumb. She was known far and wide for her beautiful flower gardens.

Stretching her arms, Ruth murmured, "Well, I'd best go see how your *mamm* is faring in the kitchen. She's working on pizza rolls for Jonny's visit."

"I told her that wasn't necessary."

"You can't host a gentleman caller without offering food. You know that." She sighed dramatically. "Perhaps I'll help with the dishes. Why, I bet she's worn herself to the bone."

Even though she knew Aunt Ruth was prone to exaggeration and teasing, Treva still felt embarrassed. "Thank you for the help, Aunt."

"Ruth, give my poor daughter a break," her *daed* called out as he finished arranging wood in the fireplace. "You're making Treva feel guilty when you know you're loving every minute of this."

"Don't feel bad, child. We're glad to help you. No lie about that."

Sitting down on the couch, Treva exhaled. "Daed, Mamm

and Ruth are being ridiculous. Jonny is coming over to visit. Not to propose marriage."

"I know. Don't let them bother you."

"They're not." When she felt his gaze rest on her, she amended her words. "Okay, I guess they are a little bit."

"Or a lot."

She laughed. "*Jah*. Maybe a lot." She lowered her voice. "I just don't understand why Mamm and Ruth have to do so much more than is necessary and then complain about the work."

"They love you, dear. That's all you have to understand."

"I should've told Jonny no."

"I'm glad you did no such thing. He might still be learning to be Amish and you might not be a fresh young girl in your teens, but it's still important to do the right thing."

"And the right thing is cleaning the whole house?"

"It is." He winked. "And making pizza rolls. I love those." Getting to his feet, he said, "What do you think? Are we ready?"

"We have a tidy *haus*, fresh-cut *blumms*, a merry fire crackling in the fireplace, and pizza rolls. I think so."

"*Gut*." Leaning down, he kissed her cheek. "Now hurry on upstairs and look busy before your mother decides that you need to change clothes or rearrange the couch's cushions."

She didn't need him to repeat that warning! As she hurried upstairs, she heard his laughter echo through the house. It combined with her mother's and aunt's chatter and made Treva feel good inside. This visit might have been unexpected, but a lot of good had come out of it already. Both her parents and her aunt were in merry spirits and seemed very pleased for Treva.

She just hoped Jonny wouldn't be too taken aback by the sight that greeted him when he knocked on the front door.

* * *

It turned out that Jonny had no idea how to come courting properly. He'd shown up with a liter of soda and a deck of Uno cards. Before Treva could think to ask why he'd arrived with such things, he'd gone and asked the whole family if they'd like to play. Next thing Treva knew, all five of them were sitting on the floor in front of the fireplace, playing game after game of Uno, sipping soda, and finishing off the entire plate of pizza rolls.

"Uno!" Aunt Ruth called out.

"Argh!" Jonny groaned. "Ruth, I canna believe you won again."

Her grin widened. "I did at that." As if something had just occurred to her, she murmured, "You don't mind, do you?"

"Losing five games in a row? Not at all."

"She's a card shark, that's what she is," her *daed* complained. "Ruth, is this why we don't play Uno anymore?"

"Maybe." As Ruth shuffled the deck with the expertise of a Las Vegas blackjack dealer, she added, "Or maybe it's because you're a sore loser."

"Never." Hefting himself to his feet, he held out a hand. "Just for that, come help me put these glasses in the kitchen, Ruth."

"Fine."

Watching the two of them walk out of the room, each holding two glasses, Treva shared a smile with her mother. The entire evening had been so much fun and so different from the times when Reuben had called and the two of them had sat awkwardly on the couch while sipping lemonade.

Climbing to her feet as well, her *mamm* said, "It's getting late. It's time we let the two of you have a few moments to yourselves. Jonny, thank you for bringing over the soda and the cards. I don't remember the last time I laughed so much."

"You're welcome," he replied as he also stood up. "Thank you for the pizza rolls, too. They were wonderful."

"I'm glad you enjoyed them," she said as she picked up her glass. "Treva, will you see your guest out in thirty minutes or so?"

"*Jah*, Mamm."

When they were alone at last, Treva glanced up at Jonny, who was now sitting on the couch. "How did you know to bring cards?"

"What do you mean?"

"It was the perfect icebreaker."

"I just thought it would be fun." He wrinkled his nose. "It's probably not a good idea to tell you this, but I'm not a huge fan of sitting around doing nothing. I get bored easily."

"Given that every other time we've talked, we've been doing something, I'm not surprised." Realizing that she was still sprawled on the floor like a teenager, she sighed as she moved to stand up.

Jonny was on his feet in a flash . . . and was holding a hand out to her. "Here. Let me help you."

Slipping her palm into his, she easily sprang to her feet. "Thanks."

"No problem." He didn't release her hand, though. Instead, he reached for her other.

And there they were, standing across from each other in front of the warm fireplace, fingers linked. His hands were far bigger than hers and slightly calloused. She liked how they felt and hoped he wasn't in a big hurry to let her hands go.

"I'm glad I came over. Tonight was fun." His blue eyes sparkled. "And by that, I mean I enjoyed being with you, Treva. Not just letting your aunt beat me soundly at cards."

"I had a lot of fun, too." Looking at his shirt, which was a faintly checked button-down that was tucked into jeans, she realized that such an evening was probably far different from when he'd gone out with other girls. English girls in his past. "Did you date a lot in high school and college?"

"I did." He shrugged. "No more than most guys, I guess."

"Did you have a girlfriend?"

"I did in high school. I dated Leigh most of my senior year."

Leigh? "Were you two serious?"

He dropped her hands and stuffed his into his pants pockets. "A little bit."

Missing their connection, she folded her arms over her chest. "What does that mean?"

"I don't know." He flashed a smile. "I walked her to class and drove her to school in the mornings. We ate lunch together when we could." He shrugged. "I took her to prom. You know, stuff like that."

That was the problem, though. She actually didn't know stuff like that. She had never been inside a high school and didn't exactly know what walking to class together would look like. And though she knew *prom* was a dance where a lot of girls wore fancy dresses, she didn't understand the significance of it.

Or if it didn't mean anything at all.

Hoping she looked far more disinterested than she was, she added, "What about in college?"

"Well, by the time Leigh and I graduated, we knew we didn't have a future. She had gotten a scholarship to an Ivy League school up east. So, we broke things off." He shrugged. "I didn't date anyone special in college."

"Why not?"

"I don't know. Maybe I was tired of having a girlfriend? Then, there were my classes. I took a full load those two years. Between those classes and my friends, I didn't have any interest in dating."

"Oh."

He stepped closer. "Why all the questions?"

"I . . . I realized that you know all about Reuben, but I don't know much about your past relationships."

He chuckled. "Leigh was great, but neither of us were in love."

"You didn't like her that much?"

Jonny looked even more uncomfortable. "I liked her, Treva, but Leigh was a star tennis player. We both knew that she was going to get a college scholarship. And, like I said, she did."

Reaching out, he ran his hands along her upper arms. "Treva, don't worry, okay? I might have dated other women, but I came over here with my eyes open."

She wasn't sure what he meant by that. "What did you hope to see?"

Leaning down, he brushed his lips against her cheek. "You. I wanted to see *you*, silly." Pulling away, he walked to the row of hooks by the front door and pulled on his jacket. "Now tell me good night so I don't overstay my welcome."

"Good night."

He grinned again as he opened the door. "I'll be at your café in the morning. See you then."

"Yes. See you then," she whispered before closing the door.

Taking advantage of the moment, she wandered back into the living room and stood in front of the warm fireplace. Thought about Jonny's Leigh and Reuben and Uno and the way Jonny smiled at her in the morning.

And how much she'd enjoyed holding his hands.

She had no idea what the Lord had in store for them, but she was excited to find out.

CHAPTER 19

Now that it was nearing the end of September the air was a little crisper and there was more than a hint of fall in the air. The sycamore, elm, and maple trees' red, orange, and gold leaves decorated the streets, and lots of English-owned houses were decorated with silly Halloween decorations or quaint-looking cornstalks and pumpkins. Treva loved every bit of it.

Those bright colors, together with the vivid blue sky, made for a string of beautiful days. Almost every customer had walked into the Trailside Café with smiles on their faces. While she made their pumpkin spice and caramel lattes, they told her all about how happy they were to be out walking and biking. It was a blessing to be able to enjoy the season.

Treva had started to get jealous.

When Jonny had come into the shop, his conversation filled with even more details about the glorious day outside, she couldn't take it anymore.

In a moment of weakness, she'd told him that she was jealous.

Which meant her aunt and mother had encouraged her to take a day off . . . and Jonny had encouraged her to finally take him up on his offer of going on a bike ride.

She wouldn't dare admit it, but she was scared. The bike was bigger than her old one at home and about a hundred times more powerful. Even though she knew deep down that she was in control—Jonny had painstakingly shown her how to work all the knobs and gadgets—at the moment she felt like a passenger on the proverbial freight train. All she could do was hang on and pray.

"You're doing so well, Treva," Jonny called out. "Are you having fun?"

"Kind of." It was more like "not really," but she was going to be very happy when the bike ride was over.

"Don't worry, Treva. Before you know it, you'll want to speed down all the hills and valleys of Walden."

"I'm not so sure about that."

Jonny's laughing response grated on her. Not because she thought he was making fun of her, but that she was pretty sure he truly had no idea how nervous she was to be pedaling next to him on the bike trail.

"How far do you want to go?"

"I don't know. A couple of miles? Watch out up here, there's a stick in the road."

Sticks? "Should I go around it?"

"You could, or just take it slow and go over. You've got good wheels, yeah?"

"Yeah." She was mumbling and she didn't even care. Spying the stick, which looked more like a dangerous obstacle, Treva gripped her handlebars more firmly.

And then *blip-blip*!

She was over the stupid stick.

"Treva, be careful now," Jonny warned. "There's no need to go so fast. We're just going out for an easy ride, yeah?"

Now he told her that? From the moment they'd set off, he'd ridden at a steady pace, dodging walkers and joggers with ease. She'd started sweating within the first ten minutes. "I'm doing the best I can," she called out. To his back. They'd started out side by side, but he'd moved in front of her when the path narrowed. She hated that. Now she not only was a ball of nerves, but she also was starting to feel like a kid following a parent or older sibling. Trying hard to keep up but not quite succeeding.

As if Jonny could read her mind, his voice gentled. "I know you're doing your best. You're doing real well, too."

"Not really." Plus, it wasn't like he could keep an eye on her from his position up ahead. He had no idea the stress she'd been feeling.

After another five minutes, he said, "Listen, there's a bench coming up in about twenty feet. Let's stop and take a break."

When she pulled to a stop where he'd designated, Jonny was already off his bike and stretching his arms. He had a big smile on his face and looked relaxed and carefree. She supposed he was.

It was too bad that she wasn't sharing even a tenth of those warm and fuzzy feelings.

"Hey!" he called out as he strode to her side. Even though she didn't need his help, he steadied the bike so she could get off and pulled down the kickstand. "What do you think?"

She didn't want to hurt his feelings, but to say she was having a great time seemed like an outright lie. "I think I'm getting the hang of things."

He studied her face. "Oh no. You're miserable, aren't you?"

"*Nee.*" Miserable was being home with strep throat. This? It was more along the lines of having a runny nose and cough one couldn't shake. Unpleasant but not horrible.

His usually crystal-clear blue eyes clouded. "Treva, you can be honest."

"Well, then I honestly have been a little bit afraid and nervous but not miserable."

"What would you like to do? Do you want to turn back?"

Suddenly she felt like a failure. And a spoilsport. Definitely selfish. Thinking of how excited Jonny had been for this outing, she knew she needed to give it another go. Bicycles were a big part of his life. What would she do if he hated coffee?

She needed to learn to enjoy bike riding. At least a little bit. "I don't want to turn around," she replied. "We can keep going."

"Are you sure?"

"I don't want this to be our date, Jonny." Just as important, she wanted to know that she gave electric bicycle riding a good try. The bike shop was Jonny's job. No, it was important to him. If they were destined to have a future together, then she was going to need to learn to enjoy riding these bikes.

Or at the very least, not hate it.

He reached for her hand, gently ran his thumb over her knuckles. "We can do something else," he murmured.

If he wasn't Jonny, Treva would've wondered if he was hinting that they could be doing something far more intimate than riding bicycles together.

But she trusted him. He was simply being sweet. Once again, her heart melted a little bit more for him. The fact of the matter was that Jonny Schrock really was rather incredible. He was night and day from Reuben and an incredible combination of English worldliness and Plain sensibilities. He also was sweet to her and accepted her for how she was.

If he could accept all of her, she knew she could try harder to be the girlfriend he wanted in life.

"There's no need to make different plans. I want to continue."

He was still holding her hand. Looking down at their linked fingers, he said, "You sure?"

"Yes, Jonny. Positive."

His smile turned boyish again. "Okay, then. Let's go another three miles. There's a pretty path that leads to a creek and . . . if we're lucky, we might even catch the gal who has an ice cream truck. I'll buy you a cone."

His plans really did sound adorable. "I can't think of a better way to spend our afternoon. Let's go."

Leaning closer, Jonny lightly brushed his lips against hers. So quickly, she didn't even have time to respond.

Except to smile up at him—and be so very glad she hadn't given in to her fears and asked him to stop.

Far too soon, they were on their bicycles again, Jonny in the lead. Treva did feel a little bit more assured, though. Even when a family coming from the other direction passed, their young children weaving slightly and not paying a bit of attention to who else was in the vicinity.

She even kept her balance and her cool when a trio of bicycle racers sped by. They hadn't announced themselves except to ring the bells on their bikes. She thought that was kind of rude.

"The stop is up ahead, Treva!" Jonny called out. "Just after the dip."

"Okay!" she replied. Smiling at the thought of walking next to him at the creek. And yes, sitting on the grass eating an ice cream cone . . . or maybe sharing a real kiss. One where she wasn't caught off guard.

Yep, she'd almost made it.

And she had . . . until a young deer ran out onto the path.

Handlebars wobbling, she braked hard. But it was too forceful and too fast. Next thing Treva knew, she'd lost her balance and fallen to the ground. The bike hit the pavement hard, sending a shrill *ting* into the air.

She might have imagined the snap she'd heard in her left arm. But the pain that followed told her a different story.

She was in trouble.

And that was the last thing she thought about before she passed out in a dead faint.

CHAPTER 20

Jonny's father had been a lifesaver. In a panic, Jonny had called him at the hotel from the bike trail. His father'd answered immediately.

Then, after Jonny had explained what happened to Treva, it was obvious that his father had dropped everything and was listening intently. When Jonny had finally stopped to take a breath, his father had quietly asked Jonny for the closest cross streets, told him to relax, then assured him that he'd be there soon.

Feeling better now that he knew help was on the way, Jonny had called the coffee shop and spoke to Treva's Aunt Ruth, who assured him that she would let the rest of their family know what happened.

Thirty minutes later, Jonny and Treva were in his father's SUV and on the way to the hospital. The two bicycles were loaded in the back.

Through it all, Treva didn't cry or appear mad at him. She simply sat quietly by his side. When he'd carefully held her uninjured arm, she'd leaned against him. Just knowing that he was able to comfort her in the smallest of ways had eased his conscience.

At the hospital, the health professionals had taken X-rays and determined that Treva's left ulna was broken. Then the orthopedic doctor had put a temporary splint on it, saying he wanted to examine it again when the swelling went down. Only then—if she didn't need surgery—would she get a cast.

Since her parents and her aunt had come with a driver and said they'd take her home, Jonny was stuck sitting on a plastic chair in the waiting room. After the stress of the last two hours, each minute felt like five as he impatiently waited until Treva appeared again. He needed to see her face when he told her good-bye.

He hoped and prayed she wasn't angry with him.

After another ten minutes had passed, he'd told Treva's aunt that he was going to step outside. The waiting room was hot and crowded. He needed some fresh air. When his father approached, his expression as stern as it had been when Jonny had gotten in trouble at school for fighting, his spirits plummeted, followed closely by a burst of annoyance. He didn't need anyone to tell him that he should've taken better care of Treva, but his father looked like he was going to tell him all about that.

Gritting his teeth, Jonny knew he was going to have to take it, too. A stern lecture about taking care of the woman he was falling in love with was nothing less than he deserved. Not only was she in pain and possibly needing surgery, but this emergency room visit also was not going to be cheap.

When his dad finally stopped by his side, he exhaled.

"How are you doing?" his father asked.

"All right."

"Really?"

Okay. Dad was going to make him say it. "Fine. I'm not feeling all that great. I mean, I feel horrible that I did such a bad job taking care of Treva."

Matt stuffed his hands into his dark-green barn coat. "Oh?"

His father was acting way different than he'd imagined. Maybe he was just waiting for Jonny to admit his mistakes? If that was the case, Jonny felt he could definitely do that. Anything to get the conversation over with.

"Look, Dad. I appreciate you picking up the phone, picking us up off the trail, and being so much help, but I don't need a lecture right now. I know I shouldn't have taken Treva so far the first time we rode bikes. I also shouldn't have ridden in front of her."

His father folded his arms over his chest. "So why did you?"

"I don't know. I guess I took her out because these bikes are important to me."

"Of course they are. Bicycles and running the shop is your job. You're supposed to care about such things."

Some of the tension Jonny'd been carrying in his shoulders eased. "Even though Treva acted a little nervous about riding, she seemed interested in it." Half talking to himself, he waved a hand. "But . . . I kept thinking that until she actually tried riding one of those electric bikes, she wouldn't completely understand what they were like. I mean, standing around in a bike shop without riding is like standing in a bakery without trying any of the stuff in the cases."

"I would imagine so. Now, did you force her to get on that bike?"

"Force her?" Affronted, he glanced at his father. Met his blue eyes. When he didn't see anything but curiosity, he replied. "Of course I didn't."

"And when she was riding, did she tell you that she wanted to go back? Did you ignore her wishes?"

"No." Being completely honest, he added, "I mean, I know that riding the electric bikes wasn't her favorite thing to do. When we stopped earlier, I even asked if she wanted to go back."

"You gave her the choice again."

He was feeling more frustrated by the second. "Dad, what do you want me to say?"

Matt's eyes warmed. "Something along the lines that you realize that Treva is a grown woman who obviously knows how to make decisions, since she owns her own business. And that she simply had an accident. Nothing more."

"I know all that."

"Are you sure? Because you sound like you're happily taking all the blame for something that was out of your control."

"Dad, I—" Jonny stopped as he realized his father was right. Very right. "Okay, maybe I am."

"There you go."

As much as he appreciated his father's support, he still resented it. "Knowing that I'm taking responsibility doesn't help me one bit. I still feel guilty for her accident."

"I understand. Feeling guilty is a natural reaction."

"You think so?"

He nodded again. "Jonathan, you obviously care about her. I'd be surprised if you didn't."

Since he'd been expecting a long, drawn-out lecture, Jonny was taken aback. Sitting down on a bench, he stared up at his father. "That's it?"

His father studied his face. "Sorry, but now I'm not sure what you mean."

"Come on. You always have something to say about everything." Often, his father's lectures had also been critical and unhelpful. At least, it felt like it had been that way lately.

Exhaling, his father sat down on the barricade next to him. "Is that really how you think of our conversations? Like I'm just talking *at* you?"

As much as he really didn't want to go down the emotional memory lane with his father, Jonny was tired of always holding his tongue. "Do you think of them as any different?" When his dad still looked taken aback, he added, "Dad, what was the first thing you told me when I said I was taking a break from college?"

He answered immediately. "I told you that I thought you were making a big mistake."

Glad his dad wasn't remembering the conversation differently, he nodded. "That's right. You said that before you even gave me a chance to explain. Then, just seconds after that, you pointed out that you were paying for part of my tuition, so you were entitled to an opinion."

"Was I wrong?" Matt swallowed. "I don't want to argue, but your tuition wasn't cheap. I felt like it was money wasted."

"It wasn't."

"Okay . . ." It was obvious he was biting his tongue in order not to pass any more judgments.

"I don't know if you were wrong as much as you talked over me. I barely got a word in edgewise."

"I guess I did go overboard," he murmured.

"And that's not the only example. You did that with sports and with my choices during the summer and even with the way I get along with Kelsey, Martin, and Beth."

Matt rubbed a hand over his face. "I don't know what to say."

"I don't expect you to say anything. I'm just trying to tell you what I think and how I feel. You don't have to agree with me."

Lines of concern marred his father's forehead. "You've been thinking these things about me for a while, haven't you?"

As much as he and his father hadn't been getting along, Jonny still didn't want to intentionally hurt his feelings. "Kind of."

"Jon, you might as well tell me the whole truth. I can take it."

"All right. Then, yes, I have."

"And the others? Martin and the girls . . . Do you think they feel the same way?"

No way was he going there. As far as he was concerned, his father could have this discussion with each of them. "I don't think I'm the only one who feels that way."

"I see." He swallowed. "Jonny, I don't know what to say other than I'm trying."

"Yes, sir."

Matt's eyes turned shadowed before they lit up with a smile. "She's out, bud."

Jonny turned to the door and saw his father was right. Treva was walking toward him in her light-gray dress, the white *kapp* that somehow still looked fresh, and now with a white bandage covering her left arm to her elbow. What caught his eye, though, was her smile.

Relief filled him. Besides the bandage on her arm and a couple of scratches on her other arm and her hands, she didn't look too worse for wear. Her parents were walking by her side, and her aunt was not too far behind. When they saw him, they looked apprehensive but not angry.

His father forgotten, Jonny strode to Treva's side. "Look at you. Okay?"

"I am."

"Are you sure?" Suddenly thinking about how her long dress covered her legs, he lowered her voice. "Are you okay to walk? Are your legs and knees bruised?"

"Beyond a couple of nasty bruises, they're fine."

He held out an arm. "Do you need help walking?"

She chuckled. "Jonny Schrock, calm down!"

"I'm calm."

"Not very. You must stop worrying so much about me."

"I'm not going to be able to do that." Looking at her parents, he said, "I hope everyone treated you well back there? Do you have any questions?"

"We're good, Jonny," her father said. "Maybe a sight better than you, I reckon."

"I was just telling him almost the same thing," his *daed* said. "That's not a surprise, though. I think Jonny was a born worrier."

"Not usually." He shifted uncomfortably.

"Perhaps you only worry about some things, hmm?" Treva's mother said.

"I have my truck," his *daed* said. "I'll be pleased to give you all a ride back to Walden."

"It will be a tight fit," Jonny warned.

"We already have a driver waiting on us, but there's no need for us all to ride home in it," her mother said. "What do you want to do, Trev?"

"A ride with Matt and Jonny would be nice. *Danke*," she added shyly.

His father grinned. "Excellent. I'll pull the truck up."

"We can walk," Treva said.

"No reason to do that," his dad said before Jonny could. "Might was well give your body a rest."

She shrugged but didn't argue.

Feeling like he and his father had ended things on a bad note, Jonny said, "Hey, Dad, I'll go with you."

Meeting his gaze, his father seemed to convey a dozen thoughts his way—especially that he still loved him. "No reason, son," he said in a gentle tone. "You stay with your girl, yeah?"

Luckily, his dad walked off before he could respond. It was just as well, anyway. All he wanted to do was be near Treva. "Are you in much pain?"

"They gave me some medicine but warned it would probably get worse when it wears off."

"Do you have some pain reliever?"

"We have ibuprofen at home, plus the doctor gave me a prescription in case it feels worse."

He nodded. There wasn't anything to say about that except to apologize, and he'd felt like he was starting to sound like a broken record.

"Hey, Jonny?"

"Hmm?"

"Before I forget to ask . . . would you like to come over tomorrow for a bit? I won't be able to work in the coffee shop."

"I'd love that."

"*Gut.*" Chuckling, she said, "I promise my whole family won't be hovering the whole time."

"I wouldn't care if they did." Jonny leaned in, intending to kiss her cheek but then remembering that both of her parents and her aunt Ruth were standing nearby. Something about Treva was starting to make him forget about everything else.

He had a feeling his mother would call that love.

CHAPTER 21

Three hours had passed since Matt had dropped off Treva and Jonny at the Kramers' house. After a quick thanks and hug, his son had waved good-bye and focused solely on his girl. Matt didn't blame him one bit. Treva was adorable and sweet. She also looked at Jonny as if he was the answer to her prayers—and maybe he was. Matt was glad his youngest child had found someone like her to be in his life.

After making sure they got safely inside, he'd pulled out of the driveway feeling at a loss of what to do. Because he hadn't intended to visit his parents for another day or two, he elected not to stop by. Not only did he not feel right about dropping by unannounced, he also was still reeling from the frank conversation he and Jonny had exchanged.

If he was being completely honest with himself, none of what his youngest had said was a surprise. He had been taken aback, however, with how honest Jonny had been. Historically, Jonny was usually his most easygoing child. Martin had questioned, Beth had been vocal about her opinions, and Kelsey would let her opinions be known in a handful of silent but very obvious ways. Jonny, on the other hand, had always been the child who had gone with the flow. He and Helen used to say that he was their little gift after giving birth to three rather demanding kids.

Now he was going to have to come to terms with the fact that Jonny hadn't been all that laid-back.

And then there had been Jonny's terse "Yes, sir." On the surface, there wasn't anything wrong about that. He'd taught his kids to say "sir" and "ma'am" to elders. Granted, all four of them were grown-up adults now, so it wasn't the same.

But that phrase coming out of his son's mouth had felt like Jonny had put up the barrier that had been slowly sliding down as they'd become closer.

"You are upset because he took control of that barrier," he told himself in his empty SUV. "Jonny isn't messing around anymore. He is no longer going to be okay with talking about the weather and you pretending to be involved. And he's really not going to put up with you having opinions about Treva. Not at all."

So that was where they were.

"Where are you going to go, then?" he asked himself. And yes, he was speaking in both the literal and figurative senses.

Back home? To his parents? Pop in on Kelsey and hope she didn't have the sudden need to lecture him about his parenting faults?

His phone ringing on his Bluetooth speaker came as a relief. "Hey, Harrison."

"Hey," one of his junior executives answered. "I'm sorry to bother you, but do you have a few minutes to discuss something, Matt?"

"Of course. What's up?"

"We've got some issues going on with the Wilson account."

"I've got all the time you need," he said. "But I'm in the middle of Amish country. If I lose you, hang in there and I'll call you back."

"No problem. Um, why are you there?" Matt could hear Harrison tapping the keys on his computer. "Did I miss a scheduled vacation on my calendar?"

"No. No, not at all. I decided to work remotely for a while." He hesitated, then figured he might as well be honest about his roots. "I'm from here."

"What do you mean? You grew up on a farm?"

"Yeah. And I mean I grew up Amish."

"No way."

Harrison's voice was so incredulous, Matt couldn't help but grin. "Yeah."

"Wow. I'm floored. You seem so smart."

And that criticism hit him in the center of his chest. On the heels of his irritation, he reminded himself that Harrison grew up outside of Detroit. He'd probably never seen a horse and buggy outside of the movie *Witness*. To him, the Amish were completely foreign. "Thanks," he said in a dry tone.

"Sorry. Did I, uh, offend you?"

"By putting down my heritage? What do you think?"

"Wow, you're right. I'm sorry. I wouldn't put up with that for a minute. I don't know why I was so insensitive."

"Don't worry about it. The mistake wasn't all yours. It's mine, too. I've spent the majority of my life reinventing myself." Taking in a breath, he added, "And . . . none of this is why you called. What's going on?"

"First off, the Wilsons don't like how Erin is communicating with them. They say that Erin isn't getting back to them in a timely way. That she takes forever calling them back."

"What does Erin say about that?"

"She's defensive. She takes notes about her phone calls, but I looked back at the e-mails she exchanged with the Wilsons, and they might have a point. Erin does get back . . . but usually not for twenty-four hours."

"So, it's a matter of defining 'timely'."

"I think so." Harrison cleared his throat. "They also said that she could've been a lot more forthcoming about some of the investments they were interested in."

"I don't understand what they meant by that."

"Well, it seems like Mr. Wilson reads a lot of broker magazines and journals and then wants to get on every new, um, horse, if you will. Erin shuts him down."

"But let me guess. Some of the ideas he's mentioned have ended up doing pretty well?"

"Yes." He took a breath. "You know how that goes, Matt. Everyone loves to talk about the stock that got away."

"You're right. All of us have a story like that. But what I don't understand is how you got involved. Did Erin or Mr. Wilson reach out to you?"

"Mr. Wilson." Sounding more aggrieved, he added, "And then Erin. Lots of hurt feelings going on around."

"I can imagine." Thankful to be alone in his car instead of in a boardroom, Matt rolled his eyes. So many people acted as if different rules applied to business relationships when thousands of dollars were in play. But actually, nothing was any different than when his father was at the auction and buying livestock. "What do you need me to do?"

"Let me know what else I need to look into so I can fix this," he replied without missing a beat.

Matt's respect for Harrison grew even more. He wasn't attempting to toss the problem in Matt's lap. He wanted guidance so he could handle the situation well—and learn from it. "What is your gut telling you about Erin, Harrison?"

"That she might be doing just fine but it's not good enough."

Matt nodded. "I agree. See if you can find some feedback about how her other clients are feeling about her communication skills. And you don't need to make the calls yourself. Have Janice call. Just to say she's checking in to make sure no one is having any issues."

Harrison was tapping notes on his computer again. After a second or two, he asked, "What should I do if Janice gets good responses?"

"Then tell Erin that. But then give her some suggestions on what to do with the Wilsons."

"And . . . if the reports aren't all that good?"

"Then offer her some coaching."

Matt could hear Harrison typing more notes. "Matt, I'm five years younger than Erin and have been with the company half the time."

"I know."

"So . . . what if Erin doesn't want to take any of my advice? What if she just says no?"

"Give her a day or two and circle back. If she still won't consider changing . . . then start the process to let her go."

Harrison groaned. "So what you're saying is I'm on my own here."

"Nope. What I'm saying is that I'll speak with Erin if you need me to, but it will mean more—and be more effective—coming from you."

"I guess I can see it that way," he said in a grudging tone.

"Harrison, I'm here for you, but I think you're ready to have more responsibility." He wondered if Harrison was realizing that Matt was offering him the same thing that he would be offering Erin.

"Understood."

"Harrison, I'll be heading back into the office on Tuesday. Call Janice and get on my calendar in the morning. We'll discuss this further then. I'm not going to leave you on your own."

"What about the Wilsons?"

"Give them a call. Tell them that you're involved and offer to bring them in for an in-person meeting."

"Okay. All right. I'll get to work."

"If it's any consolation, I have a feeling Erin is going to be willing to make things better. She's good. Her pride might be bruised, but I have a feeling she'll get over it."

"I hope so." Sounding far more relieved, Harrison said, "Hey, Matt, thanks for taking my call."

"Anytime."

After they hung up, he realized that the conversation they'd shared was more honest and open than a lot of the ones he'd had during the last couple of years with his kids.

One day, with the Lord's help, he hoped he'd be able to have that kind of relationship with them. He needed to keep doing what Harrison was going to tell Erin to do. Keep trying.

Speaking of trying, he texted Kennedy.

Any chance you'd like to come down to Walden? There's a great B&B nearby. I'll be happy to get you a room. We could do some hikes, and I'll show you around.

Will I get to meet your family?

Absolutely.

Staring at the word, Matt realized that he'd just written it without thinking. But did he mean it? Yes. Even though she was probably too young for him and there might even be a dozen other reasons why they would never work out—likely all of them his fault—Matt wanted to introduce her to this part of his past.

No, to his life.

And that was it, wasn't it? If nothing else, the experiences over the last month had reinforced his belief that he no longer had time to wait and hope for better relationships with his kids. If he didn't act soon, then there was going to be nothing left.

Nothing but himself as an empty shell of a man. Wishing for people in his life to fill his soul.

His phone rang. When a familiar and very welcome name appeared on the screen, he couldn't resist grinning. "Hi, Kennedy."

"Hi. Are you busy?"

"I'm not too busy to talk. Is everything okay?"

"Hmm? Oh, sure." She chuckled self-consciously. "Sorry, but I wanted to hear your voice when I asked you something."

Leaning against the back of his seat, he said, "Ask me anything you want."

"Okay . . . what do you think about me coming tomorrow afternoon and leaving the next day?"

"I'd think that it's a great idea."

"Are you sure?"

"More than sure." Honestly, it was all he could do to sound calm and collected. His insides were practically doing a celebratory dance.

She exhaled, like she'd been afraid that he would've said no to her. "Okay! Well, text me the name of the place and I'll—"

"I'll get you a reservation."

"I don't want you to pay. I might not—"

"Honey, we both know I can afford it, right?" He didn't want to brag about his wealth, but he wasn't going to let her pay for a single thing when she was with him.

"Right."

She sounded both resigned and amused. At least, he hoped that was the case. Boy, he wished he could see her. Maybe then he'd be able to know for sure how she felt. "Then don't make a big deal about it."

"So, um . . . you'll text me all the info?"

"I will. And I'll call you tomorrow when I know what we're doing for supper."

"Supper, huh?"

He knew Kennedy was smiling ear to ear, and who could blame her? There was nothing wrong with saying "supper" unless it was out of his mouth.

Because he probably hadn't called dinner "supper" in years. "Old habits die hard," he said, teasing her. "I'm so glad you're coming. It's going to be great."

"Wait—Don't go yet."

"What's wrong?"

"Do I need to wear anything special?"

"Well, it's warm but a little cooler in the evenings—"

"I meant, around your family." Sounding a little panicked, she added, "Do I need to wear a long dress? I don't want to offend anyone."

"No long dress is expected. Just wear whatever you feel comfortable in." Teasing her, he added, "Anything is fine, except maybe not your shortest shorts or a tank top."

"I would never!"

He chuckled. "Then you're gonna be just fine."

"Okay. Oh! Thank you. Did I say thank you?"

"You just did. And you're welcome. See you tomorrow."

"Yeah, see you tomorrow, Matt." Her voice sweetened. "I can't wait."

"Me, neither." Boy, he meant that, too. Kennedy had become important to him.

Grinning, he got on the phone and started looking for the number of the best inn in the area.

He had a reservation to make.

CHAPTER 22

After Matt had dropped off Treva and Jonny at her house, Jonny had come inside and stayed for a glass of lemonade. Then, after gifting her with a sweet, very gentle hug, he'd gone on his way. Jonny had known how tired and emotionally drained she was.

Just as she was about to escape to her room with a cup of herbal tea, their doorbell had begun to ring.

All too soon, their large kitchen was packed with people.

So many people!

Nee, they weren't just *people*, they were *family*, Treva corrected herself. That was different.

The problem was that she had such a large family. It was humongous. When word had gotten out about her bicycle accident, everyone had come running. With food and flowers and books and even a rather itchy shawl stitched together with an unfortunate shade of yellow yarn.

The item also smelled faintly of mothballs, which was a sign that it had been made by one of her aunts or great-aunts as a gift of comfort and eagerly pulled out for Treva's use.

Never mind that she'd been out bicycle riding in the sun and both their house's living room and her bedroom were warm. Even the prettiest and sweetest-smelling wrap was unnecessary.

There was nothing to do but keep the shawl spread out on her lap, however. It was a gift, and it had been given to her in love. She was grateful.

But what she really would've been grateful for was a hot shower and some peace and quiet in her room.

That wasn't to be.

Nope. There was a party going on in their kitchen, and her parents and Aunt Ruth looked delighted about it, too. She was going to have to smile and look alert for as long as possible. Anything less would hurt someone's feelings, and she couldn't do that.

"Treva," her cousin Summer said, "so far, I've heard about your visit to the hospital, riding an electric bike, and your thoughts about both broccoli soup and taco casserole. But what I haven't heard about is the boy."

"The boy?"

"Jonny," Summer replied. "Jonny 'I Want to be Amish' Schrock."

The moniker spurred a burst of laughter from her parents. And though Summer's words were true, they still made Treva feel vaguely uncomfortable. "Jonny is more than that," she said. "He's a lot more."

"I knew it!" Aunt Ruth exclaimed. "All this talk about you and him being just friends in spite of the fact that he paid you a call . . . and just this morning took you on a date."

"He took her on a bike ride where she got hurt," Treva's cousin Penelope pointed out in a cross voice. "There's a difference there."

Aunt Ruth shrugged. "Perhaps, but still. He did seem

mighty concerned when he sat with her on the couch and sipped lemonade."

"Jonny seemed concerned because he actually was concerned," Treva blurted.

"So you think," Summer said.

Her mother interrupted. "*Nee*, Treva is right. Jonny was very attentive at the hospital. And sitting here in our living room."

"Well, he certainly should've been," Penelope said. "Why, it's his fault she's gonna have a cast on her arm."

"*Jah*, but I don't think he meant for her to get hurt," Ruth said.

"How could he not have expected it, though?" Penelope asked. "We all know Treva isn't the most graceful of girls." Looking far too full of herself, she added, "You weren't very graceful even as a child, cousin."

Why was her cousin even there? They'd never been especially close. "Neither were you, Pen."

"Treva," her *mamm* said.

"Sorry," Treva said, though she wasn't sure who she was actually apologizing to. She supposed it didn't matter.

"What we need to figure out now is what happens next," Aunt Ruth said, as she gave the counter a firm swipe.

Her mother rearranged two of the casseroles on the counter. "No, what we need to figure out is what to do if Jonny Schrock wants Treva to go out bicycle riding again."

As if half the women in the kitchen had been waiting for such a statement, the entire room filled with excited chatter.

After thirty seconds had passed . . . and then sixty, Treva couldn't take it anymore. "Stop," she blurted, unconsciously muttering what she'd been thinking to herself.

Her mother and aunt stared at her in surprise. "Stop what?" her mother asked.

"Stop talking so badly about him. Stop acting as if me falling off a bike has anything to do with Jonny."

"Sorry, but it has *everything* to do with Jonny Schrock. Why, if it weren't for him, you wouldn't have been on a bike in the first place," Penelope said.

"Hush, Penny. You weren't even there."

"Well, I was at the hospital with ya, so I think I'm allowed to have an opinion. And I think that Jonny shouldn't have bullied you to get on the bike," Aunt Ruth said.

"He didn't bully me."

On a roll, Aunt Ruth waved a hand. "Furthermore, I don't know how he treats all those English girls he must have dated, but he shouldn't have treated you that way."

What English girls? "Once again . . . Jonny did not bully me. Going on the ride was my choice."

"Perhaps," her mother allowed. "But I have a feeling you were a little reluctant to go."

Her mother was right. She had been reluctant and scared and had made no bones about it to herself and her family. "I think I needed to get pushed out of my comfort zone. Even though I broke my arm, I'm glad I tried something new."

"We'll see how you feel if the doctor tells ya that you need surgery," her mother said.

Treva simply couldn't take any more of the awful, gossipy conversation. "I'm too tired to do this anymore right now. I'm going to go lay down."

Immediately, her mother hurried to her side. "You're right. This was the wrong time to talk about the whys and what happened."

"I'm glad to hear you say that, Mamm. You didn't raise me to be so judgmental, you know."

Looking even more shamefaced, her mother nodded. "You're right. Now, what do you need? A blanket? More pain reliever?"

"No more blankets. I took some an hour ago. It will kick in soon."

"How about a bag of ice? Or a hot water bottle?"

"Neither, but, um, thank you."

"All right, dear. Now, try not to worry, okay? We'll get everything figured out in no time at all. After all, there's a time and a season."

A time and a season? For what? "I know." As far as she was concerned there wasn't going to be a right time for her mother and aunt to sound so spiteful, but no way was she going to say that. "See you in a little while."

Her aunt hurried to her side. "Want some help getting to your room?"

Treva took a deep breath in order to not remind Aunt Ruth that she'd injured her arm and not a leg. "*Danke*, but I am fine," she said. Without looking back at the group of women, she climbed the stairs with more power than she actually felt was inside of her.

Even though she'd been looking forward to taking a bath, suddenly, that sounded like too much trouble. Instead, she closed her bedroom door firmly, unpinned her *kapp* and set it on her dresser, then crawled into bed.

Her arm was throbbing, but she reckoned the worst of the pain would lessen as soon as she relaxed. The conversation and the company down in the kitchen had been stressful.

Carefully moving to her side, she rested her broken arm on the outside and closed her eyes. Reflected on all the things her aunt and Penelope had been saying . . . and tried to decide if they'd had a point.

No. No, they didn't.

Sure, she'd been a reluctant rider, but she hadn't been scared to death. And Jonny had been nothing but supportive and encouraging.

Furthermore, she knew he did care about her. Just as she

cared about him. Was she sure that they were heading toward a more serious relationship? Did she think they might marry one day?

She had no idea, but as her body settled into the covers, Treva decided that she didn't need to know that answer. What mattered to her was that Jonny Schrock had stared at her like she was something special.

No, like she had his heart.

That, to her, was all she needed to think about.

She fell asleep thinking about his very blue eyes gazing into her own.

CHAPTER 23

Alan had sounded surprised when Jonny had called him the night before. It was no wonder—he had told Jonny a few days before that he was going on a vacation to Florida with his family. Jonny wouldn't have called if something wasn't important.

Then, he'd stayed silent as Jonny had relayed how he'd closed the shop for a few hours, then had been forced to keep it closed for the rest of the day and into the evening.

Admitting how irresponsible he'd been had been hard. Even though Alan had told him time and again to keep his own hours and not to feel badly if he needed either a morning or evening off, Jonny rarely had done such things.

Until yesterday.

However, his boss hadn't seemed shocked by Treva's accident, annoyed by Jonny's decision to accompany her to the hospital, or upset that he'd kept the store closed for the rest of the day and evening. Actually, Alan's only response had been to ask him if he needed anything.

Jonny hadn't known what to say to that. He wasn't the one who was hurt. Treva was.

But he didn't argue the point or remind Alan that he'd not only caused a young woman to have an accident but the bike she'd been riding was now sporting a good couple of scratches, too. And his boss had only told him to get some rest and let him know if he was going to need to take off the next day, too.

Relieved that the phone call had gone as well as it had, Jonny had spent the rest of the evening in the barn. There was a small storage area filled with bags of feed, medicines for animals, excess wire, tools, and wood. It was a hodge-podge of abandoned scraps from the past. With two flash-lights illuminating the space, he cleaned, dusted, discarded, and sorted the mess. Bugs and dirt, and even a mouse had scurried by.

Honestly, it was a thoroughly unpleasant job, and most of the time he would've done just about anything he could to put it off. But this time it felt fitting. He needed to do some-thing hard because otherwise he would do nothing but sit and chastise himself for being so self-centered.

He'd been thankful both of his grandparents had been in bed when he'd walked back in the old farmhouse and taken a shower. Mere minutes later, he'd passed out on his bed.

When he'd woken up a little after eight that morning, he'd been shocked that he'd slept so long. After quickly getting dressed, he'd hurried downstairs to help with the morning chores.

There, he found his grandparents sitting at the kitchen table sipping coffee.

"*Gut matin,*" he said.

"Ah, here you are," Dawdi said. "Did you get some rest, Jon?"

"Yes." Rubbing a hand over his face, he said, "I'm sorry I slept so late."

His grandmother stood up and rubbed her hand up and down his spine. Just as it had when he was a little boy, her touch felt soothing and sweet.

"I'm glad you slept, son. You were exhausted. Sit down and I'll get you a cup of *kaffi*."

He didn't move. "You don't need to wait on me, Mommi."

"Ach, I know that. Don't be stubborn. Sit down."

He knew that tone. He sat. "*Danke*," he murmured when she handed him one of her thick stoneware cups filled to the brim. Taking a tentative sip, he sighed. His grandmother's coffee was strong and piping hot. Although it wasn't fancy like Treva's, it tasted just as delicious. Probably because there were memories in the mixture.

Memories of being comfortable in this kitchen. Of talking with his grandparents without feeling a bother. Of good conversations and hearty food and no pressure to be anything but himself.

His grandfather chuckled. "Boy, you always look like you are tasting a slice of heaven whenever you take your first sip of your grandmother's coffee."

He smiled. "That's because it feels like it. I love it."

"No need to butter me up, Jonny. I have it on good authority that there's another woman's coffee that has claimed your heart." His grandmother winked. "Rumor has it that you've been paying her at least twenty dollars a week for it, too."

It was more than that, but as far as he was concerned, it was worth every penny.

"I do like Treva's coffee, but I love sitting here with the two of you in this kitchen. Mommi, your *kaffi* reminds me of being twelve years old and sitting at the table with Martin, Beth, and Kelsey. And the two of you, of course."

"Those were some noisy mornings, for sure and for certain," his *dawdi* said. "The four of you started each day with either an argument or some type of outlandish plans I would have to find a way to shut down."

This was news to him. "I don't remember that any of our plans were that out of the ordinary."

His *dawdi* grunted. "Mommi and me buying a herd of goats?"

"Cutting up my sheets so you all could go trick-or-treating?" his *mommi* added.

"Or how about my personal favorite . . . the idea of making a maze out of my wheat field?"

Jonny laughed. "I had almost forgotten that idea. It was Martin's, by the way."

"It doesn't matter who had the idea, the other three of you leaped on it with great enthusiasm," his *mommi* said with a smile. "You four kept your grandparents on pins and needles, for sure and for certain. We never knew what the four of you were going to dream up."

Leaning back in his chair, his *dawdi* said, "I used to tell your grandmother that I needed to take a vacation whenever the lot of you left."

Chuckling, his *mommi* added, "One time we did just that, too. We hired a car and driver and headed to a cabin in the Hocking Hills."

"We did nothing but sleep, hike, sit in the cabin's hot tub, and enjoy the quiet." Turning to Jonny's grandmother, his grandfather said, "We should plan a trip there again. It's been so long."

"I'm sorry we were so much trouble. And I promise, I didn't mean to take you down memory lane. All I was thinking about just now was sipping my first cup of coffee in this very chair."

"I'm glad that's a *gut* memory." Mommi ruffled his hair

with her fingertips. "It was so loaded with cream and sugar, it might as well have been dessert."

"I felt so grown up." He knew now that it wasn't just the coffee that had made him feel that way. It was how his grandparents had made him feel. He'd felt loved and secure.

No, he'd felt all the things he'd wished he'd felt in either of his parents' houses.

After taking another sip of the strong brew, he said, "How are you two?"

They exchanged glances. "We're worried about you, son," Dawdi said.

"Me? I'm fine."

"I don't necessarily believe that," Mommi said in a quiet voice. "Your grandfather and I heard you come inside last night. Your footsteps sounded as if you had a mighty big weight on your shoulders."

He'd certainly felt that way. Unable to help himself, he added, "I'm not the one who has a bandaged arm this morning."

"That is true."

"I hope she's going to be okay. I don't know what I'm going to do if she isn't."

"First of all, you know she will, son. Treva has a broken arm. Nothing more and nothing less." Crossing his legs, Dawdi added, "Furthermore, I happen to know Treva told ya that she doesn't hold you responsible. Do you believe those words yet?"

It would be so easy to lie. To say the words that he knew his grandparents wanted him to say. But instinctively, Jonny knew that they'd know he was telling a falsehood. Which, of course, would make them feel even more disappointed in him. "No."

"What purpose do you hope to achieve by keeping ahold of that guilt?"

"I don't know. But I'm not thinking about me." All of his thoughts were centered around Treva.

"I might beg to differ," his grandmother said in a tart voice.

Stung, Jonny winced. "Wow, Grandma!"

"Listen to me, Jonny. Has she hinted that she feels you are to blame?"

"No. She's said the opposite. Several times."

"Yet you refuse to believe her."

"I believe her . . . but I can't help but worry if she's keeping her real feelings to herself."

"I doubt she's lying, Jonny."

"What do you think I should do? Go over to her house and see how's she's doing?"

"Perhaps you should think about giving her a moment or two," his *dawdi* murmured.

"I guess so. I don't want her to think I don't care, though." Which sounded kind of stupid. She already knew he cared about her.

His grandparents exchanged looks. "I think it's time I fed you. I bet you're starving," Mommi said.

"I am hungry."

"I'll fix you a plate of eggs, bacon, and toast. Then you may help me peel apples."

"Yes, ma'am. What are you making? A pie, by chance?"

She chuckled. "I am."

"That's great news."

"We have more news to share," Mommi said. "Your father is coming over with his new girlfriend. I thought a pie might be a way to welcome her. What do you think?"

He froze. "My dad has a girlfriend?"

"It would seem so," Dawdi said with an amused expression. "He called yesterday evening and said Kennedy was coming down for the night and wondered if he could bring her by."

"And you said yes."

"*Jah*, my dear boy. That is exactly what I said." He winked. "And now I can even show off the storage room, since it hasn't looked so good since 1962."

Jonny picked up his coffee and drained the cup. The liquid was still warm but not so warm that it stung his throat.

At least he was no longer consumed by guilt.

Now he had something far different to worry about. He supposed it was no less than what he deserved.

CHAPTER 24

It felt right. Driving along the windy, hilly roads around Landon with Kennedy by his side felt right. From the moment he'd picked her up at the Inn on Briar Creek, Matt had felt like something new and perfectly right was blossoming between them.

Kennedy had met him in the lobby, looking adorable in a long, printed skirt and a crisp, short-sleeved white cotton shirt that she'd tied at the waist. Brown leather sandals were on her feet, and her glorious dark-auburn hair was tied back in a loose ponytail.

As they stood there, he couldn't stop looking at her. Kennedy looked fresh and sweet and happy.

He loved that she looked so happy.

"What?" She smoothed a piece of hair off her cheek. "Do I have a bug on me or something?"

"Not at all. You look gorgeous," he said.

Her expression eased. "Gorgeous is a bit much, but I'll take pretty."

"Pretty it is." Though, in his opinion, she did look gorgeous. No other word for it.

"You look pretty handsome yourself."

"Oh yeah?"

"Yes." She waved a hand over his body. "I've never seen any man rock a pair of rumpled khakis, button-down, and loafers the way you do."

He laughed. "Since it's obvious that I never 'rocked' anything in my life before, I'll take that. Ready to go for a ride?"

When she'd nodded, he'd reached for her hand and led her outside. Though she wasn't petite, he still helped her into his SUV, if only to have an excuse to touch her.

"Where are we going first?"

"First, I thought I'd take you to Mary Lapp's Farm and Café."

"What's that?"

"It's an Amish farm that has the best lunches around. She also happens to have a barn filled with animals, including baby pigs, goats, donkeys, sheep, and probably an assorted rabbit or horse."

"She has lambs?" she whispered.

"She does. Fuzzy white and black ones."

"Do you think . . . I mean, are you allowed to touch them?"

"Absolutely."

Her smile could have lit up the night, it was so bright. "Matt Schrock, have I told you how much I like you?"

"Not lately," he said in a laugh. "You're a fan of sheep, hmm?"

"Of course. Well, of lambs." Looking almost hesitant, she said, "What about you? Do you like lambs?"

He bit the inside of his cheek so he wouldn't laugh. She honestly looked like she might get out of his vehicle if he said that he enjoyed eating leg of lamb every now and then. "I don't know if it's possible to not be a fan of lambs."

When they pulled into the parking lot, Kennedy practically bounded out of the vehicle. He reached for her hand, linking their fingers and taking her to the entrance. An Amish woman about their age looked up from the papers she was sorting.

"Tickets?" she asked.

"*Jah. Zwee*," he said, holding up two fingers.

Kennedy looked at him in surprise. "You know Deutsch?"

"I do. I was raised Deutsch." He continued in Pennsylvania Dutch.

"You weren't raised around here, were ya?" the woman asked Kennedy in English.

"Nope. I'm a city girl, through and through. I like it here, though. It's beautiful."

Looking out at the surrounding fields, the Amish woman nodded. "It is at that. Now, what may I help ya with?"

"I'm hoping to see the lambs. Do you have any today?"

Matt felt his insides melt a bit. He knew a lot of people in his line of work. Some of them were so jaded that only something outlandish or outrageously expensive pricked their interest. But here was Kennedy only eager to see a baby lamb.

After the woman glanced his way, her eyes warmed. "You're going to have a good time, I reckon. We've got lambs to spare." After taking his money for the entrance fee, she gestured toward the barn door. "Go on inside and enjoy yourselves."

"*Danke*," he said, then motioned Kennedy toward the barn. She led the way. And stopped in her tracks when they entered the dark space that was easily ten degrees cooler.

The barn was also very . . . barnlike. It was dusty and smelled like farm animals. He found it comforting, but then again, he'd spent a lot of time inside an Amish barn. It was the opposite of pristine and new.

In addition, straw and dirt covered the floor and animals wandered all around. Some of them even had splotches of mud or dirt stuck to their fur. It would be difficult to stay clean when one was next to all the animals.

"Wow," said Kennedy.

Some of the cozy, happy feelings he'd been experiencing evaporated. "I know it's smelly and dirty in here. Would you like to leave?"

"No."

She still didn't look certain. "Are you sure?"

"Can I help ya?" an Amish man called out, his long gray beard testament to his age and experience.

Before Matt could answer, Kennedy treated the man to a bright smile. "I'm looking for the lambs."

"Ah, then you came to the right place. Come along now." He turned and started walking, his uneven gait a little slow but steady.

Kennedy glanced back at Matt, smiled again, and set off toward a pen in the back of the barn.

Deciding to hang back for a moment, he slowed his pace. It was just too fun to watch Kennedy gaze around the barn with wonder. She really was like a kid at Disneyland.

Even from his spot behind them, he could easily locate the lambs. When one of them bleated, scampering on wobbly legs, Kennedy gasped. "Oh, look at them!"

"They're right cute, ain't so?" the older man asked.

"Oh yes." Turning, she said, "Matt, have you ever seen anything so sweet?"

When he got closer, he saw that she hadn't been wrong. There had to be eight or nine white lambs moving about in the area. A couple of ewes were laying on the straw toward the back, no doubt chewing their cud while their offspring gazed at Kennedy with as much interest as she was showing them.

She stood against the wooden fence. "May I touch them?" she asked the gentleman.

"Oh, *jah*. You may, but I reckon they'd rather eat some carrots." He dug into a pocket and pulled out a paper sack of carrot rounds. "Here ya go."

Kennedy, still looking as eager as ever, took the carrots and held one out to the bravest lamb of the lot. It ate it eagerly, then eyed her right hand as her left reached out to rub its head.

When the lamb's little ears wiggled with pleasure, Kennedy cooed.

"Oh, my word. Have you ever seen anything more precious?" she asked the farmer.

"Only the lamb standing next to him," he joked.

Kennedy's cheeks turned pink. "I guess I'm being silly. But Matt . . . aren't they cute?"

He shared a smile with the farmer. "Indeed. They are cute and perfect."

"She's a good 'un," the farmer said over his shoulder.

Matt completely agreed. Walking to her side, he reached out and gently rubbed a lamb's nose. "Lambs are surely one of the Lord's pride and joy."

"Do you mind if I stay here a minute?"

"I wouldn't have brought you here if I didn't want you to enjoy them. I'll go buy us some carrots. You stay here."

"Thanks."

"No thanks needed. Take as much time as you need."

And that was all Kennedy had needed to hear. She started talking animatedly with the farmer, fed the now eager lambs loads of carrot chips, and petted as many as she could reach.

Ten minutes went by. Then twenty. Only when a family entered did the farmer leave, and Kennedy looked Matt's way.

"Thanks, Matt. This was so much fun."

Leaning down to pat one of the lambs lingering nearby, obviously hoping for another piece of carrot, he smiled at her. "It was."

"Where do you want to go now?"

"Well, after we eat, I have another surprise for you."

"What's that?" Her smile brightened. "Please tell me we're going to get to hold a piglet."

"No piglet today, but I'll try to find you one tomorrow," he added as they headed toward the parking lot. "After we go to a favorite deli of mine, I'd like to take you to my parents' house."

Her eyes widened. "You want to introduce me to your parents?"

He nodded. Tucked his hands into his pockets so she wouldn't see how completely nervous he was. "And my son."

"Which one?"

"Jonny. My youngest."

"Oh, wow."

He studied her expression. She didn't look upset, but she did look taken aback. Matt wondered why. When he'd mentioned that he'd liked to introduce his family to her, she'd seemed fine with that.

But maybe it was too soon?

Or had he taken all their conversations the wrong way? Had he imagined there was something more in between them than there actually was?

It was his usual way to ignore the sense of unease. Pretend it didn't exist. Tell himself that if he didn't bring up something unpleasant, it could be swept under the rug like a piece of bark or blade of grass tracked in by mistake from the outside.

But he'd learned the hard way that didn't solve anything. He and Helen had gotten divorced because there were so many subjects neither wanted to discuss. They'd drifted so far apart that by the time lawyers were involved, they'd practically been strangers.

Then he'd inadvertently hurt his children by keeping too

many of his feelings to himself—and worse, expecting them to do the same thing.

No matter how much he would pretend something didn't exist, it was still there, just out of sight. And, like a snag in a finely woven rug, it would create a flaw that hadn't been there before.

And . . . maybe the only person being fooled was himself.

He liked to think he'd finally gotten smarter. "Kennedy, are you upset about that idea?"

She turned her head, her eyes wide and her lips slightly parted. "Why do you ask that?"

"I don't know." He shook his head. "No, I mean, I do know. It feels like there's new tension between us that wasn't there before."

She pulled in her bottom lip. Seemed to bite down on it before answering. "I guess that's fair."

"Okay . . . ?"

"I'm nervous."

"I understand, but there's nothing to worry about. I promise, just because someone is Amish—"

"No, Matt. It has nothing to do with them being Amish. It's because they're your family. What if they don't like me?"

He stopped himself from laughing in the nick of time. "They'll like you."

"You can't know that."

"Sure, I can. I know you and I know them. All of you are going to get along fine."

"Hopefully."

"For sure and for certain."

When her lips curved up at last, he reached for her hand and squeezed gently. "We won't stay too long. My mother is going to make dessert. We'll visit with them for a little bit and have a piece of cake or pie, then move on. We'll be there an hour and a half, tops."

"All right."

"I promise, I wouldn't knowingly put you in a position where I know you'd be uncomfortable or upset. Plus, you're going to love my parents. Everyone does. They're good people." Thinking about Jonny, he smiled. "And my youngest is easygoing. He's kind, too."

She nodded. "Okay."

"Thank you, Kennedy."

She nodded again, but only looked out the window.

As he turned on the ignition and got a quick bite, he hoped he wasn't about to make a huge mistake.

While it was true that Jonny and his parents were good people and kind, it was also true that he wasn't exactly the top person on any of their lists.

Honestly, they'd probably wonder what a woman like Kennedy was doing with him.

If that was the case, then at least they'd all be on the same page. He kept wondering that, too.

CHAPTER 25

Supper was going far better than Jonny'd expected. First off, his grandmother was now offering some healthier options to be eaten alongside her usual cheesy potatoes and soup-laden casseroles. He no longer was feeling like he'd entered a minefield every time he sat down at the table. He hadn't wanted to hurt his grandmother's feelings, but also hadn't wanted to ignore the doctor's directions.

This evening's choices had been perfect. Baked chicken, roasted sweet potatoes, fresh broccoli, and a green bean casserole. There was also a bowl of applesauce and a plate of whole wheat rolls. It had been a really good meal.

But even if the food hadn't been to his liking, Jonny knew he would've enjoyed the company. Kennedy had changed everything.

He still could hardly believe it. At long last, his father had a serious girlfriend. Jonny had never given much thought to his father's love life, mainly because their mother had fallen instantly in love with someone soon after their parents divorced. Then, several years later—and every couple of years after that—she'd fallen in love again.

One parent constantly in search of romantic happiness had been enough for him. After his father had been in a very casual relationship for one or two years that had never seemed to go anywhere, he'd seemed to have settled into perpetual bachelorhood.

Jonny remembered Beth occasionally worrying about their father, but Jonny hadn't. He'd been selfishly pleased to not have to worry about anyone new in his dad's life.

Maybe that was why he couldn't seem to stop staring at Kennedy all evening. Yes, she seemed sweet and was pretty, but Jonny knew that those things weren't what drew him to her. It was that his father was different around Kennedy. Honestly, he seemed kind of smitten.

He'd also been rather tentative around Jonny and his grandparents, too. Like he was really worried about how they got along with Kennedy.

He hadn't expected that. His father was a lot of things, but "tentative" had never been one of his traits. Without a doubt, his father was trying to change for the better.

"Jonny," his grandfather prompted, jerking Jonny away from his musings. "Did you hear your father's question?"

"Hmm? Oh. No, I'm sorry." Feeling all four pairs of eyes settle on him, he fought off his embarrassment. "What did you ask me, Dad?"

"I asked how things were going at the shop."

"Oh. All right."

"What kind of shop is it?" Kennedy asked.

Turning to her, he attempted to become more engaged. "It's a bicycle shop. We sell a variety of things but mainly electric bikes and all the items that accompany them."

Her eyes widened. "No offense, but you're far away from the city. Is there really much need for electric bikes?"

"Oh yes."

"Really? Who buys them?"

"Amish and English. They're really popular. We sell several every week." Then, remembering the way he'd encouraged Treva to give one a try, he winced. "But, ah, they take some getting used to. They aren't for everyone."

Her eyebrows lifted. "Are you warning me off of them?"

Great. Now he'd offended her. "Not intentionally. If you'd like to try one of those bikes, I'll be happy to set you up with a test drive."

His father stared at him with concern. "Are you thinking about Treva?"

"Yes. I can't help it."

"Treva is Jonny's girlfriend," Mommi added.

Was she officially his girlfriend? He wasn't sure. "She's more like a close friend. We're, um . . . courting. Treva owns her own coffee shop near the bike trail. It's called the Trailside Café." Realizing he had no choice but to continue, he added, "Unfortunately, she, uh, was just out for a ride on one of the bikes and broke her arm."

"Oh no!" Kennedy exclaimed. "Is she okay?"

"For the most part, except she might need surgery. The doctor wants to take another set of X-rays as soon as more of the swelling goes down."

"Jonny's been beside himself," his *dawdi* said.

"I'm not beside myself. Just worried." And yes, they were probably the same thing.

"She'll be okay," his father said. "Remember what we talked about, son? Accidents happen."

"I know we talked, and I believe you. But I still can't stop feeling responsible." Turning back to Kennedy, he added, "I'm sorry about the conversational turn. One minute we're talking about my job, and the next we're focusing on my guilt."

Kennedy's expression warmed. "As far as I'm concerned, there's nothing wrong with talking about things that matter."

"Well said," Mommi murmured.

"I'm sorry it happened."

"Thanks."

Turning to his father, Kennedy said, "Do we have plans tomorrow morning?"

"Not yet." He smiled. "Do you want to see more lambs?"

She chuckled. "No. But . . . maybe we could visit Jonny's bicycle shop?"

"I'd like that. After, we could visit Treva's coffee shop. Not only does she make great coffee, she's got some amazing scones and bars, too." Looking at Jonny, he added, "Is that okay with you, son?"

"Sure." And it was okay, though he was starting to feel a little like they were in the twilight zone. "Mommi, Dawdi, would you like to join us?"

"*Danke*, but I think we'll let you young people trot up and down the bike trail without us," his *dawdi* said.

"I understand," his *daed* said.

"I'm excited," Kennedy said. "It sounds like a lot of fun."

Taking a sip of water, Jonny tried to wrap his head around the changes that were taking place. Somehow, over the last couple of months, he and his father had gone from speaking on the phone once a month to meeting each other's girlfriends. They were talking about things that mattered instead of the weather.

And how could he forget that not once had his father mentioned that he should be going to college instead of living at his grandparents' house and managing a bike shop?

And, while he was at it, shouldn't he be concerned about how his grandparents were taking everything? So far, they hadn't acted as if anything was different or out of the norm. But everything was!

Maybe it was time to regroup. "Since Treva has a splint on her arm, I doubt we'll actually see her at the café."

"That's perfectly understandable. But you'll be at the store, right?"

"Yes."

"Good. Let's plan on it, then."

Jonny didn't want to make things more awkward for each other than they already were—especially not with Kennedy watching their exchange. "Okay. Sure. Do you have a time in mind?" He didn't suppose it actually mattered, but he needed to find some kind of control in the situation.

His father turned to Kennedy. "Is nine o'clock too early for me to pick you up in the morning?"

Her smile was bright. "Not at all. I'll be ready."

"Looks like you three are all set, then," Jonny's *mommi* said. As she stood up, she frowned. "Well, what do you know? I could sure use a hand carrying some of these cups to the kitchen. Would you mind helping me out, Kennedy?"

"Of course not."

Now what was his grandma up to? Jonny glanced at his grandfather, but he was acting like his wife asked for help all the time.

Only when they were out of sight did he speak.

"I'm proud of you two boys," he said in a low tone. "It's time to put aside your worries and differences. It's much better to concentrate on the future than the past." He stretched his arms out in front of him. "And your relationship. One step at a time."

"I'd like for us to do that, Jonny," his dad said in a quiet tone. "Not only are you my son, but you're a good man. I want to know you better. I want to know all of you better."

"I want that, too."

"How about we continue to give it a try, then? One step at a time doesn't sound too difficult."

"I can do that."

Standing up, his father walked right over and hugged him tight. "Thank you."

"Nothing to thank me for, Dad. I love you."

"I love you, too."

When his father walked to his grandfather's side and whispered in his ear, Jonny felt a lump form in his throat as his grandpa lumbered to his feet and hugged him tight, too.

God was at work in their family. He was helping all of them, one step at a time.

And the blessings that were occurring were amazing.

CHAPTER 26

As she carefully walked down the path from her home's front door to the café, Treva took time to pray. She gave thanks for the fact that she wouldn't need surgery. She gave thanks for the many notes, bouquets of flowers, and sweet cards her friends, extended family, and customers had sent—each one wishing her well and a speedy recovery.

She prayed for her parents and Aunt Ruth and the nurses and the home care provider who had taken care of her so well over the last three days.

But most of all, she asked the Lord to help her be thankful for her well-intentioned mother, aunt, and father. Instead of closing the café for a couple of days, they'd elected to take over. Her aunt had baked, her mother had manned the espresso machine, and her father had taken over orders and payments.

To her surprise, they'd never complained about the additional work. If anything, the three of them seemed delighted to be more involved. Her father had even shushed her the other evening when she'd dared to suggest that he didn't need to be on his feet all day long.

From what her friends had whispered when they'd visited, the three of them had done a good job, too. The coffee drinks were almost as good as Treva's, and the banter between the three of them was entertaining. When she'd reviewed the receipts for each day, she'd been pleasantly surprised to see that the sales had been steady.

If she hadn't been so grateful, she might have even been a little bit jealous of how well things were going. There had been more than a moment when she'd liked to believe that she was irreplaceable.

Besides, how could she cling to such a thing when her family had dropped everything in order to step into the rigors of the café? Over and over, Treva reminded herself that this café had been her dream, not theirs. She was thankful for them, too.

They were the best.

But now, as she stood at the entrance, listening to the three of them argue and fuss and take altogether too long to do anything, Treva knew that it was time to step in. Otherwise, the novelty of their antics was going to wear off fast.

As their voices rose, she winced. Maybe it already had.

"Hello!" she called out, deciding to make a grand entrance on the off chance that someone had spied her lurking just outside the door.

"Treva, you're back!"

"*Jah*." She grinned.

"It's so *gut* to see ya," Mary Borntrager said from her spot in line. "We were told you wouldn't be here for several more days."

She held up her arm, which was covered in a jaunty-looking purple cast. "I might not be able to do all the tasks, but I can definitely help out." Noticing the dirty countertops, filled with stains from the coffee grounds, foaming milk, and who knew what else, she grew alarmed. If someone from the county came to inspect her establishment, they were not going to be impressed. She was certainly not going to be happy when she was given a fine.

She'd arrived in the nick of time.

Slipping into the side entrance to the counter area, she grabbed the first green apron she saw and placed it over her head.

All three members of her family were gaping at her.

"You should not be here, daughter," her *daed* said. "You should be at home. Resting."

"I have rested. I've rested a lot. But now that my arm is safe and sound in its cast, I can be here. Tie the sash, wouldja please?"

Her father didn't move. "Daughter—"

"We have a lot of customers and the counters are a mess," she said under her breath. "Please don't make a scene." As in any *more* of a scene.

"Fine."

Though he tied the sash, she knew he was frowning. "*Danke*, Daed." Joining the three of them behind the counter, she scanned the area, mentally debating where she could do the most good.

"We had everything handled, Treva," her *mamm* said, as she began to make a mocha coffee.

Ach. Her mother's feelings were hurt. "I know you all are doing a *gut* job, but I can't stay away." Picking up a clean dish towel and a fresh sponge, she set them on the counter and began making everything spic-and-span again. "Ah, that looks mighty nice, Mamm."

The line between her mother's eyebrows eased. "Not as nice as yours, but I'm trying my best."

"That's all that matters, ain't so?" Treva murmured with a wink.

Looking even more relaxed, her mother grinned. "Indeed."

Treva might have been imagining things, but the atmosphere in her little café seemed to lighten a bit. Her father began taking orders more efficiently, her aunt treated the baked goods with more care, and her mother talked less and worked the machine more.

She did her part by praising everyone, washing spoons, plates, and cups with one hand, continually cleaning the countertops, and greeting almost everyone by name.

In doing all that, her spirits lifted.

Until Jonny walked inside with his father and another woman. The moment he saw her cast, his expression tightened. The strange woman patted his shoulder and whispered something to him.

When he smiled at the woman and murmured something in return, Treva felt a burst of jealousy. It was as unwelcome as it was a surprise.

"Oh, look who's here. Your beau, Treva!" Aunt Ruth said excitedly. She'd also spoken loud enough to be heard over the steamer on the machine. "And isn't Jonny Schrock looking mighty handsome today?"

Two customers next to the counter turned to stare.

Treva was sure her face was beet red. "Shh, Ruth."

Ruth turned to her. "I couldn't hear ya, sweetie. What did you say?"

"She said to hush about Jonny's good looks," her *daed* said. "Treva don't want you commenting on her beau in front of all these people."

"All I was saying was that he looks handsome. Don't you think so, Emma?"

Her mother turned around. "Who?"

"Treva's beau. Jonny. Jonny Schrock."

She stopped looking at the milk frother and craned her neck. "Jonny's here? Where?"

"In my line," her *daed* said. "Get busy and make that drink, Emma."

When Jonny's father winked at her, obviously amused by her family's antics, Treva wished she could melt into the floor. She'd been embarrassed before, but this was a whole new level.

Worse, there wasn't a single thing she could do to make things better. She was stuck, and if she did try to get them to stop, everyone would know exactly what she was doing.

Including Jonny.

The pair of college-aged girls at the counter giggled and shot her a sympathetic look.

Yes. Her humiliation was now complete.

Right then and there, she knew there was only one thing to do. Pretend she wasn't mortified at all.

"I'll be right back," she told her father, as she tossed down the dishcloth she was holding and headed toward the line.

Jonny watched her every move.

She couldn't exactly discern his expression, but it sure seemed like a combination of worry and wariness.

"I was hoping to see you here, but I didn't think you'd be working," Jonny said.

"I'm not working very hard. I just arrived." Smiling at the woman, she said, "Hello. I'm Treva."

"I'm Kennedy. I'm very pleased to meet you. Jonny told Matt and me about your café last night."

"He did?"

"Kennedy came in town last night to see Daed," Jonny explained.

"Oh!" Finally, it made sense. Kennedy might be a bit

younger than his father, but she was definitely seeing him and not Jonny. That was such good news.

Jonny's father held out a hand. "Good to see you again, Treva. I hope you're feeling better?"

"I am, thank you. In no time, it'll be good again."

"And no surgery?"

She shook her head. "Nope, and I'm so glad about that. I'll only have to have on this cast for a month, and then I'll hopefully be as good as new."

"I'm glad to hear that, Trev," Jonny said. "I've been worried about you."

"I know, but there's no need for you to do that." As they moved up in line, she turned to Kennedy. "Have you been to Holmes County before?"

"I haven't."

"I trust you are enjoying yourself?"

"I really am." Looking at Matt fondly, she added, "The first place he took me was an Amish farm."

It was a popular tourist spot. "And what did you think?"

"She likes the lambs," Matt said.

"There were lots of them, and each one was cuter than the next," Kennedy said excitedly. "They must have had six or eight."

"Or a dozen," Matt added under his breath.

"They were so cute and sweet. I even got to pet them."

Jonny smiled. "I don't know anyone who can resist the sight of a baby lamb."

Treva agreed. "Did you see any other animals?"

Kennedy's smile grew. "Baby pigs, a bunch of bunnies, and some tiny goats."

"You're making it sound so fun," Jonny said. "I should go back again. I haven't gone there since I was a little boy."

"When did you go?" Matt asked Jonny.

"When we all stayed with Mommi and Dawdi for the

summer. Visiting there was always a highlight." His eyes lit up. "Beth loved seeing the baby animals. Have you gone there lately, Treva?" Jonny asked.

"You know what? I haven't been there in years. I'd love to visit soon."

"How about I take you later this week?"

"Well, I don't know. I've already missed so much work."

Jonny glanced over at her parents, who were currently bantering with each other, her aunt, and three of the customers. "I hate to break it to you, but your parents are having a grand time."

"They are, and despite a few hiccups, they're doing a good job, too." They deserved her honesty, even if that meant coming to terms with the fact that she wasn't indispensable.

"If you don't mind me giving my two cents, I think you ought to look at the silver lining for a spell," Matt said. "Before you know it, you'll have that cast off and be working all the time."

"He's right," Kennedy said. "A career is not a life." After a pause, she added, "Besides, just because you give yourself some time off doesn't mean that you can't be here either before or after your excursion."

"Looks like everyone is trying to wear you down, Treva," a lady in front of them said.

"I think it's working, too."

Jonny's expression brightened. "Does that mean you say yes?"

"*Jah*." Looking into his eyes, she realized that he made her feel good and special. Like she was worth his time and his attention. It was so different from the way Reuben had treated her, it was almost laughable.

"Treva, we've got a problem!" her father called out.

"Uh-oh. I'd better go see what he needs. See you in a minute." Aware that the people in line were all watching her join her *daed*, she made sure to keep her voice low when she got to his side. "What's wrong?"

"We need more ones and fives, dear. Do you need to go to the bank?"

"Uh, *nee*. I keep some money in a safe in the back. I'll be right back."

As she walked into the back room, she caught sight of herself in the mirror. There she was. Cranberry-colored dress, white *kapp*, same brown hair, and her striking green eyes.

New purple cast on her left arm.

But there was something new in her expression. It was hope and excitement . . . Two things that had nothing to do with the café, either. Instead, they were all because of the addition of Jonny in her life . . . and the fact that she wasn't exhausted and trying to do everything herself.

Remembering something Kennedy had told her in line—that a career is not a life—she realized that she was exactly right. She enjoyed her job and was proud of its success. But it wasn't all she was or all she hoped to be.

Ironically, when she'd finally given up control, she'd realized that she had everything she'd been praying for.

"*Danke, Gott*," she said. "Thank you for looking out for me by not giving me everything I was asking for. Thank you so much."

Her door opened. "Where's the money?" Aunt Ruth asked. "Your father needs some change, badly."

"Oh, sorry." She bent down, punched in the code in the safe, then pulled out two envelopes. "Here you go."

Watching her aunt disappear once again, Treva followed at a much slower pace.

There was no reason to hurry.

CHAPTER 27

Their twenty-four hours together had gone way too fast. Standing next to Kennedy against her car, Matt struggled with himself. Even though he knew they both had to return to their lives, he wasn't anxious to do that. Instead, he wanted to do nothing more than drive around the back roads of Holmes County, visit the restaurants, wander around shops, and simply relax.

He'd even visit a few more farms and pet animals if it would keep Kennedy nearby.

Should he offer to do that? Was there a way he could possibly convince her to stay one more day together?

Of course there wasn't.

Not only did she have her jobs to return to, but they also weren't at that place yet. Both of them had stepped outside their comfort zone by spending this much time together. Asking Kennedy to stay longer or pressing her to change her mind wasn't going to make things better between them. If he pushed too much, it would probably make things worse. She wouldn't like him pressuring her.

Looking down at her face, enjoying the way her hazel-colored eyes looked almost green in the afternoon sunlight, Matt pulled himself together. Saying good-bye didn't mean they were breaking up. That wasn't going to happen. Not if he could help it.

Her chuckle pulled him back to the present. "Matt, you look like you're having the biggest debate with yourself."

"That's probably because I am," he answered.

"What's got you so spun up?"

"Nothing important."

She studied his expression. She must have found something concerning because she said slowly, "You sure about that?"

"It's nothing." Definitely not anything that she needed to know about! He settled for doing the right thing. Doing what she needed him to do. "I'm glad you came down here."

Her smile brightened. "Me too. I had a good time. It went too fast."

"I felt the same way." Deciding he had nothing to lose by telling her the truth, he said, "To be honest, I was just wishing there was something I could do to get you to stay longer. It's in my nature to cajole and pressure to get something I want, but I don't want to do that to you." He rolled his eyes. "I bet you're wishing you hadn't asked, after all."

"I'm very glad I asked, as a matter of fact." Reaching out for his hand, she added, "I'm glad I'm not the only one who wishes our break could have lasted longer. But . . . I've got a Great Dane waiting on me. Believe me, you don't want to keep Danny waiting."

He chuckled. "Danny the Great Dane?"

"I watch the dogs. I don't name them," she joked. "Seriously, this was so fun."

"I thought so, too. Maybe one day next month we could

come down again." He paused, realizing what he had said. He'd made it official. He wanted to see her again soon.

Her expression warmed. "I'd like that. I really enjoyed meeting your family, Matt."

"I'm glad you got to meet my parents and Jonny, too." Sure, he would've loved for Kennedy to have met Kelsey and her husband, but he hadn't wanted to push things. It was enough for her to have met his parents. The fact that she and Jonny seemed to have gotten along—and Jonny had been agreeable for them to spend time with Treva and her parents—well, that said everything. "They loved getting to know you."

She smiled up at him. "Well, I guess I better get going."

Wrapping her in his arms, he once again appreciated how perfect she felt there. Unable to stop himself, he leaned down and kissed her. It was sweet and heartfelt but not too over-the-top. He didn't want to make her uncomfortable, yet he needed to convey his feelings.

"Do you know what's happening between us?" she whispered when he pulled away.

He thought they were falling in love. But he didn't want to scare her. "I think I do. What about you?"

"Maybe." She bit her bottom lip. "Part of me is a little scared. I've gotten tired of hoping, you know?"

"Yeah, I do." He knew that exactly. After everything that had gone on with Helen, he was still emotionally scarred. The day he'd been forced to move out, leaving all four kids with her, was still etched in his mind. That had been a really bad day.

Knowing it was finally time to say good-bye, he leaned down and opened her driver's-side door. "Text or give me a call when you get home."

"I will." Reaching up, she hugged him one more time, then got into her car. Seconds later, she was gone.

"Matt?"

Turning, he saw Martin's friend Patti coming his way. "Hi, Patti."

"Hi. Was that your special lady friend?"

"Yes. Her name is Kennedy."

After a second, she asked, "Like the president?"

He smiled. "Yes. It's a nice name, don't you think?"

"To be sure. I'm sorry I didn't get the chance to meet her." Looking bemused, she added, "I had coffee with your *mamm* this morning. She was singing her praises."

He laughed. "That makes me happy. My *mamm* doesn't take to strangers all that easily."

"She didn't act as if your lady was a stranger at all. For what it's worth, I don't think you have anything to worry about. Your parents thought she was wonderful."

"For what it's worth, I thought the same thing about you. Martin is blessed to have you in his life." When her cheeks pinkened but she didn't say anything, Matt added, "I . . . listen, I didn't introduce Kennedy to a lot of people because she wasn't here very long. I thought maybe a few introductions at a time would be best."

"I didn't expect you to throw a big party or anything."

"You're different, though. You and Martin are close. If Martin had been here and she had more time . . ."

She waved off a hand. "Don't you be thinking a thing about that, Matt. I didn't bring Kennedy up just to make you feel guilty."

"I know." He chuckled. "I've been on my own for a while now, and I haven't dated anyone so seriously in years. I've been trying to take things slow. Plus, I was worried about overwhelming her with my past."

"Your past?" She wrinkled her brow. "You mean your children?"

"Not at all. I was referring to the fact that I used to be

Amish. I hadn't told Kennedy that until right before she came down."

"Why did you keep it from her?"

"It wasn't from her specifically. Most people don't know that."

Her frown deepened. "You keep your childhood a secret?"

"No. I just don't talk about it because most people who I deal with don't have any concept about what my life was like. But in my defense no one I work with spends much time discussing their childhood."

She seemed to think about that. "I guess most people don't, do they?"

"Patti, thanks for saying hello. I'm glad I got to see you. Martin is a lucky man."

Her expression softened. "I'm the one who is blessed. I would've never imagined that a man like Martin and I would make a good match, but the Lord seems to have put us together."

This time he was the one who was confused. "A man like Martin?"

"You know . . . he's handsome and so smart. He has all kinds of degrees and a successful job. I, on the other hand, only finished the eighth grade."

"That's all I finished, too."

"Truly?"

He nodded. "I used to think I needed a bunch of letters behind my name, but I realized over the years that classrooms aren't the only places to learn something new."

"That's true." She still looked doubtful, though.

So much so, Matt's heart went out to her. "Patti, I don't know much about relationships. Every one of my four kids would happily tell you that I'm a work in progress. But I do know one thing for a fact."

Her eyes widened. "What's that?"

"You are as worthy as anyone. Years of school and fancy degrees don't make a person. A good heart does—and you have a great one."

"Some might say the same thing about you, Matt," she said, before she walked off.

She'd struck a chord. He stood motionless for a moment, thinking about everything she said. And almost believing she could be right.

Maybe one day he actually would.

CHAPTER 28

When Jonny had asked Bishop Frank Hershberger to stop by sometime that week to visit with him, he'd assumed the man would come to the house one evening or on Saturday morning.

Not show up at the bicycle shop.

When he'd walked in, Jonny had been with a customer. The bishop had waved off his apologies. Instead, he seemed to enjoy hearing about the ins and outs of one of the latest designs.

Ten minutes later, when the shop was empty, he hugged Jonny hello.

And then he dived right in. "How are you feeling about life here?" Bishop Frank asked. "The months are passing, ain't so?"

"They sure are. I've now lived here for several months."

"You sure seem happy," the bishop added as they both sat down. "Have you found your feet here?"

It took him a second to catch the bishop's drift, but once he did, he had to admit that his statement did seem to fit him.

At first, he'd felt lost—both about his decision to become Amish and about his future in general.

He realized now that he'd been running away. Running away from school. Running away from his parents. Maybe even running away from his life. Dr. Mason's warnings had hit him hard. He'd lived so much of his life being the easygoing child and not letting too much affect him.

But maybe he'd simply been fooling himself? Perhaps things had bothered him as much as they might bother the next person. He'd needed a reason to finally deal with them.

Then, little by little, everything had fallen into place. He'd settled in with his grandparents, finding a way to help them as much as they helped him. Then there had been Alan and the bike shop. The job he'd picked up out of necessity began to mean something to him. Now Jonny couldn't imagine working anywhere else.

Finally, there was Treva. She was the biggest surprise of all. Everything about her appealed to him—and for some strange reason she seemed to like him just as much. Calling on her at her house didn't feel as much like courting as it felt like coming home.

She made him better.

Studying the older man, with his scraggly beard, faint wrinkles around his eyes, and kind expression, Jonny spoke from his heart. "I like my life here."

"Your grandparents are enjoying your help very much. Why, just the other day, a group of us men were talking and your *dawdi* came mighty close to bragging about you."

"Really?"

"Oh, *jah*. Josiah sang your praises well and loud. He told everyone about how you help with the chores without asking, brighten the rooms, and work hard." Looking more serious, Bishop Hershberger added, "He also happened to say he hoped you would never leave."

"My grandparents are good people. Dawdi would probably say something like that even if I wasn't helping out so much."

"I don't think so." He crossed his legs. "Son, I came over to catch up, but also to ask about your heart. Because you already knew a lot of Pennsylvania Dutch and were very familiar with our ways, I haven't wanted to counsel you too much. But I feel it is time to talk about things."

"I understand."

"Jonny, have you been reading our books and contemplating our faith?"

"I have."

"Do you have any questions?"

"Not at the moment." Taking a deep breath, he added, "Bishop, the Lord has given me many blessings here in Walden."

"Such as?"

"I feel this as if He gave me this bike shop to manage as a way to prove that I could be happy living Plain."

Bishop Hershberger took a moment and thought about his words. Then he blurted, "That's a funny word, ain't so?"

The older man had lost him. "I'm sorry, but what word are you referring to?"

"Plain." He waved a hand. "Outsiders use it all the time. They describe our buggies and horses and pins in dresses and reserved manner as Plain. But, to my mind, our way of life ain't very 'plain' at all. It's filled with friendships and family and community and love."

Liking that description, Jonny added, "You're right. It's filled with all those things. And work and faith."

"*Jah*. Always faith. But there's also a belief in the Lord's will and that we need to be on His schedule, not ours."

"And forgiveness."

The bishop nodded again. "*Jah*. That too." He raised one eyebrow. "Have you been thinking about forgiveness, Jonny?"

"I think I have. Forgiving myself when I make mistakes, but also when others make them."

"*Jah*. I reckon that's a *gut* start." Staring at him intently, he added, "What about when someone makes a lot of mistakes?"

"Are you asking if it's possible to forgive someone then?"

"Yes."

Jonny's voice had come out thick and scratchy. Pulled from his insides because he hated to admit to how complicated his relationships were with his mother and father. "Bishop, I've been starting to talk a lot with my father. I'll be honest. At first it was because I had a health issue and wanted to stay on his insurance, but now it feels as if we've reached a new point. We're able to talk easier, and about real things, too."

"All of this sounds positive to me. Do you see it that way?"

"I do. I mean, I want to be Amish."

"Are you certain?"

"Yes." He wasn't lying. But always in the back of his mind were his siblings. He wasn't sure if he had been honest enough with all of them about the changes that had happened in his life.

Bishop Hershberger clicked his tongue. "You might as well spit it out, Jonny. No good is going to come of you sidestepping the issue."

"Fine. I don't know what to tell Martin, Beth, and Kelsey. Or my mother." Realizing he needed to be completely honest with both the bishop and himself, Jonny added, "I feel like things could go either way. I could tell everyone that I'm ready to be baptized and they'd think that was enough."

"Or?"

"Or I could finally be completely open with them. I could tell them about what the doctor said and the reasons I originally reached out to Dad. I could tell them that I've forgiven him and Mom for not being perfect."

"How do you think they'd respond?"

"Well, they could be just fine with it . . ."

A touch of amusement entered the other man's eyes. "Or?"

"Or it could just set off a string of disagreements and then everything between us will turn worse." Thinking about that reality, he felt like shuddering. Things between the four of them could get pretty bad.

"I can see why you're worried."

Jonny wondered if Bishop Hershberger actually could. The man was a straight talker and had a strong faith. In contrast, Jonny felt like he'd been aimlessly rolling from one goal to the next. He couldn't imagine the older man being so torn about things that might happen. "What do you think I should do?"

"First, tell me why you feel you need to share your doctor's visit with the rest of your family."

"Because I've been keeping my reasons for becoming close to my father private."

"So?"

So? "So, I think if they don't understand, they might not support my decision. Eventually, it might put a strain on both my relationship with them . . . and our dad."

The corners of the bishop's eyes crinkled. It was like he was amused but trying not to laugh at Jonny.

He didn't appreciate the man's amusement.

"Look, I know my problems might seem like nothing to you, but they're weighing heavy on my heart. I need to figure this out."

"Why?"

He was getting angry. "Because I love them."

"Hmm. And do ya think they love you?"

Why was the bishop playing this game with him? "Of course they do."

"Why?"

"Why do you think?" He waved a hand. "They love me because they're my siblings. We share the same blood. We share the same roots. They're my brother and sisters."

"Jonny Schrock. There you go, son. You just answered your own question."

Now he was completely confused. "Bishop..." He shook his head. "No. I—"

"Jonny Schrock, you are loved. You are loved by God and by your grandparents and by your parents and by Martin, Kelsey, and Beth. No matter what you do, they will still love you."

"But what if they can't forgive me?"

"That is something you can't control. If you choose to let them into your life and be honest, then you are making that choice. If each of them decides to be mad at you, then that is theirs."

"You make it sound so easy." And yes, Jonny's tone was probably full of resentment, but how could it not be?

"I don't think being honest is ever easy. But I do feel that lies are even harder to live with. I don't know about you, but my lies always seem to get tangled up in the truth."

"Mine do the same."

"Jonny, I'll tell you one more piece of advice before I visit Virginia and take her up on a piece of apple pie." He leaned forward. "Opting to live a life of unforgiveness is a miserable way to live. One sees hate and hurt and neglect and jealousy everywhere. It eats into one's heart and taints other areas of one's life."

He took a deep breath as he continued. "But that said, if someone decides to live that way, only they can decide to view the world differently. And I'm using the word 'can' on purpose. You can't change their viewpoint if they don't want to change. All you can do is be in charge of your own."

"I understand."

"Do some praying, come to a decision, and make peace with it, Jon. Then move on."

"I will."

"*Gut.* Now, if you'll excuse me, I have a piece of pie calling my name."

"Of course. Thank you for counseling me."

"It was my pleasure," the bishop said as he shuffled toward the door.

Just when he opened it, he turned back to Jonny. "I almost forgot. I believe there's a pretty young woman running a coffee shop who might have feelings for ya, too. Don't forget to add her to the list of important people in your life."

And with that, he walked out.

Sitting in the empty bicycle shop, the bishop's words ringing in his ears, Jonny realized that he already had made up his mind about what to do. He'd asked the bishop for advice, but maybe it had actually been reassurance.

It was time to make some phone calls. He was going to tell everybody in his family about what the doctor had said—and about his feelings.

And then, later on that afternoon, he was going to pay a call on Treva, hopefully sit on her front porch or in her living room, and make another formal call.

Like the bishop had said, it was time to make peace with himself and move on.

CHAPTER 29

From the time Matt had walked into his house on Friday night, he'd worked. Sure, some of it could've waited until Monday morning, but he'd been in such a mood, work had been the only thing that he'd felt capable of doing.

If he'd concentrated on Kennedy, his parents, or his kids, Matt knew he'd be a lost cause. Those things were where his heart was. He didn't mind that. In fact, he relished everything about Kennedy and was loving the way he was easing into conversations with both his kids and his parents.

But he was learning to compartmentalize them when he could. Otherwise, the work would pile up, and he'd had enough of that without adding more to it. People were counting on him.

No, he had an entire company and several dozen families' financial futures in his hands. There was no way he could take any of that lightly.

He never would.

With that in mind, Matt had tried to find satisfaction in the things he usually did. He played jazz on his state-of-the-art sound system. He'd sipped his expensive French seltzer water, ate takeout from some of the top restaurants in the city, and tried to appreciate just how comfortable his home office's leather desk chair was to sit in.

Little by little, he caught up on his e-mails and forced himself to concentrate on the wealth of reports that were waiting for his signature or comments.

And when he'd felt as if he was about to go cross-eyed from staring at figures and investment portfolios, he sat on his suede couch and watched sports. Took pleasure in the way the screen captured every detail on the football fields.

He even gave thanks for his job, the company, and his clients. He did have much to be thankful for.

It was only later, when he was lying in bed, that he realized he was thankful and proud and relieved not to be letting his clients or employees down . . . but he wasn't all that happy inside.

Nope. He only felt hollow.

That was why he'd arrived earlier than usual on Monday morning—early enough to joke with the night security guard before he went off his shift at six. Throughout the day, he met with a half dozen employees, spoke with a handful of clients, and led a lunch meeting at a conference table.

He'd done almost the same thing on Tuesday.

Now that it was midmorning on Wednesday, things were starting to ease. He'd even gotten a half-decent night's sleep the evening before. Once he'd put on his white noise machine, he'd stopped listening for the sound of crickets. That had helped.

Which was why he'd picked up the phone without thinking about the consequences.

But he should have known better. His ex-wife never called just to shoot the breeze.

"Hey, Helen," he said, as he continued to glance at a printout of one of his assistant's latest reports. "This is a surprise to hear from you. Everything okay?"

"Matt, why in the world didn't you call me about Jonny?"

He took off his reading glasses. "What do you mean?"

"Oh, great," she said sarcastically. "When are you ever going to stop playing games? Why do we have to go through this yet again?"

He closed his eyes and prayed for patience. And realized that his ex-wife sounded more upset than if she was simply in a bad mood. "Helen, stop."

"Don't tell me to do anything."

Oh, boy. "Listen to me, okay? I'm sorry, but you're going to have to back up a sec and give me more information. I've been looking at financial reports for the last five hours."

She sighed. "Why did I expect you had changed?"

Feeling his patience slipping, he stood up and began to pace. "One more time, I have no idea what you're talking about. What is going on with Jonny?"

"He's been seeing a doctor about his blood pressure and cholesterol."

"Oh."

"Oh?"

He winced. "Helen, I'm sorry you didn't know. I thought he would've told you."

"He didn't. Not until last night." Sounding even more aggrieved, she added, "Matt, Jonny made it sound like I was yet another person on his list to confide in. Why didn't you call me?"

"Because he's not a child, Helen." Plus, Matt was having a hard enough time having a firm relationship with him without sharing his test results with everyone in the family without Jonny's permission.

Then, of course, there was the small matter of him wanting to do just about anything but call up his ex-wife out of the blue.

"He may not be a child, but I'm his mother."

Matt winced. She was really hurt. But the fact of the matter was that she was going to have to come to terms with her relationships with the kids just like he had.

In addition, there wasn't much he could say about her feeling like she was another person on Jonny's to-do list. He'd heard that he'd called Martin, Beth, and Kelsey about his medical issues, too. So he could understand her hurt, but he also realized that their youngest was a grown man making his own decisions.

There were two ways he could handle this. Listen to her rant and complain and then convey that he was not responsible for their adult children's actions . . . or share some of his feelings, too.

Pushing the printout to one side, he chose the latter. "I know."

"Matt—wait, what did you say?"

She sounded so surprised, he couldn't help but smile. "I said I know you're his mother. I also know that Jonny sounded like you were just another person on his list to tell because I got some of the same treatment. At first, anyway."

"What are you talking about?" She truly sounded mystified.

"Helen, I don't know how your relationships with the kids have been going, but things haven't been all that great between them and me of late."

"Matt, they all decided to become Amish," she snapped. "*Of course* we weren't going to be on their sides."

"I thought the same thing as you do . . . until I spent some time in Walden."

"You went back?"

He wasn't surprised that she sounded incredulous. There'd

been many times—especially the first few years after they'd married—when he'd said that he would never go back to Walden if he had a choice. "Yeah. I've, uh, actually gone back several times."

"Did you stay with your parents?"

"I did. For the first night. Then I found an inn. Another time I stayed in a hotel so I could get some work done when I wasn't at the farm."

"That was a good idea. Being without electricity gets old fast."

Matt could practically see her smile. Boy, she'd hated letting her hair air-dry. He'd thought her scattered curls were cute, but she'd always whispered that she didn't feel like herself. "I mainly stayed someplace else because Jonny is living with Mamm and Daed. I didn't want to interfere. Mamm and Daed had enough to deal with." He chuckled. "Besides, you know how their hall shower is."

"The minute it gets hot, it's time to get out because someone else was always waiting for their turn." She laughed softly. "Matt, I used to think that I was never going to get all the conditioner out of my hair."

"Ha! And here I thought you only missed your hair dryer."

"Oh, I did." Her voice softened. "Boy, I haven't thought about those days in years. Remember how cold the halls were when we visited that time in early March?"

And . . . just like that, the memories returned. "Beth's hands and feet were freezing."

"Oh, the drama! It didn't matter that she had on flannel pajamas and socks, she'd be near tears. Next thing we knew, she was worming her way into our bed."

He smiled at the memory. "You didn't mind too much."

"Neither did you. Even though you always got the brunt of her kicks."

Thinking about it some more, he said, "Remember when they all played chase in the dining room?"

"How could I forget! Your father told me that no Amish children would ever behave so badly."

"And I told him that wasn't true. And even brought up when my friend Thomas and I wrestled on the living room floor and knocked over the special cabinet."

"The cabinet that your grandfather had made!" Helen moaned. "But even that wasn't as bad as when the children broke your mother's favorite serving bowl. I was so embarrassed."

Sitting on the edge of his desk, he chuckled as the memories returned, each more vibrant than the last. "No worse than me. I felt like I was twelve again, especially when my mother lectured me."

"I thought your father was going to kick us out until Martin hugged his legs and told him that he wanted to be Amish, just like him."

Suddenly, that memory emerged from wherever it had kept hidden for years. "Daed got tears in his eyes before he knelt down and hugged Martin right back."

She gasped. "Matt, I had forgotten all about that."

"Me, too." Half talking to himself, he added, "Maybe I've been wrong in thinking that them wanting to live differently was out of the blue."

"Here's my confession," Helen added. "When Beth and Kelsey came over to tell me about their plans, I barely let them talk about it. I went right on the defensive, sure they were doing this to get back at me because I hadn't been a good mother."

Even though he'd had some of the same thoughts, he hated that she was so hard on herself. Some of those early years had been so hard on Helen. She'd essentially taken care of all four of the kids ninety percent of the time. He'd been so focused on making money and a name for himself. "You were fine."

"I could have been better," she said in a soft tone.

"We *both* could have been better. But we're only human."

"That's true." She sighed. "So . . . Jonny?"

"Helen, I think he's fine. He got a wake-up call from the doctor, and instead of shrugging it off, he took the warnings seriously." He paused, wanting to make sure he phrased his words in the right way. "He reached out to me because he's on my insurance. He was worried about the price of doctors' visits and lab work. I assured Jon that I would make sure he stayed on my policy as long as possible."

"I wonder what he'll do after that?"

"I have a feeling his boss at the bike shop is going to be willing to do something for him."

"Or he could call one of us to help him pay for those bills."

He nodded. "You're right. He's never hinted that he needs any help, but I think he knows we'll both do whatever he needs."

After a small pause, Helen said, "Matt, I'm sorry I lit into you the moment you picked up."

"It's okay."

"Still . . . I'm going to do better. I need to stop being so emotional and flying off the handle." She groaned. "About everything."

"Hey, you were caught off guard. I should have told you what was going on. That would have been easy to do and saved you a lot of worry."

"It sounds like we're both going to do better."

"Yeah."

"I'll let you go. And . . . I'm glad I called. It was kind of fun bringing back some of those memories."

It had been more than that. It had been awesome. "I feel the same way. Bye, Helen."

"Bye. You take care, okay?"

"I will. You, too."

After they'd hung up, he leaned back in his chair and closed his eyes. Remembered what their life had been fifteen or eighteen years ago. The chaos and the noise. The constant mess and the piles of laundry. Chicken nuggets and ice cream bars and apple slices and chocolate milk. The way all four kids had practically knocked him over when he'd walked in the door after a long day at work.

The way Helen had leaned into him when he'd put his arms around her.

He'd give anything to experience it all again.

Just for a little while.

CHAPTER 30

Treva wasn't sure why God had woken her up at four in the morning, but she didn't try to fight it. She was too awake, and her skin felt like it was tingling. Even if she was exhausted, there wasn't a chance that she'd be able to close her eyes and drift into slumber when her limbs were so determined to move around. For better or worse, she was up for the day.

Pulling on her most comfortable dress and the soft zip-up fleece that Jonny had given her as a surprise one evening, Treva padded downstairs and put on the kettle. She'd make a steaming cup of herbal tea instead of her usual strong brew. An unusual decision, but she didn't try to fight it.

While the kettle heated, she dug in the laundry basket for a pair of socks and slipped them on her feet. Five minutes later, armed with a steaming cup of tea, a flashlight, and one of her mother's *Better Homes & Gardens* magazines she'd found on the kitchen table, she was ready to go outside.

The early morning air felt as brisk as it had the previous morning. Even under her new fleece, chill bumps formed on her arms. A hint of grass and fallen leaves scented the air. It smelled like fall.

Due to the early hour, the scent wasn't accompanied by the hint of an approaching sunrise. Stars were out and the moon was still high in the sky. Faint bird calls and cricket chirps floated around her.

It might as well have been midnight.

She hesitated. Why was the Lord compelling her to do so many things out of the ordinary? She should be snug in bed. Or, at the very least, drinking her first cup of coffee at the kitchen table.

Knowing that it did no good to second guess His will, she sat down in her aunt's favorite rocking chair, cradled the cup between her hands, and stared out into the darkness. Attempted to find something within the shadows that meant something. That would allow her to understand why she'd felt so compelled to start her day in this way.

She didn't see anything, though.

Treva felt as if she might as well be sitting in a dark tunnel. She felt completely surrounded by the darkness and the cool night air.

She shivered.

And then she heard it. A faint rustle. Every nerve in her body went on alert. What was out there? She studied the bushes, the pair of pear trees, the almost worn path leading to her coffee shop barn. Nothing seemed out of the ordinary.

The rustle came again.

Her mouth went dry, and her hands shook a little as she set the half-filled mug on the ground. When she heard the rustle again, her heart started beating faster. Hard. If she was fanciful, she would believe that someone could hear her heartbeat.

Or maybe someone actually could?

A bird screeched, accompanied by the flutter of its wings.

"Hello?" she whispered. Was anyone out there?

A twig snapped. She heard something scurrying down a tree branch.

And then she saw the culprit. The ringed tail. It was a raccoon. She nearly collapsed in relief.

Seeming to sense her—or maybe it had noticed her far earlier—the raccoon met her gaze and froze. They studied each other for a brief second before it darted off.

Leaving her alone once again.

It took her a minute, but finally she relaxed. Pleased, she picked up her tea. The morning air had cooled it. The liquid was merely warm now. Its comfort had dimmed.

Instead of rushing back into the kitchen for more hot water, she settled for curling her feet under her legs and closed her eyes.

"Lord, why did you wake me up? Why did you want me to sit outside in the dark? Why did that raccoon come out to see me?"

What had brought her to this moment, where she'd stared into the night, letting her mind jump to fanciful ideas instead of remaining firmly in reality?

What were you afraid of?

"That someone was here," she replied without hesitation.

Is that what is truly burdening your heart? What is the worst thing that could happen?

"Jah." She paused. Forcing herself to be honest. She had to be—after all, she was currently having a conversation with herself, completely alone in the dark. "I'm afraid of getting hurt."

You broke your arm. You've been hurt.

"That wasn't the same. That was only bone. A cast fixed it."

You haven't ever experienced anything worse?

"Reuben," she blurted.

If his betrayal was your greatest hurt, what is your greatest fear?

Goosebumps appeared on her skin as she forced herself to think about her private worries. About the kinds of things that kept her up at night.

The kinds of things that woke her up at four in the morning.

Then she knew. "Reuben leaving me was bad, but it's not my greatest fear. It's that Jonny is going to decide that I'm not worth sticking around for as well," she whispered into the night air. "I'm afraid of the best man I've ever met, the one man I'm sure the Lord meant for me to have, is going to turn his attention to someone else."

Or to leave Walden.

Treva exhaled. At long last, she could admit it. She shifted. Perched on the edge of the chair, waiting for the Lord to speak to her again. To prod her in the direction she needed. Instead, only silence greeted her.

Treva leaned back again, disappointed. Except she realized that she was relaxed now. She'd finally, finally faced her biggest fear, and it wasn't her past or the possibility of some stranger attacking her in the wee hours of the morning. No, it was that she'd fallen in love with Jonny and was afraid he might not love her back.

Okay, he wouldn't love her as much as she loved him. That she wouldn't be worth the sacrifices he'd have to make.

"Treva?"

She turned as the door opened. Her father was looking tired and sleepy and rumpled from sleep. Same as he always did when he went to the barn early in the morning.

"What are you doing out here?" he asked around a yawn. "When did you wake up?"

"A while ago."

"How long?"

She shrugged. "Four."

Stuffing his hands into his coat, he said, "That ain't like you. Is your arm hurting?"

"*Nee*." She'd gone to the doctor just the week before. They'd taken off the cast, done more X-rays, and elected to put her arm back in a cast. The new one was smaller and lighter, though. Sometimes she forgot it was on. "Daed, I don't know what happened. All I know is that I woke up early. When I realized I was wide awake, I decided to make some hot tea and come outside."

"Ah." To her surprise, her father sat down on the chair beside her. "I know all about that."

This was news to her. "You wake up with a head full of worries?"

"From time to time, I do." He kicked his legs out. "I reckon everyone does from time to time."

"I guess they do." She hadn't really thought about that, but it did make sense.

"So . . . is everything all right?"

"*Jah*. I've been talking to God." She smiled slightly. "And watching a raccoon dart through the yard in the bushes. He scared me half to death for a minute or two."

He chuckled. "Those raccoons. They're always on the prowl, searching and scavenging. They're a nuisance, that's what they are."

"I'm surprised I've never noticed them before."

He grunted. "Lots of things are around us that we don't notice. Some good and some bad."

She smiled. "And some are just raccoons."

"*Jah*. Did your chat with the Lord help?"

"It did," she answered. "He helped me find some answers. Well, he helped me understand some of my *questions*." Some questions she hadn't even been aware that she had.

"Ain't that something? Here, we're always so worried.

Afraid to face our fears or get help. Even imagining that the Lord is so busy with floods and plagues and war and what have you that our own concerns shouldn't be bothering Him none. But He still has time."

"He's bigger than all of us."

"To be sure." Her *daed* gazed at her for another long moment then stood up. "I'd best get to the barn. Dottie won't milk herself, you know."

The air was chilly. "Do you need some help?"

"*Nee*, child. It's almost time for you to start your day, too, ain't so?"

She knew he was talking about so much more than just her morning routine. "*Jah*. I suppose it is."

"Glad to hear it," he said, as he strode out to the barn, his boots crunching on the frost-covered blades of grass.

What she didn't know was if she was as ready as she needed to be.

On the heels of that question was the obvious conclusion: If she wasn't ready to face her future, when would she ever be?

CHAPTER 31

"You have gotten pretty spoiled," Jonny told himself, as he grimaced at the bitter taste of the cup of coffee he'd just brewed. "Not too long ago, you would've thought this drink was fine. Now you're acting as if you're drinking cough syrup."

Determined to prove his point, he picked up his cup and gulped the remaining liquid. It was as acidic as he'd remembered. In addition, even though the coffee wasn't scalding, it was hot enough to make his eyes water as it slid down his throat.

And now he was not only spoiled, but he was an idiot, too.

Sitting on the stool behind the shop's counter, Jonny tried to ignore the burn. It was difficult but doable.

Just as electing to not go to the Trailside Café at his usual time had been.

Perhaps it was just as foolish?

"You need to stop worrying so much and just tell Treva how you feel," he muttered. "Once you tell her what's in your heart, you'll know where you stand. For better or worse, you'll both know where you stand. Treva won't be guessing, and you won't be stressing." Rubbing his chest, he tried that idea on for size. It felt good.

Or maybe the coffee's burn had finally dissipated? Whatever the reason, he was going with it. "Yeah, Jonathan. That's the thing to do."

Now that he had a game plan, his future was looking brighter. But did it have to include drinking poorly brewed coffee?

He could be wrong, but he didn't think there was a strong correlation.

Glancing at the digital clock on the counter, Jonny figured the last of the morning rush should be finished within the next hour. He'd stay put, maybe wipe down some shelves, and then when it was almost nine, he'd head down to Treva's shop.

Maybe even give in and finally have one of Treva's apricot bars. Just yesterday he'd received a call from Dr. Mason's physician's assistant with his latest lab results. It had been incredible. His cholesterol numbers had gone down almost twenty points.

"Whatever you've been doing, keep doing it," the physician's assistant had said.

"I will, but can I cheat every now and then?"

"What do you mean by cheating?" she'd asked.

"Nothing too crazy. Just a cookie or muffin every once in a while. Maybe have a steak?"

To his surprise, the woman on the other end of the line had giggled. "You did take Dr. Mason's orders seriously, didn't you?"

"Wasn't I supposed to?"

"Yes. Yes, of course! It's just that . . . well, not everyone is so diligent, I'm afraid."

"So, can I?"

"I think it would be fine, as long as you don't go too crazy."

Her voice hardened. "Don't you dare start eating fast food and donuts all the time."

"I won't." Still needing direction, he said, "But maybe three cheats a week?" And yes, he was acting like a kid looking forward to a pillow sack filled with Halloween candy.

"Do you really need your directions to be that specific?"

"I'm afraid so."

"Three cheats a week, then. But that doesn't mean a burger, fries, and chocolate shake count as one cheat."

"So . . . that would be three?"

"That would be three."

"What do you think about four?"

"I think I'm beginning to understand why you needed specifics," she said, teasing him. "Jonny, I feel good about telling you three cheats. If you want something different, you're going to have to go see Dr. Mason."

No way was he going to drive up to Cleveland just to be told to take care of himself better. As far as he was concerned, he'd already been there and done that. "That won't be necessary."

The PA chuckled but seemed satisfied with their conversation.

And now, here he was, thinking about Treva, her coffee, and some apricot bars.

When the door chimed, he breathed a sigh of relief. He needed a break from the thoughts about Treva revolving in his head.

But it looked like that wasn't going to be the case.

There she was in the flesh, looking fresh and delightful as always. And, even better, holding two large cups of coffee in her hands.

"Treva, I can't believe you're here."

A puzzled look appeared on her forehead. "I hope you're glad to see me?"

"Very glad," he said as he strode to her side. "Especially if one of those cups is for me?"

"It is, though you're making me feel kind of bad," she said. "One would almost think you're more excited about seeing that cup of coffee than me."

"Not at all." And before he went and talked himself out of it, he leaned down and kissed her hello. Her lips softened as she leaned close, letting him know that she welcomed it.

Pleased, he brushed his lips against hers again before moving back.

"Treva, I was just thinking about you . . . and here you are. It's a nice surprise."

"I'm glad you think so." Looking a little dazed, she handed him his cup. "Here."

He laughed. "*Danke*." Taking an exploratory sip, he sighed in appreciation. There it was. Smooth, flavorful, nonacidic coffee. Fixed just the way he liked it. "It's perfect."

"It's just a cup of coffee, Jonny."

"It's more than that. Plus, you used almond milk. Thank you."

"I know that's what you prefer. It wasn't any trouble." A line formed between her brows. Obviously, she was confused by his effusive praise, and who could blame her?

Glad they were alone in the shop, he reached for her free hand and pulled her toward the back of the shop. "Have a seat," he said. "I'll go grab another stool."

When he returned, she was half spinning on the stool, going about halfway around before returning to her original position. He noticed that her cast was far smaller and her wrist didn't seem to be bothering her any.

Today, she had on a violet-colored dress, black stockings, and some half boots. Instead of wearing a cloak, she had on the fleece he'd given her. "I like you in the fleece," he said.

"*Danke*. It's cozy and warm. I like wearing it."

When they shared a smile, tension rose between them. It was obvious that each of them had something on their minds. "Since you're here and the shop is empty, can we talk for a moment?"

"Of course. That's actually why I came. I was hoping to get the chance to visit with you during your morning lull."

"We're learning each other's schedules, aren't we?"

"I'd say so." She looked down at her lap as she sipped her coffee.

"Treva?"

She looked him in the eyes again. "Yes?"

"I need to tell you something, but every time I practice my speech, it comes out wrong."

"Why don't you just tell me what you're thinking, then? I don't want to hear something that's practiced."

She was right. Smooth, glib words wouldn't convey the same meaning as three simple words did. Setting his cup of coffee on the counter, he reached for her hand. Took a fortifying breath. "I love you."

Her eyes widened and she inhaled sharply.

For a second there, he'd been sure that she'd guessed what he'd been about to say. A flicker of unease settled back inside of him, burning his insides like that awful, acidic coffee. "Sorry if I've shocked you," he said in a rush. "Another man might have a suave way of putting things, but I've never claimed to be suave. But it's true," he continued, unable to stop himself from talking nonstop. "I love so many things about you, Treva Kramer. I love the way you treat everyone around you. I love how close you are to your family. I love how you rode that bike even though you were scared. I love how you can make a perfect cup of coffee. I love how pretty you are. Treva, you've claimed my heart."

"Jonny." Her voice sounded kind of breathless and her green eyes were damp, making the color turn to jade.

Was she happy? Upset?

"Treva, say something," he whispered. "Say something before I begin another awkward, incomprehensible speech."

"I understood your speech just fine." She squeezed his hand.

One of the tears that had been filling her eyes escaped. Unable to help himself, he captured it with his finger. "And?" he asked.

"And I love you, too."

"You do?"

"So much." She leaned forward.

That was all he needed to move closer, pull her into his arms, and kiss her lips. When her lips moved against his, he deepened their connection, enjoying the feel of her, the taste of her.

No, enjoying the feeling of being in love.

When they finally broke apart, he said, "You've made me so very happy, Treva. I love you so much."

Happiness and promise filled her eyes. "Then kiss me again."

He needed no more urging.

CHAPTER 32

Spring

Watching Kennedy dart back and forth from her closet to their bedroom like a crazed squirrel twelve hours before an approaching storm, Matt was tempted to offer advice. But he hadn't reached his age without learning a thing or two—the most important being that dressing for an important occasion was serious business. At least it had been for Helen, his girls, and now, it seemed, Kennedy.

Experience had taught him a thing or two, too. It did no good to make comments, watch the clock, or give opinions. Not even when they were asked for. All those things did was cause an argument, panic or—in Beth's case—tears.

He'd do a lot to avoid tears.

Therefore, even though they really should have been heading to the door, he leaned back in the pretty paisley-upholstered chair in the bedroom.

He also took a moment to give thanks for the hot cup of coffee in his hand. And, more importantly, for the fact that his bride of two months was in his life. Kennedy was a wonderful woman. Sometimes he couldn't believe how lucky and blessed he was to have found her.

"Matt, what do you think about this dress?"

He carefully set the cup down.

Kennedy now had on a pale rose-colored sheath. The fabric was silk, and the dress had embroidery and seed pearls stitched into the hemline. It was a beautiful dress. So were the neutral heels on her feet.

Honestly, he didn't think a woman could ever look more beautiful.

Except, perhaps, the way she'd looked on their wedding day. He'd thought she'd looked positively angelic.

But was he going to say that? Nope. Actually, he knew better than to offer any opinion. "What do you think, Ken?" he asked.

"I think I need your opinion."

Umm . . . probably not. "Well . . ."

Tapping the toe of a brand-new shoe, she exhaled. "Matthew Schrock, don't you start that with me."

"Start what?" He attempted to look innocent but was pretty sure he was failing. Badly.

"You know what. Don't you start not telling me how you really think about something."

He stood up. "Kennedy, are you sure you want my opinion? And I'm asking because you looked kind of irritated the last three times I told you I thought you looked pretty."

"That's because you were unhelpful." Before he could say a word about that, she added, "We're about to go to your son's wedding. His Amish wedding. I'm his non-Amish stepmother."

"And . . . ?" He didn't want to sound idiotic, but he truly didn't know where she was going with that.

Her eyes widened. "And I don't want to look completely out of place."

"You won't. You'll be with me."

"Matt, that is not what I meant, and you know it."

"I don't care if that's what you meant or not. I'm just being honest."

"But—"

"You're going to look beautiful, and I've got on a new navy suit that looks pretty good, I think."

"You should. You've been working out for months."

He had, both for vanity and because Jonny's health scare had encouraged him to work out more—and, of course, take up bike riding. "What I'm trying to say is that you've got nothing to worry about. We'll look great."

"You're being no help."

"Actually—"

She interrupted. "You know that this whole 'what to wear' thing is different for women."

Realizing that no amount of reassurance was going to do the trick, he took another sip of coffee and sat back down. "I reckon so."

"Are you sure I shouldn't wear a longer dress?"

"Yes."

"But what if other women are wearing them? What did you say Helen was wearing?" Turning to the mirror again, she groaned. "I knew I should've called her. Do you think I should call her?"

"Now?"

"Well, yeah."

Staring at her, Matt realized he was out of words. There was only so many compliments and reassurances words could provide. He stood up, crossed the room, pulled her into his arms, and kissed her soundly.

She stiffened, then—as he'd hoped—melted into his arms. Running a hand down her back, he deepened the kiss until he feared they were going to lose track of time.

When he lifted his head, he said, "Kennedy Schrock, you

look gorgeous, everyone is going to love your dress, my mother does not expect you to look Amish, I don't care what Helen is wearing . . . and you need to grab your purse so we can go because I'm not going to show up late to my son's wedding."

She froze. Scanned his face. And then nodded.

"Okay." She turned, reached for her bag, then headed down the hall.

He was left to follow behind, leaving the pile of dresses on the bed and the array of shoes littering the floor.

Reaching for her pashmina, he settled it around her shoulders, double-checked that he had his wallet and phone, then opened the door leading to the garage.

At last they were on their way.

EPILOGUE

"Mornings after a wedding should start at noon," Kelsey moaned as she wandered into the Trailside Café. "It's soooo early."

"Stop complaining," Jonny said. "I'm the one who's a newlywed. I should still be in bed with my wife." He grinned, liking both the way that sounded and how content he'd been lying next to his sleeping wife.

Beth covered her ears. "Jonny, you're my little brother. That is the last time I ever want to hear you talk about being in bed with Treva."

She had a point. "Fine."

"You are also the one who said it would be no trouble for the four of us to meet before you and Treva take off on your honeymoon, so don't blame me for this meeting," Kelsey said as she headed toward the counter. "Anyone need anything?"

"I do! Get me another apricot bar, Kelsey," Beth called out.

"And another scone for me," Martin said. "Any flavor will do."

"On it."

Jonny glanced behind them at the counter. Treva's aunt Ruth and one of Treva's new hires—a petite English coed out of Wooster on spring break—smiled his way.

"Do you need anything, Jonny?" she called out.

"Yep. Put the total on my tab, Nance."

"You got it," she said with a smile.

"No way. I've got this," Kelsey retorted.

Though it felt odd to accept his sister's payment, he didn't argue. Honestly, he didn't think he would argue about much. He was still on his wedding—and wedding night— high.

"Look at you," Martin said, teasing him. "I've rarely seen you ever look so pleased."

"I have a lot to be happy about. I have Treva and the wedding is over."

"It really was quite the to-do," Beth said. "Four hundred people is a lot. Sometimes all I could see was a mass of people."

"Between our grandparents and Treva's, we've got a lot of Amish relatives."

"Plus we had all of Mom's and Dad's crews from work and their neighborhoods and churches. Those people added up fast."

"Who would have thought our father would've invited like two dozen of his work friends?" Kelsey asked. "Until recently, I thought everyone at his office was afraid of him."

"I knew they weren't afraid, but I hadn't thought they were all so close," Martin said.

"And that they'd all show up?" Beth asked. "I always thought they were all stuffy, but they were nice."

"I think they had some of the best times out of everyone there," Martin mused. "I'm pretty sure I saw Dad's banker playing cards with some of Dawdi's farming buddies."

Jonny chuckled. "I was so worried about everyone getting along. I should've known better."

"Here we are," Kelsey said. "My large latte, Beth's apricot bar, and Martin's scone."

"Thanks, Kels," Martin said.

Jonny sipped his drink. Allowed himself to revisit some of his favorite moments of their wedding reception—all the toasts being one of the top five. He'd treasure them for the rest of his life.

Then, of course, his thoughts returned to his bride. "I love all of you, but can we now talk about whatever we were going to talk about so I can get back to Treva?"

"Yeah. And settle down. I'm the one who picked you up. I'll drop you off," Martin said. "And our topic is me and Beth."

"Speak for yourself, Martin," Beth chided.

"What does that mean? Have you changed your mind?"

"I'm not sure."

Kelsey put her cup of decaf down. "Beth, I'm not going to pressure you to live with our grandparents if you don't want to do that."

"I'm not, either," Martin said. "When we first discussed this idea, it all felt like a lark. I hadn't really thought about much except not having electricity. But living Amish is so much more than that."

"I know."

"Richard always reassures me that there's no 'right' way to be Amish," Kelsey said, "but I do think that there's some ways to do it wrong. Your heart needs to be ready to accept the faith."

"I know that, too."

"Okay." Staring at his sister, Jonny was at a loss for words. Beth had always been the type of person to run into a new situation and shrug off any type of obstacles or doubts.

"What about you, Martin?"

"Well, I'm kind of at a crossroads. I love Patti and she loves me. We want to be together, but we're still not sure what that life should be like. At the moment we're straddling two different worlds, and that isn't going to last too much longer."

"Are you going to move back in with Mommi and Dawdi?"

"*Nee*," Martin said. "I thought about it, but I decided not to. It just doesn't feel right." Turning to Beth, he said, "There's no timeline on your future, Bethy. If you aren't sure, you should wait."

Kelsey nodded. "That's right. It's not like we all won't still be brothers and sisters." After taking a sip of her drink, she added, "And things can change. I mean, look at our father."

"He has been the surprise," Martin said. "He and Dawdi seemed to have patched things up."

"He told me that living a life of unforgiveness would make him sad," Jonny shared. "He didn't want to do it."

"That makes me proud of him," Kelsey said. "I want to be close to our father again. To both of our parents."

Beth cleared her throat. "Did any of you spend much time with Mom?"

"I think we all did," Martin said. "She seemed good to me." Glancing Jonny's way, he added, "I know she really likes Treva."

"She's been sweet to her. Treva likes her, too."

Beth nodded, but still seemed bothered by something. "I thought Mom was good, too, but I don't know. Maybe she also seemed kind of lost?"

"Maybe," Martin said as he took a bite of scone.

"No, I think Beth had a point," Kelsey said. "Mom did seem a little bit at loose ends. But, who can blame her? I think last night was the first time she's shown up for one of our events alone while Dad had a date."

"That's true. Mom always had someone with her," Jonny said. "Some better than others."

"Do you think that's it?" Beth asked. "Do you think she was only having a hard time attending her son's wedding by herself?"

"I'm not sure," Jonny said.

"Maybe you're overthinking everything, Bethy," Kelsey said. "Mom seemed okay. And like we've all said, she did seem happy for Jonny and Treva."

"Let's all try and touch base with her more often," Martin said. "What do you think?"

"I can do that," Jonny said.

Kelsey lifted her cup and tapped Jonny's. "Me, too."

Ready to get up and get out of there, Jonny shifted in his seat. "So . . . like I said. I love you, but I want to go back to my wife."

Martin laughed. "Go on, buddy. We'll see you after the honeymoon."

"No, wait!" Beth blurted. "Sorry, but I have something to tell you all."

"What is it?" Martin asked.

Suddenly, his older sister looked a little pale and very nervous. "I . . . I've had a secret. I've been keeping something from you all."

All of Jonny's worst fears rose to the surface. "Are you sick?"

"No." She bit her lip. "I mean, not exactly."

He frowned. "Either you are or you aren't, Beth."

"Jonny's right. Tell us," Martin said.

"I'm pregnant."

Jonny was pretty sure if he'd been holding his cup of coffee, it would've just fallen on the floor. "Beth? You're sure?"

Looking miserable, she nodded. "Look, I know you all are shocked and have about a hundred questions, but hold onto them, okay? I need to say all this only once." Staring hard at each of them, she added, "And . . . maybe realize that I don't want to be grilled?"

The three of them exchanged glances. "We won't grill you, Bethy," Kelsey said in a soft tone.

Beth swallowed. "All right. Here goes. I did something stupid during a weekend with some girls from college and now I have a lasting reminder."

"So, you don't want a relationship—"

"Hush, Jonny," Kelsey chided. "She doesn't want questions."

"No, Jonny, I don't want a relationship with that guy," she said quietly. As if gathering her nerve, she added, "As hard as this is to admit, what I did didn't mean anything. I hope you all aren't too ashamed of me."

"Never," Martin said.

"Never, ever," Kelsey added, while Jonny reached over and kissed Beth's cheek.

After taking a deep breath, Beth continued. "Anyway, what I'm trying to tell you all is that this baby . . . this baby means a lot to me." Covering her stomach with her hands, she added, "I'm going to keep it. I know it might not make sense, but I've elected to wait a couple of weeks to tell Mom and Dad."

"And our grandparents?" Jonny asked.

"Jonny, hush!" Kelsey said.

Beth smiled. "It's okay, Kels. I ended up telling our grandparents last night. I figured they wouldn't be able to say much with three hundred and ninety-nine other people in the area."

"Wow," whispered Martin.

"And . . . well, they were shocked, of course. But they didn't say I wasn't worthy. Actually, they said if I wanted to be a single mother here in Walden, the Amish community would probably accept me with open arms. I think that they're right."

"What do you mean?" Jonny asked. He glared at Kelsey before she could tell him to hush again.

"It means I'm going to go live with Mommi and Dawdi after all. I had a great job, but I haven't been happy. I need to be happy. This baby is a gift from God. I think he or she is going to help me find my path in life. I'm moving in with them next week."

For a good thirty seconds, everyone stared at each other.

Beth looked apprehensive, and Martin appeared to be trying hard to bite his tongue.

Kelsey smiled.

And Jonny? Well, he didn't know what to do. Beth had surprised him, and that was no joke.

"So . . . did I just ruin everything?" Beth asked.

"No," Martin said as he stood up. "Not even close."

"You're fine, Beth," Jonny added.

And then something shifted. And once again, they became themselves again. The four of them together, no matter what. No matter how each of their parents acted. No matter if they were all at summer camp or playing at their grandparents' farm.

"What am I doing?" Kelsey said as she jumped up. "Congratulations, Beth! I love you and I'm going to love this baby, too."

"Yes, congratulations," Martin said as he bent down, kissed Beth on the forehead, and whispered something in her ear.

"I love you, Bethy," Jonny said. "I'll be the best uncle you've ever seen."

"Unless it's me," Martin joked. "I think I'll probably be giving you a run for your money."

With tears in her eyes, Beth smiled at them. "You all are the best. I couldn't ask for a better family."

"Right back atcha," Jonny said.

And . . . that was that, Jonny decided after he hugged them all good-bye, promising to call when he and Treva returned back from their honeymoon.

Life was unpredictable and chaotic and filled with sweet spots but also challenges. But no matter what, morning after morning, if the Lord was willing, the sun rose and each day began again.

No matter what, life went on.

Just as important, no matter what happened, life was good. He had his family and his darling wife. The Lord had been with him, too. He was always good. So good.

And for that, Jonny gave thanks.

ACKNOWLEDGMENTS

Once again, I'd like to share my appreciation for the many people who work so hard to make my books the best they can be. Thank you to Elizabeth Trout, Alicia Condon, and Carly Sommerstein for their editing, guidance, and advice. I'm also so grateful to Lynne Stroup, who reads the second draft of every book and writes such wonderful notes about every one of my characters. Lynne, my books would be a mess without you! In addition, I'm so grateful for the members of my Facebook group, the Buggy Bunch, who form street teams, write reviews, come to book signings, and share my novels with friends and family members. It's because of all of you that I'm still writing books that fill my heart.

Read on for a special preview of *New York Times* best-selling author Shelley Shepard Gray's next Amish ABCs novel . . .

C IS FOR COURTING

Coming in fall 2025 from Kensington Publishing Corp.

You are members of God's family. *Ephesians 1:5*

Things turn out the best for those who make the best of the way things turn out. *Amish proverb*

CHAPTER 1

January 8
Walden, Ohio

It was so cold. Wrapping her grandmother's thick black cloak around herself more tightly, Beth Schrock carefully made her way over to Patti Coblentz's house. The first time she'd visited, the weather had been warm, the well-worn path leading from the Schrock's old barn to the neatly tended path in front of Patti's door was easy to find, and Beth had nothing but time on her hands.

Today was another story. Wind was blowing specks of sleet and ice into her face, and the path under her feet was slick. She also was carrying two loaves of freshly baked bread that were in danger of slipping out of her arms.

So, yes, she was uncomfortable and cold.

But she was also worried about her future and feeling guilty because her grandmother was under the weather and so far she hadn't done half the things she'd promised to do.

As another blast of wind threatened to turn her eyelashes

into mini-icicles, she grimaced. Almost two years ago, when she'd imagined living Amish on her grandparents' farm, she had thought all her troubles would miraculously fade away.

She'd been such a fool.

Patti's door opened just as Beth reached the front steps.

"Beth, I canna believe you!" she scolded, as she hurried down the steps and reached for her arm. "You should not be out in this weather."

After allowing Patti to pull the loaves of bread out of her arms, she attempted to defend herself. "I didn't think it was that bad out."

"You couldn't have looked out the window?" Patti asked, as they climbed the three steps.

"Ouch. That's kind of harsh."

"You're right. I'm sorry," Patti said, as she closed the door behind them. "I just hate the thought of you slipping and falling."

She would hate that, too. "I was careful."

"Come into the living room. I've got a fire going. We'll take off your cloak in there. Then you can stand in front of the flames and warm up while I get you some tea."

"You don't have to go to the trouble."

"Don't you worry about that. Or about drinking anything caffeinated. The tea is decaf, I promise you that."

"Thanks."

Patti shrugged as she continued to get Beth settled. "After you warm up for a spell, put your feet up and rest a bit."

Going directly to the fireplace, Beth almost moaned in contentment. The heat coming off the grate felt heavenly. Continuing to face the fire, she called out over her shoulder, "Sorry, but I can't stay long. I need to get back."

"You will stay long enough to rest and warm up."

Unhooking her cloak, Beth shook off the few drops of precipitation that clung to the fine wool before tossing it on the magazine holder on the ground. She'd hang the garment up properly as soon as she could feel her hands. "I'll be fine."

"Do you want some of my strudel? It's cherry."

"Thanks, but I better not. The doctor already told me that I shouldn't be gaining so much weight so fast." Looking down, she rubbed a protective hand across her belly. Within the last two weeks, she'd gone from looking a little chubby to sporting a baby bump. She wasn't going to be able to hide her pregnancy from the rest of the world much longer.

"You are not walking back," Patti called out from the kitchen. "Junior can drive you. Right, Junior?"

Everything in Beth froze. They weren't alone?

"Of course, Patti," a deep, masculine voice replied from the hallway. "I don't mind at all. We're about done now, anyway."

"*Danke*, Junior."

Feeling her cheeks heat, this time having nothing to do with the temperature of the fireplace and everything to do with pure embarrassment, Beth turned to face the speaker. Junior Whoever-he-was.

The man staring back at her from the other side of the room was a complete surprise. At least ten years older, Junior looked to be in his midthirties, was clean-shaven, and had clear blue eyes, thick blond hair, and was massive. He kind of looked like a Viking in one of her favorite television series.

What he didn't look like was a Junior.

She also couldn't figure out why he was spending time alone with Patti. She'd thought Patti and her brother Martin had something special between them.

When she realized he was taking in everything about her as well, she found her cheeks heating. Nothing like being a twenty-seven-year-old unwed mother who was currently trying to decide if she wanted to be Amish or stay English. Yep, every part of her life was in disarray.

Just as quickly, she shook off those feelings of discomfort. First of all, her personal life was none of this man's concern. Second, she might be contemplating a life in Walden, but that didn't mean she still wasn't the same woman she'd always been. She knew her own mind, and she was still tough enough to stand on her own two feet.

As the silence dragged, she cleared her throat. Then decided to speak. "Hi."

He strode forward. "Hiya, Beth. I'm John Lambright, but everyone calls me Junior."

If she'd been at work, she would have stepped forward and held out her hand. Since she was in Patti's living room, she stuffed her hands in her dress's pockets. "It's nice to meet you."

"Junior is one of my bookkeeping clients," Patti said as she carefully slid a healthy portion of strudel onto a plate. "Beth here is living with her grandparents next door."

"It's nice to meet you," he said with a slight nod. "I've heard a lot of about you and your family."

"Oh?" She glanced at Patti.

"Don't worry, Beth. It weren't nothing bad. Just normal news."

"I see."

"Pretty much everyone in the area has been following the adventures of you and your siblings," Junior said with a smile. "What with your sister marrying a preacher and your brother marrying Treva Kramer."

"Yes. I can imagine there would be talk."

"Please sit down, Beth," Patti said as she placed a cup of tea and the strudel on the coffee table. "You need to get off your feet for a spell."

And . . . there was the reminder of her pregnancy. Out

there in the open. "I'm all right." Suddenly noticing the ledgers and pair of manilla folders open on the other end of the dining room table, Beth mentally groaned. Once again she had a lot to learn about living Amish. Just because Patti was Amish didn't mean she did nothing but cook, clean, quilt, and wait for visitors to come knocking on her door. She was a busy woman with her own business.

"This strudel looks so good. I'll enjoy it while you two finish your meeting."

Patti's expression eased. "*Danke.* I don't want to be rude, but we do have a few more things to discuss."

Realizing that she would have a pretty good view of the two of them at the table, Beth said, "Would you like me to go into another room? I would understand if you'd like more privacy."

"It's up to you, Junior," Patti said.

"There's nothing too secretive about taxes or savings plans. I don't mind finishing our work here."

"Very well." After shooting a quick look at Beth, Patti sat down at the head of the table, put on reading glasses, and picked up a pencil. "Here's where I think we could make some changes, Junior."

"What about when the quarterlies are due?"

Patti pointed to an open calendar. "We could either agree to meet here, or I could give you a call and remind you to mail that check."

"You wouldn't mind?"

"Of course not. It's my job."

Beth tucked her head as she pretended not to notice Junior's grin. That smile made her feel things she didn't want to think about. Carson and the night she couldn't wait to forget. Martin and his yearning for Patti from afar.

And, unfortunately, the fact that she was even noticing such a thing. Shouldn't a man's smile be the last thing on earth she should be thinking about? Hadn't she learned anything?

Stabbing a wayward cherry on her plate, she frowned.

"Ah, Beth? Beth?"

She started. Lifted her head. "Yes?"

"Are you all right?"

"Of course. Why?"

"You were stabbing that pastry like it had personally offended you," Patti said. "Does it not taste good to you?"

"It tastes fine," Beth said.

Junior chuckled. "You worry too much, Patti. I told you not fifteen minutes ago that your treat was delightful."

Patti blushed. "It's not that. It's just that I've heard that sometimes foods taste different when one—" Obviously embarrassed, she cut herself off.

Beth might wish she had done things differently in her life, but she was long past the point of pretending that her pregnancy didn't exist. "When one is pregnant?"

"*Jah.*" Patti smiled.

"I suppose that might be true, but Junior is right. The pastry is delicious. It's . . . well, it's my attitude that is off today." Standing up, she collected her plate and undrunk tea. "I don't think I'm the best company today. I'm sorry to not have your tea, but I think it's best if I head on home."

Junior's chair scraped against Patti's wooden floor, no doubt scuffing it. "I'll take you."

"You are in a meeting."

"We're essentially done. Right, Patti?"

"That is true."

Feeling even more awkward, Beth reached for her cloak. "I appreciate the offer, but there really is no need. I'll be fine walking."

"I think differently." He voice was firm. It was obvious he

wasn't going to accept her pushing him away. Or, perhaps, burdening Patti.

"Thank you."

Ten minutes later, Beth had her grandmother's cloak back on and was sitting next to Junior in his buggy. His horse was a sturdy gelding named Arthur, of all things. He'd glanced at Beth when Junior had helped her into the buggy and then seemed to stomp a hoof. She wondered if he was anxious to go or wasn't real pleased to have yet another person to cart around.

"Ready?" he asked.

"Sure."

"All right then." He clicked. Arthur, obviously eager to be on his way, pulled the buggy forward with a lurch and then off they went.

"How long has Patti been your bookkeeper?"

"Not long."

"My brother said she's very good at accounting."

"Is he a client, too?"

"No. Just a friend." She bit her bottom lip so she wouldn't add that Martin and Patti were very close friends.

"How are you settling in at your grandparents'?"

"Well enough."

"What about your man?"

Her man? "What are you talking about?"

"You know. The father of your unborn baby."

Well, she supposed one couldn't get much more specific than that. But did she appreciate the question? No. No, she did not. Though it was tempting to say that the father was none of his business, Beth knew that he was going to be one of many folks who would either ask outright or hint around for more information.

So she decided to blurt the truth. "I don't have a man, Junior. This baby is a product of a foolish night."

Though he didn't turn his head to face her, she noticed a muscle jump in his cheek. Seconds passed.

When he spoke again, his voice was a shade deeper. "Well now. That must have been some night."

Beth was about to be offended . . . until she saw the hint of a smile on his lips. "Are you joking about this?"

"A little bit. Are you offended?"

"Not really." To her surprise, she was telling him the truth, too.

"It's, ah . . . that I couldn't help but think about how *mei shveshtah* and her husband had to try for months for their first baby. Here, you got pregnant during one evening." Twin splotches of color appeared on his cheeks. "And, I've just become very aware that my teasing was in very poor taste. I'm sorry."

"No . . . I mean, it's okay." She shook her head, not sure what to say but needing to say something. "To be honest, I was shocked about what happened, too. It was very unexpected."

About a dozen thoughts seemed to roll around in his head, but Junior remained silent.

Five minutes later, they'd arrived at her grandparents' house and he was setting the parking brake. "Stay put," he said. "I'll come around and help you down."

"I can get myself out."

"I'd prefer you allow me to help ya. It's cold, sleeting, and windy." Those blue eyes settled onto her. "If you wouldn't mind, that is."

Figuring he had a point, she didn't move until he opened the buggy's door on her side and held out a hand. Then Beth pretended she didn't notice the way his left hand curved around her waist and his right hand's fingers were slightly rough. Or that he smelled faintly of oranges, like he'd eaten one that morning.

"Thank you for the ride," she said as he escorted her up the steps.

"Anytime."

She opened the door but stood in the threshold as Junior turned around, nodded his head to someone near the barn, then climbed into the buggy and drove off.

Wondering who he'd seen, she turned to see her brother Martin in the doorway of the barn.

Immediately, her heart lifted. Now, at the very least, she wouldn't feel quite so alone and out of place.